BEG FOR MERCY

TONI ANDREWS

MERCY

BEG FOR MERCY

MIRA

MIRA

ISBN-13: 978-0-7783-2365-5
ISBN-10:   0-7783-2365-X

BEG FOR MERCY

www.MIRABooks.com

Printed in U.S.A.

First printing: September 2007

When I sat down to write *Beg for Mercy*, I found I so loved these characters that the story spewed out like water from a fire hose. I was helpless to slow down and take an objective look at whether the story even made sense, never mind compelled a reader to keep turning the pages.

As I finished each chapter, I sent it to a group of friends and family members who faithfully returned critiques, corrections and encouragement, and eagerly (or so they claimed, bless them) awaited the next installment.

So, for Sue Peek, Hilda Alvarez, Renee Branski, Mona Risk, Tina Stitzer, my brother Bob Andrews and my sister Sue Sinclair, thank you for helping me bring Mercy and the Balboa gang to life. I couldn't have done it without you.

1

I've never been certain I'm human. Oh, the X-rays and blood tests are normal, and no doctor, not even my gynecologist, has ever suggested otherwise, but it's not my body that's different. Not in any way you can see, at least. Most people have no reason to suspect I'm more—or less—than I appear to be. But none of them really know me. Sometimes I get tired of being cautious. But not so tired I let my guard down. Ever.

That's probably why I go to Jimbo's. Balboa's most notorious dive is not the kind of place that invites curiosity.

In the summertime, the population of Southern California's Balboa Peninsula swells as the beachfront condos fill with vacationing families. The trio of tiny three-car ferries circle continuously, and those who choose the longer overland route discover that the two four-lane roads leading onto the peninsula rapidly merge into one congested street and that all parking spaces are full by ten in the morning.

Evenings, when the beaches have emptied and the tourist traps have closed their doors, the heartier visitors migrate to pubs specializing in tropical drinks and steel bands. They drink Red Stripe beer and dance to reggae in their bikinis and sarongs, glowing from sunburn and tequila shots.

In the midst of this festival atmosphere, Jimbo's staunchly refuses to be festive. Its windowless single room, decorated with faded photos of men holding prize-winning fish caught half a century earlier, has little appeal to any lost tourist who stumbles into its dimly lit interior. Occasionally, some brave souls might try to blend in with the locals and sit at the bar for a draft beer and a pickled egg, but they seldom ask for a refill. If they stay long enough to need them, the bathrooms will probably scare them off. The graffiti, never painted over, is legendary.

I was sitting at the bar sipping a Budweiser—Jimbo's sells no other beer—and listening to Sukey prattle on about her latest flame, Rocko. Sukey is crazy for big, beefy guys who are long on muscles and short on brains. We definitely do *not* compete for the same men.

"He's *gorgeous,*" she gushed. "I can't wait until you meet him!"

I smiled and nodded. We'd had this conversation many times before. Sukey is the most wonderful person in the world, but she's a bit high-maintenance for most men. She'll call them twelve or fourteen times a day at work and give them adorable nicknames, often involving food. In my experience, most men don't want to be called "cupcake" in front of their drinking buddies.

"Are you supposed to meet him here?" I asked,

already knowing the answer. For Sukey, a date meant he had said he might stop in. If he showed up, it would count as the first step toward commitment. If he didn't have a girl on his arm, that is. I really hoped that wouldn't happen tonight. Sukey is usually a happy drunk, but a crying binge was not out of the question.

"He had some other things he had to do first," she said. "But he should be here soon. I'll just call him." She fished around in her massive purse for her cell phone. Wondering how many times she had already called him today, I put a hand on her arm and looked around for a means of distracting her. "Cupcake" would find out about Sukey's telephone habits soon enough. Maybe I could buy her a little time.

"Who's that guy over there?" I asked, pointing to the back of a head I didn't recognize. Sukey knew everyone in town and was an excellent source on anything male.

"Oooh, I'm glad you reminded me," she said, forgetting the cell phone. "That's Sam. He's the guy who bought Butchie's business. He doesn't come in here very much. And he's *exactly* your type."

I didn't consider Sukey an expert on *my type,* but the change of subject was welcome. "I missed Butchie's retirement party. Isn't this guy from Florida or something?"

"Key West." Sukey sipped her margarita. "His father's got Alzheimer's, and Sam came out here to take care of him. Sam's dad and Butchie were best friends in the Korean War or something. Sam's really nice but kind of boring." This meant that when Sukey had flirted with him, he hadn't flirted back.

"He's always at the coffee shop in the morning, reading some enormous book," she went on. Because I was on a first-name basis with everyone who worked at the local library and the secondhand bookstore, she assumed any man who had read a book was my dream boy. Reading probably meant he wasn't a complete moron, but it hardly qualified him as relationship material.

I was about to point this out when the man in question turned and I got a good look at him. I think I actually managed not to gasp, but this *was* my idea of gorgeous. Sort of Sam Shepard meets Matthew McConaughey. Tall, lean and wearing a chambray shirt washed until it looked as soft as a feather. Laugh lines had weathered in exactly the right way, and his light blue eyes almost matched the faded shirt. He smiled at something one of the local commercial fishermen said, and I saw the glint of white teeth against a tanned face.

Sukey laughed. I realized I had frozen when about to take a sip of my beer, and I was still holding it in front of my parted lips. I'd been staring like an idiot, and Sukey had enjoyed the whole scene.

"I told you!" she said, whacking me on the shoulder. "Do I know what you like or what?"

"This time, I have to admit you do." I raised my beer and clinked her margarita glass, causing salt to fall into my beer and raise a head of foam that dripped over my hand and onto my jeans. We laughed together, and I thought about how much I liked this silly, shallow girl. The one who was always so genuinely happy to see me and thought I had no faults. The one who was as excited as I was when I opened my own business.

No, I don't let anyone get too close, but I almost made an exception for Sukey. She didn't have a suspicious bone in her body, and her curiosity was like that of a child—easily distracted by the next pretty, shiny thing. In a million years, she would never guess my secret. And she was unlikely to make me angry.

I have to be very, very careful about getting angry.

I went to the bar to get some napkins to sop up my spilled beer and turned to find the object of my recent attention standing right in front of me. "Excuse me," he said, and we did that awkward dance where two people each try to let the other pass and keep choosing the same path.

I heard a voice behind me shout, "Sam! Meet the Newport Bitch!" Jimbo himself was tending bar tonight. He had coined the nickname on one of my earliest visits, and never tired of the joke. Resigned, I moved so Sam could put down the empty bottles he was carrying and put out a hand to shake mine.

"Sam Falls," he said.

"Mercy Hollings." He had a good handshake, and his eyes were even more arresting up close. I probably stared just a moment too long, because Jimbo started shouting again. Years of running a boisterous bar had left Jimbo with only one volume—full.

"Whoooeee, she must like you, Sammy boy. Usually she shoots 'em down like skeet." Jimbo mimed sighting down the barrel of a rifle. "Pull…*BLAM!*

Another poor bastard, shot right out of the air." Thankfully, the other customers kept Jimbo from warming to his theme, and he walked away, leaving me with Mr. Blue Eyes. I shook my head.

"If I didn't know he only insults the people he likes, I'd be hurt," I said and smiled tentatively, wondering what Sam thought of Jimbo's performance.

"He must hate me, then, because so far he's been friendly." The white smile crinkled those laugh lines again, and I felt my stomach do a tiny flip-flop.

"Give him time. He's probably still trying to think up something really offensive."

"I'll look forward to it." Again the smile. *God help me.* The tingle in my stomach moved lower. I was trying to think of something clever of my own to say when I saw the smile fade as his gaze moved to look at something behind me.

I turned to see what he was looking at and saw three men coming through the back door. I should say I was *aware* that there were three men, but one of them drew the eye so completely, the other two were mere outlines.

My first instinct was laughter. Luckily, years of caution had taught me to think before I acted, and I managed to look away before I lost control. "Holy shit," I breathed. "What *is* that?"

"I don't think I want to know," said Sam, turning toward the bar and picking up the beer Jimbo had placed before him. I tried to keep my eyes on the bar, but it was like trying not to look at a train wreck. With what I hoped was subtlety, I glanced out of the corner of my eye at the apparition at the door.

He was muscle-bound and wearing a white T-shirt with the sleeves cut off—and about two sizes too small. His black hair was slicked back and shimmered with oil, and matched his moustache and goatee. From his mirrored aviator sunglasses to his oversized diamond stud, he was a walking mass of clichés. To my dismay, his scan of the room caught my glance, and he flashed me a "you know you want me, baby" smile. I shuddered and turned away.

"Looks to me," said Sam dryly as he sipped his beer, "like a bad case of testosterone poisoning."

I did laugh this time but hoped having my back to the man would disguise the object of my amusement, who was, at this very moment, relating a story to his cronies in a voice designed to ensure everyone could hear him. "So I told him 'Go ahead and hit me, asshole. Fighting gives me a hard-on.'" His sidekicks laughed dutifully, and the walking anachronism stepped up to the bar and pounded on it with the flat of his hand, making everyone jump.

"Hey, Jimbo, you old pervert, get us some tequila shots, wouldja? And not that cheap shit, either. The Patrón Silver, okay?" To my horror, he turned to me.

"You ever try the Silver, sweetheart? It's smoother than a baby's ass. Hey, Jimbo, get a shot for hot stuff here, too." Jimbo grabbed a fourth shot glass and, just as I was about to protest, a squeal interrupted.

"Hey, baby, get me a shot, too!" Sukey squeezed in between me and the man's oily biceps—were they shaved?—and beamed. *Please, God, say it ain't so. It can't be*. But I knew better. With a sinking feeling, I saw Sukey throw her arms around his thick neck.

"Rocko, you're finally here. Oh, good, you already got a shot for Mercy. She's the one I've been telling you about." She turned to me and stage-whispered, "What did I tell you? Isn't he just *beef*?"

"Grade A," I muttered back, thinking he really would look better hanging on a hook.

"Oh, and Sam. You haven't met Rocko, have you? Rocko, get Sam a shot, and we'll all do one together."

"Rocko Peretti." Freeing himself from Sukey, Rocko reached around me and took Sam's hand in a vise grip. Sam didn't wince, but he didn't smile, either. I was impressed. Before the handshake could turn into an endurance test, Sukey pouted and grabbed his neck again.

"Honeybun, you said you'd be here at nine-thirty. I've been holding off drinking so I could keep up with you. Aren't we going to do the shots?" Rather than being annoyed, Rocko seemed pleased by the attention. He released Sam's hand and sat on the bar stool, pulling Sukey onto his lap.

"Me and the boys had some business, sweet cheeks, but Rocko's all yours now." He kissed her sloppily, and she giggled in delight.

"I really don't want a shot," protested Sam as Jimbo placed one of the tequilas in front of each of us, then set a plate of salt and limes on the bar.

"If Rocko's baby says you get a shot, you get a shot. Ain't that right, baby?" Rocko nuzzled Sukey's neck as he reached for his own shot. She wriggled like a happy pup, and I grudgingly scored a couple of points for Rocko. Any man who called me baby in public would be risking the loss of a limb, but Sukey loved the attention. At least this guy was behaving as if he really considered her his girlfriend.

"Please, Sam?" said Sukey sweetly. "Just one to celebrate—" she looked from Sam to me with arched brows and no subtlety whatsoever "—making new friends."

"New friends!" thundered Rocko, upending his shot, then slamming the empty glass on the bar. I glanced at Sam and shrugged, then tossed down my own shot. He did the same.

Smooth as a baby's ass was not the exact phrase that came to mind, but I had to admit the smoky tequila was better than I expected. I felt warmth spread from my stomach to my limbs. The sensation was pleasant, and I tried to look at Rocko with a less jaundiced eye.

Okay, so he was too loud and too macho. But he had let Sukey call him "honeybun" in public, and that earned him at least the benefit of the doubt. He and Sukey were cooing and kissing like teenagers, and I turned away to give them some privacy, such as it was.

"It was nice meeting you." Sam's half-full beer sat next to his empty shot glass, but his posture left no doubt he was about to walk out the door.

"Yes, nice to meet you, too," I said, disappointed he was leaving already. The tequila had given me a nice warm glow, and I was prepared to entertain a little harmless flirting. Also, if he left, I would have no choice but to talk to Sukey and Rocko, or leave and risk hurting Sukey's feelings. She would forgive me for ignoring her in favor of a man, but not for leaving for no particular reason.

"Well, it's a small town. I'm sure I'll see you again," he said. I nodded, and he slipped out the front door.

I turned to face the lovebirds, trying to imagine just what I could say to them. "I have to go to the bathroom." Brilliant.

I took my time in the women's room, scanning the walls for anything I hadn't read before. I finally spotted something over the mirror as I was washing my hands. *No matter how good he looks, some other woman is tired of putting up with his shit.* I chuckled as I dried my hands and headed back out to the barroom.

"Hey, Mercy, I need a partner." Lifeguard Skip was chalking a cue next to Jimbo's single pool table. The place might be a dive, but table etiquette is taken very seriously. Challengers' names are on the chalkboard, and winners call the game. A "slop shot"—accidentally knocking your own ball into an unintended pocket—results in the loss of a turn, no exceptions.

Technically, a challenger can choose any partner for a doubles game, but if the winning team is mixed, it's considered bad form for two men to challenge. Some silly notion that men are better players.

"Sure, Skip." Grateful I would not have to make nice with Rocko for at least one game, I chose a light cue and examined it carefully. Jimbo is pretty good about replacing the warped, cracked or tipless cues, but they accumulate nevertheless.

Pool is something I can do. Years of keeping people at a distance—for their benefit as much as my own—have given me a deserved reputation as a loner. But I've always been drawn to the dark, smoky bars where companionship can be had without the complications of intimacy. The best place to interact with others without personal conversation is the pool table. Over the years, a few old sharks have taught me some valuable lessons.

We won the table easily, and the other team bought us beers—the tacit wager for all games without stated bets. Lifeguard Skip is an even better player than I am. It's been thirty years since he last donned red shorts and a whistle, but he's never held a job that paid a whole lot more than minimum wage. Pool has probably supplemented his income since he was old enough to drink. I knew he was hoping the casual games would result in real bets, but there were no serious takers tonight, so we accumulated beers and a few more tequila shots. I was starting to feel the alcohol and knew I needed to get out of there.

I told Skip I didn't mind if he changed the game to singles, and he gratefully complied, putting up a not-too-convincing argument. Given the choice, no real pool player will choose playing doubles over a one-on-one challenge, no matter how good his partner. As I passed the bar on my way to the exit, I saw Sukey sitting alone. From the slump of her shoulders, I figured there was trouble in paradise.

I slid onto a stool next to her and, sure enough, saw mascara streaks on her cheeks.

"Okay, what happened?" I winced at the cynical

tone of my voice. I tried to make up for it with a genuinely sympathetic look.

"N-n-nothing." Sukey sniffed and dried her eyes with a bar napkin. "Smoke got in my eyes."

"Sounds like a song title." I smiled at her, but either she was too young for the reference or my timing sucked. I guess she wasn't ready to be cheered up yet. Too many years of being a loner had done little for my girlfriend sympathy skills. I tried again.

"What's the matter, Sukey? Where's Rocko?" Her lower lip quivered, but she bravely fought sobs.

"He had to g-g-go." She sniffed again.

"So why are you crying? Did he say something mean?"

"No. Yes. I mean…" She took a fortifying sip of a flat-looking draft beer. "He got a phone call and just left. I asked him where he was going and he said—he said—" More sniffles.

I waited, maintaining my sympathetic expression. I had once cruelly speculated that if someone had to have troubles, it was a good thing it was Sukey. At least she could *enjoy* the suffering. She had a natural knack for dramatic timing.

"He said I asked too many questions. Then he just walked out." She took another sip of the flat beer. "He didn't even pay for my drink!"

I stifled a sigh. I had heard this song before, and I knew the next verse. A good buddy would listen to it anyway, but I was new at this friend thing and my head hurt. My main problem at present, however, was the quantity of alcohol I had consumed. Not only did I hate the feeling of being less than one-hundred percent in control, but I well knew the potential consequences that lack of control could bring. I had no business being out in public one moment longer than necessary.

"Do you want me to walk you home?" I asked, hoping she would take the hint. Sukey and I both lived within a few blocks of Jimbo's, albeit in opposite directions. A walk in Newport Beach's cool night air might do us both some good.

"It's not even midnight," she said with dismay. "You don't want to go home yet, do you? I don't."

What was I thinking? You're obviously having so much fun. I should probably have ordered some of Jimbo's horrible coffee and stayed to keep an eye on her, but I just couldn't face it.

"Do you need me to pay your bar bill?" If I was going to abandon her, I could at least pay for the drinks Rocko had neglected to take care of.

"Oh, no, Jimbo always lets me run a tab."

"I'm really tired, Sukey. Will you be okay if I leave?"

"Of course." She wiped her eyes again and peered at herself in the dim mirror behind the bar. "Oh, God, I look like a raccoon. I'll just go freshen up." She hopped off the bar stool and hugged me. "Thanks for coming to meet me."

I pulled back and eyed her critically. She actually did look somewhat recovered. I told myself she would be fine. Probably.

"Call me tomorrow," I said, and headed for the back door.

Jimbo's tiny parking lot was still full. As I wove

between cars, a shiny black Firebird double-parked and Rocko got out. *Shit*. There was no way to avoid him—Jimbo kept the lot brightly lit, and I was too far from the shadows of the alley.

"Hey, it's hot stuff." He looked appreciatively at my breasts. "Where are you running off to?"

"Your date's inside, Rocko. And whatever you said before you took off didn't make her too happy."

He shrugged and did something unsubtle to make his neck and chest muscles bunch. I was probably supposed to swoon, but I missed my cue.

"Plans can change. A man needs to know when to seize the opportunity. You know of any opportunities I should be seizing?" He ran his eyes up and down my body. Ick.

"Naw, I only mate with my own species." *Shit, shit, shit*. After all that beer and tequila, my mouth was working faster than my brain. His darkening expression should have slowed me down but only succeeded in pissing me off. So I kept talking.

"Sukey is sitting in there waiting for you. And while I can't say I understand why the hell she should care about anything you say or do, she does. You let her think you were going to spend the evening together, so I suggest you sashay your ass back in there and make nice."

"Just who the fuck do you think you are?" All the seduction was gone from Rocko's voice. I already knew he liked to fight, but would he hit a woman? "Sukey and me will get along just fine without you sticking your nose into our business."

"Just see you don't hurt her or you'll regret it." I was getting mad, and fast. I should have calmed down, but the tequila flowing in my veins and Rocko's derisive snort combined to keep the fire flowing.

"What, you think I should be afraid of you?" The disdain in his voice was the final red flag.

"You should be *very* afraid of me, Rocko. Terrified, in fact."

Rocko's face blanched, and his expression changed to one of pure horror. He backed away from me, his hands lifted as if warding off a blow. His eyes flashed toward Jimbo's back door, and he darted for it.

Oh God, oh God, oh God. I could not believe what I had just done. Mentally kicking myself, I practically ran toward the alley that led in the direction of my apartment. *Oh God, oh God, oh God.*

I headed for home in a daze, unlocked the door with shaking hands and slammed it behind me. Without turning on the lights, I slumped against the wall. My head spun, and my stomach lurched like a washer on spin cycle. I bolted for the bathroom and managed to get the toilet seat up before all the beer and tequila I had consumed over the last hours made a hasty exit.

I sat on the bathroom floor, trembling. Tears ran down my face, and I choked on both the acrid taste in my mouth and a suppressed sob. *Stupid, stupid, stupid.* It had been over a year since I had lost control. I had been so sure I had it licked. Then…one night with a few too many drinks, plus one asshole, and I was right back to square one.

An inquisitive meow echoed in the dark room,

followed by a loud, rumbling purr. I felt silky fur rub against my arm and gathered Fred into my arms.

"Oh, Fred," I said, burying my face in his coat. "Mama's been a ba-a-ad girl." The purring got louder and more irregular as he licked my face with his rough tongue, encouraged by the salty taste of tears. Fred is a kisser.

"Come on, furball." Setting him down, I rose to my feet and turned on the light, searching for aspirin. I found some, then followed Fred's four-inch-wide orange tail into the kitchen for a glass of water. I forced myself to drink three full glasses with the aspirin, hoping to avoid a hangover. *I should have thrown up two hours ago.* Then I never would have let that obnoxious jerk get under my skin. Then I never would have used *the press* on him.

2

When I was fourteen, I read a book by Stephen King called *Firestarter.* In it, one of the characters had the ability to compel others to do as he said. King called it the "push." There were side effects, both on the guy doing the pushing and on those he pushed, and he could only do it when he had full control of his faculties and concentration.

I should be so lucky.

My ability is different. The good news is, I don't seem to do any damage to myself when I use it. The bad news is, I can do it any time, anywhere, regardless of my physical or mental condition. And sometimes it happens unintentionally.

It didn't start until I was an adolescent, and I had no idea what was happening. When I told another kid at school to shut up, he didn't speak for months. I hadn't a clue that the weeks of psychological testing, expulsion from school and the ridicule from other kids he had to endure were all due to my vehemence at the moment I said those two words.

I had *pressed* him. I could have saved him and his

parents months of agony by saying, "Okay, you can talk again" with equal intensity, but I neither knew that I could nor did I have the opportunity once he was taken out of school. Nor did *he* know why he was unable to speak, or that I had anything to do with it. Poor kid. Eventually my instructions wore off, but he never caught up with the rest of his class and ultimately graduated a year late.

Not that I was still in the same school by then. My adoptive parents had given up soon after the first time I almost killed someone. The foster homes—and there had been many—were mostly situated far from the pleasant suburban communities with their pleasant suburban schools I had attended until I was in fifth grade.

As I readied myself for bed, I forced my mind away from the ugly memories tonight's slipup had raised. After washing my face and brushing my teeth, I made myself do the short relaxation exercise I had learned in yoga class. My mind cleared as much as possible for now, I got into bed and invited Fred to join me. He did me the honor of agreeing.

One little image sneaked in before I drifted off into alcohol-enhanced slumber. The look on Rocko's face when I told him—pressed him—to be afraid of me. My last thought was the reason I was really so upset about losing control. It was because making that asshole frightened of me had felt *good*. And that feeling was what I was really afraid of.

The sleep that comes from tequila is not the same thing as real slumber. When I awakened to a horrible, piercing sound, it took me a few long seconds to identify its source. It was my cell phone, which I had remembered to put in the charger next to my pillow, but failed to reduce the ear-splitting volume setting I used for bars and other crowded, noisy settings.

I picked it up and punched the button but forgot what I was supposed to say. So I said nothing, and a voice at the other end asked, "Is anyone there? Hello?"

"Yes, I'm here." *Shit.* Aspirin or no, my head hurt.

"May I speak to Mercedes Hollings?"

"Speaking." I sat up, wondering who the hell would call me at…what? Three-forty-five in the morning.

"Ms. Hollings, I'm calling from the emergency room at Hoag. There's a Susan Keystone here. Your name is in her wallet as one of the people to call in case of an emergency."

"Sukey? Is she all right?" My mind raced. Had Rocko beaten her up? Had she been in an accident?

"She's being moved to intensive care." This was not an answer to my question, but you don't move corpses to intensive care.

"I'll be right there." I punched the off key and jumped to my feet, causing Fred to make a protesting sound. I no longer felt any effects of the alcohol, other than a pounding in my head as I leaned over to find a clean pair of jeans in my bottom drawer.

Less than two minutes later, I was driving down Balboa Boulevard at well over the speed limit. I hoped I would not get pulled over—this was a notorious speed trap—but I figured I could talk my way out of it under the circumstances. Hell, the cops probably all knew Sukey, too. She loved uniforms.

The Hoag Memorial Hospital parking lot was almost empty at this hour, and I was through the emergency room entrance in moments. "I'm here about Susan Keystone. I got a call—"

"Ms. Hollings? I'm the one who called you." The woman behind the desk smiled warmly. People who say hospital staff members are impersonal or unfriendly have never been to Hoag. I swear they must send their personnel to hospitality management classes. "She's in intensive care. We're only supposed to let family in to see her, but she asked for you, and you were the only number we were able to reach on her emergency list."

"Her father's out of the country," I said, remembering. "One of her sisters lives in San Diego, though. I'm sure she'll want to come up. What happened to her?"

"We left a message with a Regina Keystone at a San Diego area code. I'm not authorized to tell you any medical details, but if she's told the doctor it's okay to talk to you, you can get the details from him. Let me tell you how to get to the intensive care reception desk." She handed me a brochure with a map. Hoag hospital has more in common with a good hotel than just friendly staff.

I found my way to the elevator and the seventh floor intensive care reception. The male nurse behind this counter was just as professional, if not quite as friendly, and led me down the hall to the room where Sukey was visible through a glass wall, hooked up to monitors. I told him I would like to see the doctor whenever possible, then went into the room to stand next to the bed. Sukey was sleeping, and I looked her over critically. I saw no bruises or bandages but got no other clues. I searched for a chart but didn't see one. Sighing, I took the chair next to her bed and sat to wait.

Patience is not my strong suit. I hadn't brought anything to read and I've never been able to sleep sitting up, so I spent the time on a couple of my favorite pastimes: guilt and self-retribution.

I never should have left her alone in the bar. Which was ridiculous. Sukey was thirty years old. I knew because I had contributed toward the stripper at the surprise party. She had certainly made it the two blocks home in much worse condition than I had left her in. But if I had stayed…

If I was going to press him anyway, I should have told Rocko to stay away from her. This was really insane. First, the press had been totally unplanned. Second, I had no right interfering in Sukey's love life, even if it was a train wreck. Rocko was a throwback but, for all I knew, he might have really cared for her. If Sukey had asked me for help, that would be different, but she hadn't.

Maybe pressing him caused him to do something to hurt Sukey. Here it was, the real crux of the matter. Rocko's fear of me in the parking lot had been genuine. He had practically pissed himself. A guy like that doesn't much like being afraid. Maybe as soon as he got inside he got mad at himself. He would have been confused, with no idea why he suddenly found me terrifying. He would have resented it and might have looked around for someone to take it out on. And since Sukey had introduced us…

My empty stomach churned uncomfortably. There was a very real possibility my stupid loss of control had resulted in Sukey's current condition. This was why I couldn't allow myself to have friends or let anyone get too close to me. Because I always ended up hurting them.

"Ms. Hollings?" A softly accented voice interrupted my internal litany of self-loathing. I looked up into a pair of chocolate-brown eyes in a smooth face.

"I am Dr. Patel," said the young man. "Ms. Keystone was awake for a while and asked for you. I told her you would be called and asked her for permission to speak with you about her medical details."

I nodded my understanding.

"Please, won't you step out where we can talk without disturbing her?"

I stood and followed him to a comfortable waiting room. A jigsaw puzzle was partially completed on the table, and a big-screen television was dark in a corner. Books and magazines filled shelves and tables. We sat in upholstered chairs.

"What happened to her?" I asked.

"It appears to be a drug overdose. Heroin, most likely."

"Heroin? *Sukey?*" I shook my head at this impossibility. "Sukey would never use heroin. She's terrified of needles." I had gone with her once to get a tetanus shot, and she had been a wreck.

"She appears to have inhaled or smoked it," he replied. "And it was probably cut with something that did her no good, either. Probably diphenhydramine, which sometimes triggers breathing problems, especially with asthmatics or people with allergies. Someone dumped her on the curb in front of the E.R. and took off."

"I see." I didn't see, not really. Sukey liked to party, but heroin was way out of her league. She would never do it on her own. And though I thought I remembered her mentioning something about allergies one time, I hadn't really paid attention, so I couldn't say whether they were the problem.

"Rocko." I didn't realize I had spoken aloud until I saw the inquisitive look on the doctor's face. "Nothing. I was just thinking about—" I shook my head. "Is she going to be okay?"

"She should be. We are going to keep her here at least twenty-four hours to make sure. She should be out of intensive care and in a regular room later this morning."

I nodded, and asked another question. "Does this have to be reported to the police?"

"Not unless they ask." He smiled gently at me. "Ms. Hollings, you seemed very surprised to learn your friend had used heroin. How well do you know Ms. Keystone? Is it possible she has a problem with the drug?"

I shook my head emphatically. "If Sukey took heroin, it was because she didn't know what it was. You can take my word for it." I meant it—meant it enough to press, just slightly. I had a firm policy of not pressing anyone without their permission, but exceptions could be made in the case of extreme emergencies. This definitely qualified.

Dr. Patel gave me a speculative look. He nodded and stood. "Ms. Keystone did ask that we call you, but I am reasonably sure she will not wake up for several hours. Perhaps you could get some rest and come back later." He excused himself and left the room.

I decided to wait it out but desperately wanted a cigarette. I call myself a social smoker, which is pretty funny when you consider my social life. What I mean is, I don't smoke every day or even every week. But when I do smoke, I may smoke an entire pack in a night. It all depends on my mood. I was pretty sure I had an almost full pack of Marlboro Lights in my glove compartment. The current situation had awakened dormant cravings.

I went out to the car, found the pack and lit up. The tobacco was stale, but I wasn't really smoking for the taste. I had parked in a spot shadowed from the spotlights by a large royal palm, and I leaned against the side of my car and looked out over the lights of the Pacific Coast Highway and Newport Island. Dawn would not come for another couple of hours, and anyway, it took a long time to peek over the mountains to the east, which were rarely seen through the coastal haze.

Movement at the other end of the parking lot caught my attention. A sleek black Firebird cruised near the emergency room entrance, and although I could not see through the tinted windows, a rush of adrenaline made every nerve tingle. *That son of a bitch. Too chickenshit to take her inside, but hanging around to see if she doesn't make it and the cops show up.*

I completely forgot that less than four hours ago I had promised myself I would not use my abilities in anger ever again. *I'll press you this time, you cock-sucker. I'll press you right off a cliff into the Newport Harbor.* Mindless of the consequences, I took off in a run after the black car. If I could just get within earshot before he saw me....

Unfortunately, my Birkenstock sandals were not designed for sprinting. The car had turned, exposing Rocko's face through the open driver's side window, and I just had time to see the look of pure terror take over his features as he saw who was pounding across the parking lot toward him. Tires squealed as he accelerated toward the exit.

Shit! I reversed directions, heading back for my Honda. He had a good start on me before I squealed my own tires, but fortunately the short, curvy drive leading down to the street did not let the larger engine of his muscle car give him an advantage over my more maneuverable vehicle. I was right on his tail when he hit the Coast Highway, but I had no chance to catch him on the straightaway.

To my complete astonishment, the moron turned onto Newport Boulevard and headed down the peninsula. This was like a scene from *World's Stupidest Criminals*. There were only two ways off the peninsula, and after Labor Day—two weeks ago—the Balboa Island Ferry stopped running at two in the morning. Rocko was heading toward a dead end, and I was right behind him.

I kept my foot on the accelerator, but there was no way I was going to catch an eight-cylinder muscle car. It didn't matter as long as I could see his taillights, and I wanted to hang back in case he tried to turn down one of the side streets and circle back behind me. I was hoping his panic wouldn't wear off until he had driven too far down the peninsula for there to be a good place to turn around.

You should be very afraid of me, Rocko. Terrified, in fact. My own words echoed in my head. I had been sick and furious with myself for losing control. Now I just wanted to get close enough so I could press him again. If I could just get him to hear me yell "stop," that would be enough.

Any other day of the year there would be one or two police cars lurking on the tiny side streets, waiting for incautious tourists to violate the twenty-five-miles-per-hour speed limit, but Rocko's taillights continued to pull away. *Shit.* If he made it all the way to where the peninsula widened at the Wedge, it would be harder to trap him.

I breathed a sigh of relief when I saw his brake lights flash as he slowed and made a fishtailing left turn toward the Balboa Island Ferry ramp. He must not have known it was closed. I took a turn down an alley and then went the wrong way down a tiny side street, cutting off his last chance to get around me and head back toward the mainland. I came around the corner in front of Jimbo's, expecting to see Rocko's car on the ramp to the ferry. It wasn't there.

Damn, where is he? I cruised slowly around the block, looking for the vehicle, but nothing was moving at this hour. As I pulled up along the main boulevard again, I caught a flash of movement in my rearview mirror. I twisted around just in time to see Rocko disappearing around a corner on foot, heading toward the silent and dark arcades and junk-food stands of the Fun Zone. The street was too narrow for a U-turn, so I made a couple of lefts and came around the tiny block, trying to cut him off. If I could just get where he could hear my voice…

I pulled up as close as I could get to the string of arcades, slammed the car into Park and jumped out. The boardwalk was still and empty. Suddenly I heard the loud rumble of a boat's engine starting up. *Jesus, why didn't I think of that?* I ran out on the tiny public pier, nearly slipping on the steep ramp.

Where was the rumbling coming from? I scanned the smallish boats moored at the marina, but all were motionless. Then I saw a larger, darker movement beyond the still marina. *I don't fucking believe it. The moron is stealing the Balboa Island Ferry.*

I ran back to my car. There was no way I could make it back around to the tiny bridge before Rocko got the ferry over to the other side, then slipped into the warren of alleys and side streets of Balboa Island, but maybe a quick 911 call could get a reception committee there in time. As I threw the car into Reverse and backed toward the alley, I fumbled for my cell phone but hesitated before punching the number.

Did I want to call the police? They would trace the call and might want to know what I was doing on the boardwalk somewhere after four in the morning. I didn't want to tell them anything that would lead back to Sukey, and I definitely did not want them around while I had a private chat with Rocko. But since it didn't look like my chances for having that chat tonight were very high, I wouldn't mind at all if he ended up spending the night in a cell.

I screeched to a halt in front of the liquor store and ran for the payphone. I dialed 911 and got an answer on the first ring. Newport Beach, California, does *not* suffer from a shortage of law enforcement resources.

"Someone just stole the Balboa Island Ferry from the Fun Zone. He's heading for Balboa Island."

"Who's calling, please?" I slammed down the receiver, wiped off the handset with my sleeve and was back in the car within ten seconds. *Calm down, girl. You can't get to him tonight. Just take a deep breath and get your ass back to the hospital....*

Before I could take my own advice, the unmistakable sound of an enormous crash sent a frisson of apprehension through my limbs. "Holy shit!" I pulled out of the parking lot and looked around. I thought the sound had come from the direction of the ferry ramp, and I turned that way. I couldn't see the source, but the loud *crump* of an explosion told me where it had to be. I screeched to a halt at the base of the ramp and saw I was right.

Rocko had driven the ferry directly into the gas dock in front of Butchie's Balboa Boat Rentals, and the outlines of the burning pumps could be seen through the dancing flames on the ferry's deck—now jammed between the pilings of the ferry ramp and the rental slip entrance, half over the floating dock. I smiled grimly. The single-screw ferries were notoriously difficult to steer, especially when it was windy, and the idiot hadn't even made it to the opposite side of the channel. He had made an arc right back into the shore where he'd started.

The live-aboard residents in the marina were popping out of their boat cabins like groundhogs. They were on the other side of the ferry slip, away from the danger, but one figure charged toward the flames like an Olympic runner. I just had time to realize it was Sam, naked except for a pair of boxer shorts, when another fast-moving figure caught my eye. It was Rocko, running in the opposite direction.

As they say in the police reports, I gave chase. Abandoning my useless sandals, I took off like the sprinter I had wanted to be in high school. I passed Sam, seeing him check as recognition registered in his eyes, but neither of us stopped. I rounded the corner and saw Rocko crossing the boulevard in the direction of the Balboa Pier.

"Rocko, stop!" I shrieked, pressing with all my might, but he was too far ahead of me to understand my words and intent.

He headed out onto the pier. *What is it with this guy and dead ends?* I didn't have time to argue with miracles. I slowed down, knowing this time he really had nowhere to go, unless he jumped into the frigid Pacific. As I caught my breath, I reflected I really wouldn't mind if he drowned or got eaten by one of the great white sharks that are occasionally reeled in by anglers fishing off the pier. But I knew that when my fury wore off, I would not want to have a man's death on my hands, even if that man was scum. So I slowed to a fast walk, hoping a slower pursuit would prevent him from panicking.

The pier was well-lit, but the retro diner poised at its end hid the farthest portion from view. He was probably huddled on the far side of the building, waiting for the big, bad, boogey-person to get him.

"Rocko, come out where I can see you," I shouted over the wind and crashing waves. I didn't know for sure if I could press without visual contact, but I tried anyway. I figured he could probably hear me now. Sure enough, he came around one side of the building and stood under a light. I could see him trembling as I walked closer.

"D-d-don't do anything to me," he said in the tone of a scared child. With his bulging muscles and deep voice, it was eerily incongruous.

"Come over here and stand out of the wind," I said, continuing to press. He did as he was told, still shaking. I could have told him to stop being afraid. I didn't.

"I want to talk to you about Sukey. Do you understand me?" He nodded, and I could see the whites all the way around the dark pupils of his eyes as his face caught the lamplight. "Tell me what drug you gave her."

"Heroin." The expression on his face told me it caused him pain to speak, but he was compelled to do so.

"Why did you give it to her?"

"To make her be quiet." He licked his lips and swallowed, looking at me like a rabbit caught in front of a coyote.

"Why did you need her to be quiet? What was she making noise about?"

"She wouldn't shut up. She kept crying."

"Why was she crying? Did you hurt her?" If I had been entertaining any thoughts of giving Rocko a break, they evaporated.

"She said I only wanted to fuck her."

"And did you?" When Rocko didn't answer immediately, I realized he needed a clearer question. This guy really was a moron.

"And did you have sex with her? Did you force her?"

"I didn't have to force her. She wanted to."

"She wanted to before the heroin? Or was it after?"

"Before...both."

I took a few minutes to think about it, while Rocko stood jittering and shaking like he was freezing. I had a pretty good idea about what had happened, even if I didn't have a lot of details. They didn't really matter, anyway, and I could get them from Sukey later. Right now, I just wanted to get rid of this guy.

"Where's your car?"

"Jimbo's." I hadn't even checked the parking lot, but it made sense he would abandon it somewhere he had been before.

"Here's what you're going to do. Are you paying attention?" He quickly nodded, moaning in a combination of eagerness and terror. "When I say you can go, you are going to go get in your car. There are probably going to be a lot of police around the ferry and the marina, and I want you to get to your car without any of them seeing you. Can you do that?" He nodded, and I continued.

"Then, you are going to get into your car and drive

carefully out of town. You are not going to speed or do anything that might get the police's attention. Pick up any of your things you need, and then go far, far away. Never come back. Never call Sukey or anyone else from this town. Never tell anyone where you have gone. Flush all your heroin and any other drugs you have hanging around down the toilet, gas up your car and leave. You understand me?"

Again that rapid nodding.

"Good. Now go."

It was as if I had fired the starting pistol at a track meet. Rocko shot past me toward the base of the pier. As he ran by, I could smell his sweat and urine. He had pissed himself.

I watched until his dark form reached the boardwalk, then vanished between two houses. I walked over to the edge of the pier and, making sure the wind was behind me, vomited for the second time in less than five hours. There wasn't much left to come up.

3

By the time I got back to my car, I had my story as straight as I was going to be able to get it. I knew Sam had seen me, and I had left my car in the middle of the brightly lit ferry ramp. As I rounded the corner, my view of the ramp was blocked by a fire truck. I hoped they hadn't pushed my car into the bay to get it out of the way. I had insurance, but I didn't relish filing that particular claim.

Flames no longer lit the sky, but lights from more than a dozen emergency vehicles made an artificial cone of daylight. I could see Sam, who had found a pair of jeans, talking to a man with a notebook. There were no television trucks, so Sam's companion was probably a detective. My stomach gave another lurch, but there was nothing for it. I headed straight for the pair.

Before I could reach them, Sam spotted me and pointed a finger. "There she is," he said loud enough that I could hear anger in his voice. He advanced toward me before the detective could get his notebook shut. "Where the hell have you been? And why were you running away?" He looked like he wanted to strangle me, and I really couldn't blame the guy. The gas docks were part of the operation he had just bought from Butchie.

"Ms. Hollings?" The detective moved smoothly into my path in front of the advancing Sam. "I'm Detective Gerson. Mr. Falls says you ran past him right after the explosion. Is that correct?"

"Yes, that's correct," I said shortly. Sam, who had been about to say something else, closed his mouth abruptly. He had apparently been expecting denial.

"Can you tell me why you were running away from the scene?"

"I was never at the scene. I heard the explosion and saw a man running away from it. I took off after him."

"Why did you do that, Ms. Hollings? It might have been dangerous."

"I thought maybe if I could get a good look at him, I'd be able to identify him later. I don't think he even knew I was chasing him."

"Did you? Get a good look at him, I mean."

I shook my head. "He was too fast, and I never got close enough. He lost me at about Tenth Street. I didn't have my running shoes on, and he must have turned down an alley."

I hoped Rocko had made it back farther than Tenth, and that the police hadn't blocked off the foot of the peninsula. We have a pretty high cop-to-citizen ratio in Newport Beach, and they're capable of mobilizing a lot of resources even for small crimes. I'd always considered this a good thing, but tonight I just wanted

Rocko to get out of town before the cops connected him to Sukey.

"Your registration says you live less than three blocks from here, Ms. Hollings. Why were you driving around in your car at this time in the morning?" This guy was no idiot.

"A friend of mine had to be taken to the emergency room earlier. I was on my way back from Hoag when I heard the explosion." I realized I had just raised the very topic I had been trying to avoid and silently prayed he wouldn't tug that particular thread.

"What's your friend's name?" *Shit, shit, shit.* I paused long enough to see who was listening. Sam had been called over by a fireman and was gesturing at the damaged roof of the boat-rental building. I took a deep breath. *One last time.* I really hated this.

"My friend's name is not important, and my story seems completely plausible." I pressed very gently and was relieved when Detective Gerson nodded. I could see Sam was done talking to the fireman and was coming back, so I continued quickly.

"You don't have any more questions for me right now, and I'll call you if I think of anything."

Obediently, Detective Gerson took a card out of his wallet and handed it to me. He turned and started walking toward one of the uniformed policemen.

"That's it?" Sam was incredulous. "He's already done talking to you?"

"There wasn't much I could tell him," I said. "I saw the guy take off and ran after him. He got away before I could get a good look."

"You were gone a long time." I could see soot on his face, and his hands were shaking. "I thought you…I hoped you…" He trailed off. "Look, I'm sorry. When I realized you had nothing to do with it, I guess I just hoped you would know who did this, and why." He ran dirty hands through his hair and sat heavily on a park bench. "It's just that I haven't got the insurance all straightened out yet, and I don't think this is going to be covered."

"Maybe the ferry company's insurance will cover it."

"Maybe." Suddenly his gaze sharpened. "How did you know it was the ferry? I heard you say you were never at the scene."

"The detective told me." I hoped he could not see my flush in the flickering light. I had forgotten to be careful, but the adrenaline of the evening was wearing off, and I was starting to feel the exhaustion. I would *not* press Sam. I would *not*. I turned to face him, not surprised to find he was still looking at me with a speculative expression. I willed my face to remain neutral.

"How did you get here so fast?" I asked. This seemed like a safe change of subject.

"I've been living on my boat part-time." He gestured vaguely at the marina. "I sort of woke up when I heard the ferry start up. It's usually my alarm clock."

I nodded—I lived only three blocks away, and on quiet mornings I could hear the ferry's horn give its characteristic three toots as it finished each run.

"I'd almost fallen back to sleep when I heard the crash. Then the explosion." He shook his head again.

"I just can't believe it. I mean, the rental business makes some money, but it's the gas that keeps the place going."

My heart sank. The local tourist economy was extremely seasonal, and businesses that relied too heavily on the cash spikes of the summer months seldom lasted through the quiet winters. The long-surviving businesses, like Butchie's, relied on year-round residents to make it through the slow months, and none of them had a big enough profit margin to stand much of an interruption. Sam was just starting out, and now he couldn't pump gas and sell supplies to the small fleet of commercial fishermen who worked all year.

If I hadn't pressed Rocko, this would not have happened. A few minutes ago, Sam had apologized for blaming me. Little did he know it really *was* my fault.

"How bad is the damage to the store?"

"The windows are blown out, and the roof took some debris. They haven't let me go inside yet. I have no idea what I'll find in there."

"Jesus, Sam, I'm sorry." He nodded, and I could tell by the slump in his shoulders that he was taking this as a statement of sympathy rather than an apology. Just as well. He got wearily to his feet.

"I'm going to go make some coffee. Once these guys let me back in, there's going to be a lot of work to do. And everyone in town will probably show up to gawk and ask questions." He gestured toward his boat again. "You want some?"

I shook my head. "No, I need to get some sleep." I knew I should probably stay and help him, but I had done enough damage for one night, and I needed to get back to Sukey.

He walked off toward his boat without saying goodbye, for which I was actually grateful. None of the policemen made any objection when I started my car and drove it off the ramp, for which I was even more grateful.

I resisted pulling into the parking place that went with my apartment and drove past it and back to the hospital in time to see dawn start to lighten the skies. Sukey had been moved to a regular room but was still asleep. I sat in the chair next to her bed and looked out the window at the five-star view of the Pacific as it reflected the subtle pinks and grays of a California sunrise.

"Mercy? Is that you?"

I blinked and tried to get my bearings. A sheet was covering my face, and I pulled it down. Sukey, her face directly opposite mine, was lying in a hospital bed a few feet away. Sometime after dawn I had crawled into the other bed in the room. I hoped Hoag wouldn't charge for it.

"Hey, kid, how are you feeling?" I asked, sitting up and trying to disentangle myself from the bedclothes.

"Like hammered shit." Sukey groped for the automatic controls of her bed, and I stood up to help her. Between the two of us, we succeeded in getting her into a sitting position. "Thanks for coming."

"No problem. It's the least I could do." I did not add, *especially since it was at least partially my fault.* I looked at my empty wrist—I hadn't taken time to put on a watch this morning. "I wonder what time it is."

Sukey moved some items around on the opposite bed stand, revealing a digital clock. "It's nine-thirty."

I groaned. "Well, at least I missed my hangover."

"Yeah, well, I didn't." Sukey rubbed her head, wincing. "Did they tell you what happened?"

"Yes. Do you remember?"

"Sort of." She grimaced. "Rocko came back right after you left, and he was really anxious to get out of Jimbo's. I don't know why."

I did. "So you went with him?"

"Yeah, we went to the Keg for a while. Then to his place. Then we…we snorted some speed." Sukey knew I didn't approve of recreational drugs but was usually frank about them when asked.

"It wasn't speed."

Her eyebrows rose in alarm. "Rocko said—"

"Sukey, it was heroin." There was silence as I watched this fact sink in. Her eyes filled with tears.

"Rocko gave me h-h-heroin?" Her lip trembled, and I handed her the box of tissues from the bed stand. "I can't believe he would do that to me." She blew her nose loudly.

"Good morning," a bright voice interrupted. "Are we feeling better?" A nurse stuck her head around the corner. "I stopped by earlier, but you were out cold, so I decided to just let you sleep," she said to me confidentially.

"Thanks. I hope there's no problem with me taking the other bed. I couldn't keep my eyes open, and I was afraid I'd wake up crippled if I fell asleep in the chair."

"It was so nice of you to stay here all night," said

Sukey. I was afraid the nurse would contradict this assumption, but her shift must have started too late for her to know I had been gone for a couple of hours. A very busy couple of hours.

"Let me see if I can track down some coffee and a doctor. We'll find out when you can get out of here."

The nurse directed me to a coffee machine and offered to page the resident on duty, who came within a few minutes. After a lecture on recreational drug use, he agreed Sukey could check herself out as long as she did not stay alone.

I surprised myself by saying she could bunk with me for a couple of days. No one—but no one—stayed at my apartment. The fact that I even had a spare room was…well, I had picked the place for its location, not its square footage. By the time we got all the paperwork handled and Sukey installed in my car, it was noon.

Sukey fell asleep about thirty seconds after lowering herself into my guest bed. I closed the door to prevent unauthorized cat visits and stepped out to pick up a few things from her apartment. On the way back, I found my feet on the route that would take me by Sam's gas dock. A few locals were still standing around, exclaiming over the damage and sipping coffee. A *Closed* sign hung on the undamaged front door, but I could hear the sounds of activity inside, so I sidled around the narrow strip of pier to the back.

I found Sam struggling to hold up a piece of plywood over a back window with one hand while hammering with the other. I put down Sukey's duffel bag and grabbed the corner he was about to drop. "Jesus, Sam, there are probably about ten people in Jimbo's who would help you for the price of a couple of drafts."

"I'm not sure I can even afford that." He hammered in the nail in three expert strokes. He was shirtless, and I could not help but admire the grace with which he performed the task. The effortlessness was probably an illusion, though, considering the sheen of sweat that coated his tanned torso. I averted my eyes.

"Have you been in touch with your insurance agent?"

"Left a message. About six messages, actually. And a few pages." He shook his head. "The law requires insurance on the pumps, but it's for liability, not loss. I'm not sure if the building insurance covers the dock and pumps. I doubt it."

He turned and leaned against the small portion of the back wall that was undamaged. He looked exhausted.

"Did you get any sleep at all?" I asked him.

"I tried, but there was too much noise. I kept picturing someone coming in through the back and picking up whatever was left. So I got Lifeguard Skip to go get me some plywood, and here I am."

I was surprised Skip hadn't stayed to help, but with no chance of beer money, he had probably sought greener pastures.

"Look, Sam, if you're not going to get any sleep, let me buy you a cup of coffee." I gestured at the coffee shop within a clear line of sight. "We can sit outside, and you can keep an eye on the place."

"Why do you want to do that?" His tone was more tired than hostile, but it still pulled on my guilt strings. If he only knew.

"Because you need it. Because I'm your neighbor. Because I'm just about to open my own business, so I can imagine what you're going through." All of which was true.

He looked at me for a moment, then nodded and put the hammer inside. The back door was propped open, attached by only the bottom hinge. He made a half-hearted attempt to close it, gave up, found his shirt hanging on a rail and put it on. Ah, well. It was probably a little too cool to be bare-chested in the shade.

I bought us each a latte and brought them outside. It was a perfect fall Saturday afternoon, and a few day-trippers were headed to the afternoon reggae spots, which were relatively quiet after the end of the tourist season. The sound of the steel band from the bar at the Newport Landing filtered down as we sipped our coffee in silence. I tried not to stare at Sam's perfect profile. I had no business looking at this man with lust in my heart when I had just destroyed his business.

"Even if the insurance comes through and I'm able to get a new tank and fix the pumps and lines," he said as if completing a thought, "there are about a hundred federal, state, county and city agencies that have to sign off before I can legally operate again."

I nodded. I knew one local business that had spent six months fighting the city over an illuminated sign. I could imagine what would happen when dealing with a product with environmental considerations. "How about the store? What's it going to take to get re-opened?"

"Not too much. Wood, paint, a little electrical repair. I already did a lot of damage to my credit cards taking the place over. I can probably manage the supplies, though, if I do all the work myself." He took another sip of the cooling latte.

"Can you make enough on the boat rentals to keep going until the gas business is up and running?" I was afraid I already knew the answer, but I had to ask.

"Maybe now, while the weather is still decent. But if I don't have everything operational before it gets too cold for pleasure boating, I'm going to be in trouble."

I reached for a straw. "Can you get a loan?"

"Not another one." He looked at me with a painful smile. "Unless you have thirty or so grand lying around you'd like to lend me."

I winced. "Nope. My business opens on Monday, and I'm leveraged to the eyeballs." I made a decision. "But I'm a pretty good hand with a paintbrush. Tell you what. I'll go stick my head in Jimbo's and promise one of the boys a few beers later if he'll keep an eye on the place for an hour. You run up to the hardware store and get whatever supplies you need to get started. I've got to run by my house and check on something, but I'll meet you back here. We have about five hours of daylight left, and I can probably borrow some spotlights from my neighbor. Could you open the boat rental business up tomorrow if we get enough done?"

During this speech, I watched the expression on

Sam's face change from surprise to disbelief then to outright astonishment. "You don't have to—"

I interrupted. "No, I don't. But I'm going to. Now hurry up and go get the stuff before I change my mind." I marched off in the direction of Jimbo's before he could argue.

It was a simple enough matter to find someone who would sit on the bench and watch the store for an hour, and Sukey was still sound asleep. I left a note beside the bed explaining where I was, changed clothes and put my cell phone in my pocket. The mirror was not my friend, so I ignored it. Within an hour, I was back at the tiny store and hard at work.

It wasn't as bad as it looked. Once we picked up all the debris and swept up the broken glass, the casualties were listed as one glass case with assorted fishing lures and other tackle, three windows, one door, the shingles from about a quarter of the roof—there was a hole all the way through in one place—and a section of the back wall. The electrical box was miraculously undamaged, but some of the wires leading out of it had been severed when the wall was knocked in. Sam decided to wait until morning, when he would have better light and a clearer head, to tackle the wiring.

Once we started working, the owners of other businesses stopped by, and we borrowed ladders, saw-horses and a few other tools. Sam had a basic kit in the shop, including some ancient but serviceable carpentry tools, but now modern power tools material-ized, along with a few hands to wield them.

By four in the afternoon, Matt had finished hosing

down his charter fishing boat and was on a ladder measuring the hole in the roof for a patch. Lifeguard Skip was holding the ladder and taking down measurements. Beth Ann, a day-shift waitress at the Landing, was sorting through the debris pile for salvageable fishing lures and other small items that only needed to be dusted off.

By six-thirty, the two guys who rented out bicycles and pedal-carts had locked up their shop and were cutting two-by-fours to reframe the door. Skip was re-attaching the hinges and had put on a new knob. Matt was nailing shingles over the tar paper he had spread earlier.

By nine, I was putting the finishing touches of paint on the new door frame, and everyone was picking up their various pails, ladders, brooms and power tools. Jeff the electrician had stopped by on his way home from work and promised to return at seven-thirty the next morning to help with the wiring fixes.

At ten, Sam locked the new latch on his back door with his shiny new key, then slowly turned to look at me. A dazed smile was on his face. "This has been the most amazing day of my life. All these strangers..." Words failed him.

"Yeah." I didn't tell him I was probably more blown away by the experience than he was. I had lived in this neighborhood for five years, and I knew everyone's face and first name. I could say hello, chat about the weather, even share the occasional beer or coffee. But I had always kept people at arm's length. Maybe I had underestimated what I had given up to keep my secret safe.

"Come on," I said. "If you don't stop by Jimbo's for a beer tonight, you're going to disappoint a lot of people."

It was a short walk, and it no longer mattered that I looked like twelve miles of bad road. So did everyone else—paint spattered, sweaty and dirty. The cold draft beer tasted like the nectar of the gods, and Mario brought over some large pizzas—on the house—from the stand across the street.

Jimbo refused to let Sam pay for the beers. "You save your money, Egghead. You'll need it."

"Did he just call me Egghead? Nobody says egghead anymore." Sam looked at Jimbo's retreating back.

"I guess you're officially a local," I said. "You have a nickname."

"I'm honored. But did it have to be *Egghead?*" We laughed together.

"Look, I have to get home. I have a sick friend staying over, and tomorrow is my last day to get things ready before my office opens." I drained the last of my beer and got to my feet.

"You never said what kind of business you're opening," said Sam.

"Oh. Well, it's—"

"Excuse me, but are you Mercy Hollings?" A deep voice interrupted, and I turned to see who was talking. It was a stranger. A very tall, very handsome stranger.

"Yes, I'm Mercy. Who's asking?"

"Allow me to introduce myself. My name is Dominic Dellarosa."

He held out a manicured hand, and I took it automatically. He was wearing a beautifully tailored suit and still managed to look comfortable surrounded by patrons in paint-splattered T-shirts.

"I was told you might be able to help me find someone."

"Who?" I felt caught in his gaze, like a hawk's prey.

"My cousin," he said in a velvety voice. "Rocko Peretti."

4

"Rocko Peretti?" I avoided wincing at the nervous squeak of my own voice. Could he have told someone what I had done to him? I stammered as I answered, even as I frantically tried to remember my exact words to him. "W-what about Rocko?"

"I understand you spoke with him last night." I swallowed, and my knees suddenly felt like rubber. "Here, in the parking lot."

I almost sagged with relief. That had been hours before I had told Rocko to get out of town.

"I saw him on my way out. He was coming back in here," I said. Sam turned around in his chair and was eyeing Dominic carefully.

"So I understand. To meet with a young lady he has been seeing. I believe her name is…Sukey." Dominic purred out the name like a big jungle cat. He was like a panther—big and sleek and powerful. And dangerous.

"Yes, she introduced us earlier." I eased back against the bar stool I had just vacated and sat down, hoping he would take my cue and do the same. He would be less scary sitting down. He didn't oblige.

"They left together, I'm told. But I have not been able to get in touch with her. She doesn't answer her phone," he said.

"How did you get her number?" I asked—too quickly.

Dominic's eyes narrowed with suspicion. He was the one asking questions, and he did not seem to relish having the tables turned.

"It was easy. Everyone seems to know her." A chill slid down my spine, and I wasn't sure why. He hadn't done anything that was even remotely threatening, but I did not want him to know where to find Sukey. Had she called anyone and told them she was staying with me? If Dominic had charmed her phone number out of someone, it would probably be just as easy for him to get that information, too.

I shrugged noncommittally. "I'm sure you have the same phone number I have. But didn't you say you wanted to talk about Rocko? What does this have to do with Sukey?"

My tone must have taken on some hostility, because he seemed to readjust his posture. Suddenly he was no longer intimidating. It was as if he had shed one persona and put on another. He seemed to shrink an inch or two, and then he sat on the bar stool opposite Sam, to whom he turned.

"Forgive me for interrupting. I'm Dominic. And you are…?"

"Sam." I couldn't feel the grip, but I could tell that unlike Rocko, Dominic wasn't engaging in any macho strength tests. Just a normal, charming handshake. He turned to me and grinned. It was actually disarming. *This is one smooth dude.*

"I have to apologize again if I seem rude. It's just that my Aunt Celeste is driving me crazy. She was expecting Rocko to take her to lunch today, but he didn't show up, and his cell phone doesn't seem to be working. So she asked me to check on him." He signaled Jimbo and ascertained the house's best Scotch, managing to do so without sounding pretentious. He offered Sam and me drinks, but reacted with grace when we both declined.

"When I couldn't reach him, either, I stopped by his place. It looks like he moved out in a hurry." He smiled again. "Rocko is kind of the family screwup, but I try to keep an eye on him for his mother's sake. He's really not a bad guy at heart." He wore the long-suffering expression of someone who had a lot of experience apologizing for his loveable-but-troublesome little brother—or cousin, in this case.

"I wish I could help you, but I really have no idea where Rocko could be." This last part was true. I had just told him to go far away, to the best of my recollection.

"It was a long shot." He drained his Scotch and stood up. "Thank you for your time…may I call you Mercy?" I nodded automatically, and he repeated it. "Mercy." He took my hand and looked deeply into my eyes. *Man, oh man.* It may have been a well-practiced move on his part, but that didn't make it any less effective. "Do you mind if I give you my card? Just in case you remember anything else."

"Sure." I was a freakin' font of eloquence. He took a gold case out of his inside breast pocket and handed me an embossed card. *Dominic Dellarosa, Purveyor of Fine Antiques.* A Corona del Mar address was listed.

I wasn't sure whether he was on the level, but I decided it might be a good idea to take out a little insurance. Just a tiny bit. Looking into his eyes, I summoned a very light press. "You should stop looking for Sukey. She won't be able to tell you anything about Rocko."

"Maybe not, Mercy. But I have to try. I promised Aunt Celeste, and I never break a promise." Nodding at Sam, he turned and walked away, leaving me stunned. *The press hadn't worked!*

I had accidentally pressed people on numerous occasions, but I had never before failed when the press was deliberate. *Just who is that guy?*

"Just who is that guy?" Sam's echo of my thoughts startled me out of my trance.

"Rocko's cousin," I said mechanically.

"Yeah, I got that. What I meant was, what is a guy like that doing around here? Doing the whole 'come with me to the Casbah' routine. It was a little over the top, don't you think?"

"I guess." I shook myself and got back to my feet. "Look, this time I really do have to go. I didn't spend any time in the office today, and my opening reception is in two nights."

"Yeah, I should go, too. I could really use a shower, but the idea of a cold one isn't too inviting." Sam looked at his dirty shirt and pants.

"A cold shower?"

"I usually shower in the shop. I don't use the shower in the boat if I don't have to. It empties the freshwater tank too fast. And with no power in the shop, the hot-water heater has had—" he looked at his watch "—eighteen hours to cool down."

"You could use mine." *Did I just say that?* Dominic's visit must have put me more off balance than I'd realized. I lived less than three blocks from Jimbo's, but the vast majority of the regulars didn't even know my exact address.

"I just might take you up on that. If you don't mind waiting while I run to my boat and grab a change of clothes." He headed for the door.

"I'll meet you outside." In five years, I had never left Jimbo's with a man. In this tiny town, it would take about fifteen minutes for everyone to know it if I did so tonight. I waited about five minutes before I strolled out the back. He was just coming around the corner under the streetlamp. I admired his lanky grace as he strolled toward me, then fell in beside me as I rounded the corner toward home.

It occurred to me that I had spent more time with Sam in the last thirty or so hours than I had with anyone in years. I should be itching with discomfort, but I wasn't. I had offered to help him with his repairs out of a sense of responsibility. *Or had I?* Would I have been so eager to help if he didn't make my thighs clench every time I got a good look at him?

It was a short walk, and I asked him to wait in the living room while I checked on my still-unnamed sick friend. Sukey was asleep but woke up when I came into the guest room and shut the door behind me.

"Whassup?" She blinked sleepily at me.

"Just got back. Sam's here—he doesn't have power at his place, so I said he could use the shower."

"Sam's here?" She almost sat up, but I eased her back down. "You invited him home with you? You never do that! Where's he going to sleep?"

"In his own bed, Sukey. He needed a hot shower, and I offered. I'm just being neighborly."

Her expression told me she wasn't buying it. "If you ask me, you should grab him before someone else does. He's a prime catch, and all the girls in town are going to be sniffing after him."

"I didn't ask," I chided, but I smiled as I did so, and smoothed her hair back. "How are you doing, kid? You scared the shit out of me, you know."

"I know, and I'm sorry." She sniffed, but it was mostly for effect. "I don't know why I keep going after guys like Rocko, but he seemed so sweet…" She sighed heavily. "I just want a boyfriend. Is that too much to ask?"

"Of course not. But you sell yourself short, Sukey. You need to wait for a guy who deserves you. You're too good for an asshole like Rocko."

"I wish I believed you. I really do."

I looked at her closely. "Do you mean that?"

"Of course."

I considered this. If she really wanted to change her self-image, and I was one-hundred percent certain she meant what she said, I could help her. But I wasn't going to do anything on the basis of the word of someone suffering from a combination of the blues and a drug hangover. If she still felt the same way tomorrow, I would do something about it. Maybe.

"Well, I'm going to give Sam some towels and let him get started. I just wanted to warn you so you wouldn't wander into the bathroom while he was naked."

"Maybe *you* ought to wander in while he's naked."

"Sukey…"

"I know, I know. I've already been to the bathroom, and I'm going back to sleep." She yawned hugely and unconvincingly. "Don't worry about disturbing me. I probably wouldn't hear it if a train ran right through the middle of the apartment."

"Right." I grinned at her, turned out the light and shut the door behind me.

Five minutes later, Sam was in the shower and I was sitting on a towel I had spread on the sofa. I was so filthy I hadn't wanted to soil the cushions. Fred appeared from wherever he had been hiding and landed on my lap with a substantial thump. As my hands found his favorite itchy spots, he purred noisily.

"So, Fred, what the hell is going on in your house? Sukey is sleeping in your bedroom, and there's a strange man in your shower." I didn't kid myself about who the apartment really belonged to. As far as Fred was concerned, I was the hired help. "Are you wondering who I am and what I've done with your mama?"

The purring increased. He didn't care how weird

it was for me to have midnight guests. More slaves for him.

But it was *extremely* weird. I tried to remember if anyone other than Fred had actually ever slept in my so-called guest room. I had put my old single bed in there when I splurged on the new queen. But the room mainly functioned as a spare closet. And as for someone other than me using my shower...

Before I could obsess further, the bathroom door opened and a cloud of steam puffed out. Followed by a damp, shirtless man wearing a perfectly faded pair of jeans. *Damn, I should have showered first.* Suddenly I was self-conscious about my own grubby appearance. Sam with shower-wet, tousled hair, and emitting the smell of soap and clean man, was more than I'd counted on. *Wow.*

I must have been gaping, because he said, "You look like you're ready to pass out. I forgot you haven't had much more sleep than I have."

I closed my mouth and tried to look like I still had an active brain cell as he continued. "I've been so wired with adrenaline and caffeine all day, I thought I would never sleep. I think the shower helped me wind down. You should try it."

I was torn between the sudden, desperate need to be clean and reluctance to let him out of my sight. If I got in the shower, he might leave. *Which I wanted him to do, right? Didn't I?* Apparently not, because I said, "Look, why don't you hang out while I shower? I've been pretty strung out all day, too, but I haven't hit the wall yet. There's beer and wine in the kitchen."

Babble, babble, babble. When had my mouth disconnected from my brain?

"Okay." That easily, Sam wandered past me toward the kitchen, wafting Zest and pheromones. I abruptly dumped Fred off my lap and fled to the bathroom.

I had a little mental chat with myself as I peeled off my paint-splattered clothes, stepped into the shower and began the process of scrubbing away the physical evidence of the last thirty-six hours. I was still trying to figure out just exactly what I wanted or expected to happen with Sam when I exited the shower, smelling at least as good as he did. Okay, so I used the Sensual bath gel I had bought at the Body Shop, and maybe I moisturized more thoroughly than usual. All of which meant *absolutely nothing.*

Wearing my bathrobe, I skittered down the hall toward the refuge of my bedroom, then tried to figure out what one put on in this situation. I had a ridiculous flash of an old Marilyn Monroe movie when she slipped into something more comfortable. I snorted at the thought of me in a marabou-trimmed peignoir. Not in this lifetime.

I finally decided on a T-shirt and loose shorts. I didn't want to look like I was trying too hard. Because I wasn't. Really.

I found Sam on the sofa with a glass of wine in one hand and a large orange cat in the other. He had opened the shades and turned off the lights, which was good. Otherwise, the apartment became a fishbowl at night. This way we weren't on display to late-night walkers on the facing boardwalk, but could see the moon and even the tiny wedge of the Pacific visible from my apartment.

"Nice cat. He licked my face."

"Yeah, he's a fickle beast." I plopped down on the opposite end of the sofa, expecting Fred to abandon Sam's lap for mine. He didn't.

"I poured you a glass." Sam nodded toward the coffee table, and I self-consciously picked up the glass of cabernet. I wasn't accustomed to being served in my own home. Hell, I wasn't accustomed to any of this. I sipped in silence, trying to think of something to say. This wasn't exactly uncomfortable. After the day we'd both had, it was nice just to do nothing.

"One more detail," I said, standing. I walked over to a wall switch and flicked it. With a whoosh, the gas flames in my fireplace ignited and curled around the fake logs. I turned and grinned. "Vintage seventies, I think. It doesn't make much heat, but it has a certain tacky charm."

"A switch-on fireplace. I love it."

Sam smiled, I returned to my seat, and we sat once again in companionable silence, watching the dancing flames. "How's your friend?" he asked. I still hadn't told Sam the sick friend's identity.

"She's better. Sleeping." I watched as Fred started to creep up Sam's chest. Lucky for him, he had put his shirt on. I'm not very good about trimming Fred's claws.

"Friendly cat."

"Careful, he's a mouth kisser." Fred had climbed up until he was level with Sam's chin. "If he starts to gaze into your eyes and turn his head, it means he's going for tongue."

"I'll keep that in mind." He took another sip of his wine, and I surreptitiously watched the firelight on his face. A sudden and amazingly strong tingle spread through my nether regions, and I stifled a gasp. I had to get him out of here before I jumped him. It had been way too long since I had sex, but that was nothing new. I usually just put it out of my mind, but right now my mind wasn't cooperating.

He must have heard my intake of breath, because he was looking at me. He gently disentangled himself from Fred, drawing a minor *prrrt* of protest, and leaned forward to put his empty wineglass on the table. His gaze deepened, and a frisson of fear shot through me. *Oh, shit, he's going to try to kiss me.* Suddenly terrified, I looked down at my own wineglass, surprised to see it was also empty. Following my gaze, Sam took the glass from my hand and set it next to his. I avoided his eyes, so I was looking down when he took both my hands in his and stood, drawing me to my feet.

Standing, he was almost a head taller than me. I found myself staring at his collarbones. His perfect, smooth collarbones, meeting under a lightly stubbled chin. With a cleft.

"Mercy." His voice drew my eyes to his, as had no doubt been his intention. "Thank you for today." *Gratitude?*

Relief flooded me—gratitude I could handle.

"It wasn't me, it was—" I was interrupted by his kiss.

Kissing Sam was like falling into deep, warm water. Too bad I hadn't had a chance to take a breath first. My knees would have buckled, except I felt oddly weightless.

He tasted wonderful—a delicious man with a cabernet tongue. As his hands came around to the small of my back and pulled me closer, every sex-starved nerve in my body awakened. I think I had an orgasm right through my denim shorts.

Suddenly I could breathe again. My eyes came open, and I broke away, gasping and taking a quick step back. Sam stared back, a sardonic smile forming on his face. His eyes fairly crackled with electricity— or was it just reflected firelight?

"Wow." Again my eloquence knew no bounds.

Sam laughed. "Wow is right. I didn't plan to do that. It just felt right." His smile turned sheepish. "I hope I didn't wear out my welcome."

"Yes. I mean, no." I took a more normal breath. "I mean, you are still welcome, but I'm not ready to… to…"

He laughed. "Neither am I. But I'm not sorry I kissed you."

"No. I mean, I'm not, either." *Shit.* My powers of speech were devolving by the moment.

Sam broke away from my gaze and picked up the two empty wineglasses from the coffee table. Without comment, he walked to the kitchen and rinsed them out in the sink. *Damned if he isn't housebroken, too.*

"I'm going to head back to the boat. You have a big day tomorrow, and you spent all day on *my* business."

He retrieved his dirty clothes from the hook in the bathroom, and opened the side door and started to walk out, then paused. "By the way, you never did tell me what kind of business you're opening."

"It's…um…well. Yes. I'm a hypnotherapist."

"No kidding! Interesting." He leaned forward and kissed me lightly again before I could react. "A hypnotherapist, huh? I'll bet you're a good one." So saying, he closed the door behind him.

He had no idea.

5

I know, I know. Here I've been ranting and raving about how I hate to use the press, and yet when I chose to open a business, it's pretty obvious I picked one that was a thinly veiled excuse to use my unique talent. Believe me, it was a decision that had taken a long time. Years.

It didn't appear my ability was ever going to go away, and I had entered, wallowed in and passed through the denial stage by the end of my teens. Self-pity had taken up my early twenties, to be gradually overtaken by an obsession with control, where I had pretty much stalled out at the ripe old age of twenty-nine.

So with thirty looming, I had experienced a small epiphany. I had this talent. Could there be a reason? I'm not particularly spiritual, but I abhor waste. I could help people, and a teeny little voice inside me told me I might just be able to help myself in the process. But since the control freak was still very much in charge, I had come up with a strict set of rules.

1. Never use the press without the subject's permission. Okay, so the subject didn't know about the press, so technically they couldn't ask me to use it. But they could say, for example, "Please help me stop smoking," or "Help me have more confidence when I ask my boss for a raise."

2. Never use the press to get an unfair advantage for personal gain. You may be asking, "Oh, so you weren't planning to charge for the hypnotherapy sessions?" Of course I was. That would be compensation for value received. I meant I couldn't use it to get the landlord to reduce the rent on my office. While wading through the endless bureaucracy of opening a new business in Newport Beach, I'd been tempted to violate this rule more than a few times, but had not succumbed.

3. Never use the press without exploring the consequences. This was the trickiest one, because it made me have to walk a thin line with rule number one. Let me explain.

   Suppose a woman who is slightly overweight comes to my office and asks for help with weight loss. What if she's actually a recovering anorexic? It might be better for me to instruct her to love her body the way it is. Or if a woman tells me she wants help to stop fighting with her husband, when the truth is she is trying to figure out how to stop making him so mad that he regularly beats the crap out of her. She needs a whole different set of directives. So rule number three sort of gives me permission to stretch the bounds of rule number one. It allows me to ask: Why?

You may already have seen the gaping hole in my business plan. It's that I'm going to be such a terrific hypnotherapist that I'm not going to get a whole lot of repeat business. So I had decided that one-problem-per-visit was a fair policy. Most people have more than one thing in their life with which they are dissatisfied. The other was that, after careful self-examination, I had also concluded it would not be a violation of rule two to end a session with a gentle press saying, "If you are happy with the results of this visit, and it will not embarrass you to discuss it with others, please recommend me to your friends." Wouldn't any good hairdresser do the same?

My soon-to-be-opened office was on the Lido Peninsula, easier to access from the mainland than Balboa and in an area still considered artsy. It was next to a municipal parking lot, which was a big plus. It was also across the street from my favorite coffeehouse, which was another. Without caffeine, I have no personality whatsoever.

I had installed Sukey at my desk, where she was happily browbeating caterers, florists, valets and other assorted people expected to arrive the following evening for the opening gala she had helped me plan.

With my desk phone in one hand and her cellular in the other, she was also calling everyone on the *Yes* RSVP list and reminding them about the event. Half listening as I went over my notes, I realized she was calling the *No* respondents as well, and asking them to reconsider. Actually, nagging would have been a better word.

She disconnected from both phones more or less simultaneously. "I've already increased the guest list by seventeen people. By the end of the day I'll bet I can get at least that many more." Ah. That explained why she had been cajoling the caterer.

"How many people are we expecting?" I looked at our surroundings.

"Sixty-seven, so far. Which reminds me…" Within a few seconds she was on the phone with the party rental place, explaining why they should give us more folding chairs at no notice and with no extra cost. And I thought *I* was good at convincing people to do things.

Sixty-seven people? My stomach took a not completely unpleasant lurch. *For the opening of a hypnotherapy office?* Well, I had wanted a successful business launch, and I guess now I was going to have one.

"Take a break after this call, would you?"

Sukey motioned she had heard me and finished sweet-talking the poor schmuck on the other end of the phone. "What's up?" she asked when she got off.

"I want to talk to you about a job."

She smiled. "You mean you want me to be your office manager? Part-time for now, then full-time later?"

I gaped, and she laughed, then continued, "I had already thought about that. I was going to tell you after the grand opening."

"Tell me? Not ask me?" Her audacity knew no bounds.

"Well…I figured you'd get around to asking eventually. I just thought a little push in the right direction wouldn't hurt. I already told the restaurant I may need to cut back on my shifts."

"You know, Sukey, if you showed half the confidence about your love life as you do when you're making a business call…"

"That's totally different."

"Not really." I sat down on the desk and faced her. "Last night you said you wished you believed me when I said you deserved better than Rocko. Do you really wish that?

She sighed. "Of course I do. You always tell me stuff like that, but when I start thinking about a guy I really like, I get all stupid and scared, and afraid he'll think I'm fat or uneducated or something."

"You are *not* fat, and you are pretty damned smart when you want to be."

"I know that with my head, just not with my heart. I really wish I had more confidence when it comes to men, Mercy. Like you."

"Like me?" I snorted. "Whatever gave you the idea I have confidence with men?"

"Well, you act like it doesn't matter what they think about you. That's probably why they all want you so much."

I was struck dumb by this statement, which Sukey took as her cue to continue.

"They're always talking about how hot you are, and how great your body is and stuff. *And* how smart you are."

The look on my face must have shown my incredulity, because Sukey started to laugh. "You really have no idea, do you? The locals around here are just waiting for someone to get into your pants. A few even thought you might be a lesbian, but I set them straight."

"Gee, thanks." I was so dumbfounded by this turn of the conversation, I almost forgot why I had started it. Almost. "Look, Sukey, the reason I brought this up is I was wondering if you would like to be my first customer. Free of charge, of course."

An enormous smile split her face, totally outshining the dark circles that still lurked under her eyes. "For real? I've been *dying* to be hypnotized! Can you make me do anything you want?"

"The idea is to make you do something *you* want."

"You mean like grow a spine where men are concerned?"

"That," I agreed. "Or something else important to you. Come on, it will be good practice for me."

"Excellent." Sukey jumped up with more energy than she had shown since Friday night. She went into my office and plopped down on the sofa. "Should I lie down? Or do you need me to look into your eyes or gaze at a swinging watch or something?" She tried various positions on the sofa, then moved to one of the comfortable chairs.

"As long as you're relaxed and able to listen to my voice, you can sit or lie down anywhere you want, including the floor." I was touched by her puppyish enthusiasm.

"I want you to do everything exactly the way you would do it with a real customer." She went back to the sofa and lay down with her hands folded on her chest. "Just pretend you never met me before." She closed her eyes.

"When someone comes for the first time, I plan to start by telling them what to expect."

"Okay."

"I'm going to start by helping you reach a state where you feel very relaxed and safe. Then I am going to ask you a few questions about why you are here today and what you hope we will accomplish."

Sukey opened her eyes and looked at me. "What if they already told you? Like they just came to quit smoking or something?"

"Even if you have already told me your reason for being here, I need to ask you again after you're in the relaxed state, so I'm one hundred percent certain about your needs. We'll have a very brief interview to make sure you're happy with your decision to be here and I understand exactly what you want."

"Oh, that's a good policy." Satisfied, Sukey closed her eyes and settled more deeply into the sofa.

"Once we conclude the interview, I'll deepen your hypnotic state, and then I'll make the suggestions that will enable you to reach the goal we discussed. When I believe the suggestions have been successful, I'll bring you back to a fully alert state, doing so in a manner that will make you feel rested and content. Do you understand everything I've explained?"

"Yes. Can we start now?"

"Yes, if you're ready."

"I'm ready."

"Okay, let's begin."

What I had described to Sukey was the normal cycle of a hypnotherapy session as taught at the West Coast Institute for Healing Arts and Sciences. After spending almost a year waiting on tables nights, studying during my breaks and living on Top Ramen and coffee, I had been astonished to learn that California doesn't require hypnotherapists to be licensed. To paint someone's toenails, you have to be certified by the California State Board of Barbering and Cosmetology. To poke around in their psyche, you only need the balls to hang out a sign.

To be fair, most of those practicing hypnotherapy in the state go to a legitimate school to learn how, and I had been to the best. My diploma hung on a frame over the desk in the other room. I had originally gone to the school thinking I would have to struggle to keep an open mind, but I had been happily surprised by the classes and the earnestness of both instructors and students. If I did not exactly employ their techniques, I had modeled my structure and a great deal of my professional ethics on their training.

"Let yourself relax completely," I began, with only the barest trace of a press. "It feels good to let all the tension leave your muscles, doesn't it?"

"Yes." Sukey's voice was already taking on the dreamlike quality of the entranced. The technique of following an instruction with a validating question was straight from the institute's basic training class.

"Tell me what you want to change about your life."

"I want a boyfriend." No hesitation.

"You are a good person, and you deserve a boyfriend." Light press. "You believe you are a good person, don't you?"

"Yes."

"You are a good person who deserves to be treated well, and to have friends and loved ones who care about you. You know this is true, don't you?"

"Yes."

I was surprised not by her answer, but by how gratified I was to receive it. I was using my talent, and I was making someone happy. I was doing something good. I could get used to this.

"You don't have any reason to allow a man to treat you badly or without respect, do you?"

"No." Her brow furrowed slightly, and I wondered if she was remembering Rocko. I decided I might as well put that particular demon to rest.

"You don't have any strong feelings about Rocko, and you don't care if you never see him again. He gave you heroin, and you don't want to be with a man who treats you that way." I swallowed, realizing I was stretching the limits of what Sukey had agreed to. "Are you over feeling bad about Rocko?"

"Yes."

"You are not worried because you don't have a

boyfriend right now. You know you can wait until the right person comes along, and you are happy in the meantime. Are you happy now, Sukey?"

"Yes!" Her voice was like that of a joyful child.

I smiled. "You are glad we had this session. You feel confident about yourself. You know you are attractive and that others are attracted to you. You are relaxed and happy. Do you feel good?"

"Yes, I feel great."

"Okay, Sukey. That's all for today. We're done now."

Her eyes blinked open. "That's it?" She looked around. "I thought I wouldn't remember anything, but I think I remember everything. Sort of."

"People usually remember what takes place in a hypnotic trance," I told her. "That 'you will remember nothing after I count to three' crap just happens in the movies."

"I remember you told me to feel happy. And I do! I feel really happy." She smiled. "How long until it wears off?"

"Oh, not for quite a while." I grinned. "Come on, let's grab some dim sum. I'm famished."

"Can we have it delivered? I have some more phone calls to make." She stood up and returned to the desk. "Which reminds me—did you invite Sam to the opening?"

"Sam? I don't think he's the gala-opening type." I pretended to look through some magazines on top of the filing cabinet.

"Tell me again why he left last night." Despite her

assurances about trains in the living room, Sukey had been wide awake when Sam left, and had come out to investigate when she heard the door close.

"Because it was midnight, he had been up for twenty hours after four hours of sleep, and also because I did not invite him to stay." *But I might have if he had kissed me again.* "We hardly know each other."

"You spent all day yesterday together. *And* you saw him Friday night."

"For fifteen minutes and one tequila shot." When I was pressing her to stop worrying about getting a boyfriend, I should have ordered her not to worry about finding one for me, either. "We haven't had what you could call a date or anything."

"If you invite him to the gala, then that would be a date." She was digging in her wallet and pulled out a rumpled card with a flourish. "Ta-da! I just happen to have his business card right here. Butchie was handing them out at his retirement party. I'm sure Sam's at the store right now—it's perfect weather for sailboat rentals."

I groaned, but took the card. *Balboa Boat Rentals— Sam Falls, Owner.* "Okay, you win. You call the Ho Sum Bistro, and I'll call Sam."

As Sukey happily ordered various dumplings and the world's best Chinese chicken salad, I stared at my cell phone. I had never asked a man out in my life. Not to a movie. Not to a party. Hell, I had never even *had* a party. I heard Sukey wrapping up her call and knew I had better start dialing before she hung up.

The phone rang five times, and I was about to hang

up when the answering machine switched on. "This is Sam. I'm helping other customers right now, but leave a number and I'll call right back. Or, for our hours and rental prices, press two now." A tone told me it was time to speak.

"Hi, Sam, it's Mercy. Listen, I, uh…told you my hypnotherapy office is opening tomorrow. Right. Well, there's a little…well, I guess it's not so little…" I paused, wondering what I should call it. Reception? Event? The pause went on too long, and the machine ended the call.

"Shit!" I looked at the phone in my hand. Seeing Sukey's inquisitive glance, I explained. "The machine cut me off."

"So call back." Simple. Except I hadn't been expecting a machine and had sounded like a babbling idiot. Mercy Hollings, paragon of self-control. What had Sukey said? *You act like it doesn't matter what they think about you. That's probably why they all want you so much.* Right. Little did she know I was standing here worrying about the impression I had made on a freaking answering machine.

It was unavoidable, so I hit Redial. This time I was ready for the beep—Sam must be helping someone rig up a sailboat or something—and did a little better. "Hi, it's me again. I got cut off before. I'm having an opening reception at my new office tomorrow night at six, and I thought you might like to come. It's on Thirty-first Street, sort of across from Alta Coffee. Just look for the balloons." I paused, wondering how to sign off, and again the machine made the decision for me. I had been planning to say something like *hope to see you,* but it would have been too Sukey-like to call a third time for something so redundant. It would have to do.

I turned to Sukey. "Satisfied?"

She nodded vigorously. "Now, you have a date. What are you going to wear?"

I shrugged. "I hadn't really thought about it. Whatever I wear to the office. Black pants and my beige blazer, probably." I needed to give a little thought to my wardrobe if I was going to be keeping regular office hours.

"No way! What about the pictures?"

"Pictures?" I hadn't budgeted for a photographer—not that I recalled.

"For the paper. I've got the *Register,* the *Orange County Business Journal* and *OC Weekly* coming."

"What? For a hypnotherapy office opening?" My head spun. This was getting out of control.

"Hey, I give good phone."

I shook my head. "You should forget being my office manager, Sukey. You have a promising career in publicity."

"Do you really think so? Maybe I could start up my own business on the side. That office on the other side of the courtyard is going to be available in a few months."

Jesus, that confidence suggestion might backfire. Or not. With a little experience, Sukey would make one hell of a publicist.

"But back on the subject of clothes, what have you

got that's a little more glamorous?" She wasn't going to let it drop.

Glamorous? I mentally searched my closet. I had spent my adult life trying *not* to be noticed. My closet looked like a black hole—literally. Black jeans, black slacks, black T-shirts. I grasped at a straw. "I have a black dress."

"The one you wore to Jennie's funeral?" I nodded, and she grimaced. "It's fine for funerals, but it has no shape." She looked at her watch. "Look, the stores at Fashion Island are open for four more hours. As soon as we eat, you run over there and find something." She narrowed her eyes. "Can I trust you to go without me? You won't buy something that makes you look like a prison matron, will you?"

"I'm not sure what to look for," I protested.

"I know! Go to Nordstrom and ask for Gina. She's Matt's sister. You know Matt?"

I nodded.

"I think she works Sunday. I'll just call her and tell her you're coming. What size are you?"

"Sukey, I can't afford anything at Nordstrom. My credit cards are still screaming in agony from the reception expenses."

"Are they maxed?"

"No, but…" She was already dialing.

"Look, Gina will find something fabulous *and* on sale. And by the time the bill comes, you'll have a zillion paying customers…. Hello, can I speak to Gina in better sportswear? Thanks." She turned to me. "Mercy, you are the most gorgeous woman I know, and you never show it off. If I had your tits... No, Gina, not *your* tits." Sukey laughed.

"It's Sukey. Listen, my friend is having this big gala opening tomorrow night and has nothing to wear. I think she's a size ten." She looked at me questioningly, and I nodded. "Yeah, she'll be there in about an hour. Try to talk her into a dress—she has *killer* legs. And don't let her leave without shoes, okay? Okay. Love ya! Bye." She hung up the phone, a smug smile on her face.

"There. You're going to have a hot date and an even hotter outfit." She frowned suddenly. "Now, what am *I* going to wear?"

The door buzzed, signaling the arrival of lunch. Suddenly I was not hungry. My stomach roiled.

Tomorrow would be my first day of business, my first party, my first date with Sam—assuming he showed up—and my first time in the newspapers. Plural. What the hell was I getting myself into?

6

Flash. Judging by the white spots blinding me, I had at least managed not to blink during the picture this time. I wasn't getting any better at smiling, though. I wished they would just take pictures of the guests and leave me alone.

Although I had to admit I didn't look too bad. The Diane von Furstenberg blood-red wrap dress fit me like a glove. I don't think I'd *ever* worn red before, unless I was too young to remember.

When I had said goodbye to my last customer at five-thirty, I had found François waiting in my office. He was a semi-retired Hollywood makeup man who owned a chic salon in Corona del Mar. He worked one or two days a week and charged outrageous prices.

"François, you're early for the party."

"I'm not here for the party. Well, not *just* for the party." He held up an industrial-size tackle box and a duffel bag. "Sukey told me you bought a red dress but don't even own a blow dryer or any decent makeup. I could not allow this to happen."

I wondered what Sukey had promised to get him

here but had no opportunity to argue as he swept me back into the hypnotherapy room and went to work.

"I've wanted to do this for years," he said, taking my hair out of the ponytail I had thought so tidy and professional.

I seldom visited salons, as my all-one-length straight hair requires little maintenance and I'm too uncomfortable being touched by strangers to permit a manicure or a facial. Sukey was right that my makeup supply was pathetic. I had never learned how to use the stuff and was at a complete loss about what to buy on the rare occasions when I found myself in the cosmetics aisle at the local pharmacy.

François had my hair up in enormous hot rollers, "just for volume," faster than I could repeat the phrase. I watched, more mesmerized than my clients, as he removed a series of mysterious items from the case. He took out what looked like a regular painter's palette and started spreading various flesh-toned substances on it. He unrolled a cloth package containing brushes, chose one carefully and began painting my face.

"You have fabulous cheekbones. Are you part Native American?"

"I'm not sure," I said truthfully. "I never knew my parents."

"I didn't know that." Sukey's voice came from the doorway. "Why didn't you ever mention that before?"

"It didn't come up."

Sukey came around to stand in front of me, and she looked terrific, if a little over-accessorized. I may not know about fashion, but some of Sukey's outfits make me a little dizzy. At least she knew enough about makeup not to require assistance. She watched François work for a few minutes, then nodded her approval. "You're going to look *unbelievable*. François, are you going to be done soon? Guests should start arriving in fifteen minutes."

"Perfection takes time," he said. "It's okay if she makes an entrance. You never want to be the first one at your own party."

"I'll remember that," I said, and he remonstrated that I must stop moving my lips until he was done. Chastised, I shut up.

"Well, clean up when you're done. The refreshments are all set up in the courtyard, and the brochures are in the front office. But people are going to want to see this room, too, before the night is over." Sukey peeked in the closet, sighing with relief when she found my new dress, underwear and shoes in there. My sensible cotton bras and panties would *not* have worked with the clingy dress. "Did you remember to buy pantyhose?"

"Gina says I don't need hose."

Sukey sighed. "No, I guess you don't. You've got that smooth, hairless skin thing going on. I should be so lucky." She borrowed a hand mirror out of François' duffel bag and examined her teeth to make sure she didn't have lipstick on them, as she so often did. "Okay, then I'm going to go downstairs and greet anyone who shows up. Call me if you need anything." She left, leaving me to fend for myself under François' ministrations.

An hour and a half later, I had to admit I was glad I had submitted to the mini-makeover Sukey and François had engineered. I have never liked having my picture taken, but if there was no way to avoid it, I felt better knowing professionals had picked my outfit and done my makeup. It would take more than a makeover, however, to teach me to smile every time someone aimed a camera at me. *Flash.* Damn, I was just getting my eyesight back from the last one.

Someone grabbed my arm and dragged me up the outside stairway for privacy, and I was relieved to see it was Sukey. "You are not going to believe this," she whispered, turning me to look at something. "But get a load of your *date!*"

Blinking, I tried to see clearly through the spots left by the most recent round of flashes. And then I saw him.

"Wow," I breathed, and Sukey giggled.

"Yeah, he cleans up nice, doesn't he?"

Nice was hardly the word for it. I didn't know enough about fabrics or brands to put a name to what he was wearing, but it looked like it had grown on him. It was some kind of lightweight suit in a pale beige, and his blue shirt, open at the neck to show his tanned skin, was exactly the color of his eyes. As he negotiated the crowd that filled the courtyard to reach the bar, every woman—and a few of the men—turned to stare at him.

Before he reached the bar, he looked up and caught sight of Sukey and me on the outdoor landing between the first floor and my office. He did a double take, then a smile lit his face. I felt as if I had been hit in the chest by a hard blow. He changed his route, grabbing two glasses of champagne off a tray on his way to the stairs. I swallowed convulsively as he came up to the landing and handed me a glass.

"You look…amazing," he said, and I could see his eyes move over my face and body. At a stifled giggle from Sukey, he looked at her and hastily added, "You both do."

Sukey laughed outright. "I know I'm not the belle of the ball tonight, but that's okay. I made her buy the dress. Doesn't she look *killer?*"

"She does at that," said Sam, handing each of us a flute of champagne. "That color is perfect for you."

"Thanks. You look pretty killer yourself." I sipped the champagne with what I hoped was a nonchalant expression. I managed not to inhale it and choke, so I figured I was doing pretty well in the finesse department.

"Who are all these people?" Sam looked over the crowd in the courtyard below, eating canapés and checking out one another's clothes.

"I have no idea," I said.

"Mercy, I've introduced you to at least half of them." Sukey sighed in exasperation. "Haven't you been paying attention?"

"I've been trying, but it's all becoming a blur." I eyed her with suspicion. "How do *you* know all of them, anyway?"

"I don't," she said. "Or at least not all of them. I mostly got their names from the society page. Charity events and stuff. I just called their offices or social secretaries or whatever." She shrugged, as if anyone could have rounded up the local A-list with a little gumption. "I know a few of them from the restaurant, of course, and I dropped their names like crazy."

"Hey, there's someone I know." I pointed to a bright pinkish-red head bobbing in the crowd. "Is that Hilda?"

Sukey nodded.

Hilda was our local merry widow. She had done what so many poor girls dream of and few achieve—she had married a ridiculously rich man who had obligingly developed a terminal illness and died within eighteen months of the wedding. "Smiling Sal" Bennington had owned a few dozen automobile agencies around the state and had been famous for his hokey commercials. To hear Hilda talk, the dearly departed Sal should have been canonized for sainthood, and his untimely death had ended one of the world's great romances. According to most others, their tempestuous marriage would likely have ended in an ugly divorce if Sal hadn't gotten sick.

According to Hilda, Sal had told her that she should have a good time with his money once he was gone. She had taken him at his word, or at least tried to. She was rumored to be sixty or so, but a considerable investment in cosmetic surgery had at least delayed some of time's ravages. She typically had a younger man on her arm but appeared to be dateless tonight.

"Mercy!" She waved at me. I went down the stairs to meet her, amused as she looked Sam up and down unabashedly. "So, you're finally open. I need an appointment right away. Tomorrow, if possible."

"You'll have to talk to Sukey. She's in charge of my schedule." I didn't precisely like Hilda, but I didn't have anything against her, either. Until she had too much to drink, which did not appear to be the case tonight.

"Can't you work me in one way or the other? I was thinking two or so." I was about to explain that I planned to keep a strict schedule in fairness to all my customers when Sukey, who had come down the stairs behind me, smoothly stepped in and took her arm.

"I'm pretty sure I still have something open, Hilda. Why don't we go up and check? I really want to get your opinion about the hypnotherapy room. You have such an eye for decorating."

This was a shameless lie, or at least I hoped so. Sukey had once dragged me to a party at Hilda's ostentatious, overdone house. Yuck.

I was pleased that Sukey had rescued me from Hilda, but I now felt adrift in a sea of unfamiliar faces. Everyone seemed to know who I was, and they all had at least one question. How long had I been practicing hypnosis? How much would I charge? Could I help with a daughter's eating disorder? A son's lack of enthusiasm about getting into college? I tried to answer each question thoughtfully and honestly, but I was starting to feel claustrophobic. I was about to bolt when I felt Sam's light grip on my arm.

"You okay?" he asked when there was a momentary break in the revolving interrogation. I shook my head.

"I'm not used to all this…interaction." He looked at me questioningly. "I mean, I know I'll have to interact with my customers, but that'll be one at a time." *And under my control,* I added silently. "But first I have to *get* some customers, if I'm going to make a success of this."

"I am sure your new venture will be a great success," said a familiar smooth voice, and I shivered as an icy sensation went down my spine. I also felt Sam stiffen, and I turned to see Rocko's cousin, Dominic.

He was, if possible, more handsome than the last time I had seen him. His suit was so black that it seemed to absorb the light around him, and the courtyard's fairy lights illuminated the sculpted features so that everything surrounding him seemed dim by comparison. His eyes...

Hey, I'm the one who hypnotizes people here. I pulled myself away from his gaze with an effort. "I'm surprised to see you here. You didn't mention coming when we met."

"I didn't know about it then. A friend invited me just today, although she seems to have disappeared at the moment."

I expected him to scan the crowd, but he kept that disconcerting stare directly on me. I remembered with relief that I was not alone.

"You remember Sam," I said, stepping back so that Sam's right hand was free. He took his cue and held it out to Dominic.

"Of course. It's good to see you again." Dominic smiled, and I wondered if teeth could be that white naturally. I doubted it. I looked at the two men standing together. They made an amazing study in contrasts.

Both men were tall, athletically built and drop-dead

gorgeous. There the similarity ended. Sam was all cool ocean breezes and sun on the water. Dominic was velvety city moonlight and barely restrained power. Standing this close to both of them at the same time was like trying to tread water in a whirlpool— the force of it threatened to spin me around.

"There you are, Dom." Hilda's strident voice sounded from the stairs, and she and Sukey came down to join us. Hilda grabbed Dominic's arm possessively. "I guess you've met Mercy."

"But not this charming lady," he said, holding a hand out for Sukey's. Panic jolted through me. I almost pressed and shouted *freeze* before I caught myself, and then I felt Sam's hand on my arm. He must have picked up on my agitation, even if he didn't know the reason for it.

"I'm Sukey," came out of the "charming lady's" mouth before I could figure out how to avert disaster. I saw Dominic's perfectly arched eyebrows lift in surprise.

"Not Rocko's Sukey," he said, pausing with her hand halfway to his lips.

"I know Rocko, if that's what you mean." She smiled pleasantly, and Dominic recovered quickly enough to finish kissing her hand.

"Aren't you his girlfriend?" Dominic looked puzzled.

"No. I used to see him, but not anymore. He gave me heroin without telling me, and I don't want to be with a man who treats me that way. I deserve to be treated better." She said this in much the same tone as she would have used to explain where she got her hair cut, or to give directions to the nearest gas station.

Sam and Hilda both gasped, and I groaned inwardly. Dominic looked at a complete loss for words, which I had a feeling was an unusual state of affairs for him. Again, it did not take long for him to regain his balance.

"Can you tell me when you saw him last? I've been trying to find him for several days."

"I haven't heard from him since he dumped me at the emergency room after I passed out from the heroin. I mean, I guess it was him who dropped me off. I don't really remember anything after he gave me the drugs." She turned and smiled brilliantly at the four of us. "Would anyone like some more champagne? I'm going to go check on the caterers."

"I'll have some," said Hilda. The rest of us just stared as Sukey walked away.

Hilda rounded on Dominic. "Who is this Rocko person? Why would you be looking for someone who gives heroin to nice young girls without their permission?" she demanded.

"Would you excuse us for a moment?" he asked smoothly. Sam and I nodded, and Dominic guided the indignant Hilda away, quietly speaking into her ear. I guessed he was giving her the story about Aunt Celeste and his troublesome-but-not-really-a-bad-kid cousin. I saw him smoothly grab a glass of champagne from a passing waitress's tray and figured he would have Hilda believing everything he said within about three minutes.

I turned to Sam, who was eyeing me speculatively. "So Sukey's the sick friend who was staying at your house, which means you knew about Rocko giving her heroin when Dominic came into the bar looking for him." No fool he.

"Well, er, yes." Defensive under his scrutiny, I added, "I figured what happened between her and Rocko was private, and I didn't have any business telling this guy anything about it. I don't know who he is, or even if Rocko is really his cousin."

Sam shrugged. "Does it matter? You don't have any reason to protect Rocko, do you?"

"No. But I didn't want anyone bothering Sukey until she felt better."

"She seems to be okay now." He grinned. "You could have knocked me over with a feather when she came out and told Dominic about the heroin, right in front of all of us."

"Yeah, she's much better." Looking at his grin, I finally saw the humor in the situation and choked back a small laugh. *If only he knew how much better.* Then I sobered—Dominic wasn't stupid, either. As soon as he got Hilda calmed down, he was going to realize Sukey would have told me about the heroin incident, as well, even if he didn't know she'd been staying at my apartment. And that I hadn't called him to tell him about it. Oh well, I didn't owe him an explanation.

While I was considering this, another bevy of well-wishers enveloped me, and began peppering me with personal and professional questions. I forgot all about Dominic—almost—and was soon back to wishing the endless evening would wind down and all these people would go home.

When the crowd finally thinned, Sam told me he had to leave. "I sleep over at my father's house Sunday through Thursday. He has a caregiver on the weekends, but tonight's one of his nights off. Butchie stopped by this afternoon, but he's probably gone now, and I don't like to leave Dad alone too long."

I told him I understood, thanked him for coming and surprised myself by hugging him. If he hadn't been there that evening, I didn't know how I would have gotten through it.

I sat down on the steps and took off my high-heeled sandals. They were more comfortable than I had expected—Gina had explained that fit was more important than heel height when determining comfort—but I wasn't used to standing on my toes, and my feet were screaming. Sukey was saying goodbye to the last guests and making sure the caterers were doing a good job cleaning up and stacking chairs and tables. The party rental company would collect them in the morning.

The fairy lights in the courtyard went out, and I stayed where I was, enjoying the stillness. All in all, the evening had gone pretty well.

"Still here?" Dominic's voice startled me so much that I knocked my shoes off the stairs and into the flower bed underneath. He chuckled and retrieved them for me.

"Where's Hilda?" I asked, surprised my voice worked. Suddenly my throat felt very dry. Why did this guy make me so jumpy? Guilt over Rocko's sudden departure? It certainly felt like more than that.

"I took her home. I think she'd had a little too much champagne."

I realized he was going to sit next to me on the step, and I rapidly moved over to give him as much room as possible.

"I, on the other hand, hardly had a sip. I was too busy keeping an eye on her all night. She's a dear lady, but she really needs a keeper."

"Applying for the job?" I winced at the acid in my tone, but his answering laugh held no malice.

"No, I'm afraid I would make a very bad gigolo. I'm not very good at playing to the whims of others." He stretched like a big jungle cat. "Where's Sam? Not about to pop out of the bushes and demand what I'm doing with his woman, is he?"

I considered lying for a split second but was more annoyed at being referred to as someone else's possession than I was afraid to be alone with Dominic. "He had to go home. And I'm not *his* anything."

"I am greatly relieved to hear it."

He turned to regard me, and the flickering glint from the streetlight filtered through to the courtyard and caught his eyes. They seemed to glitter, and I shuddered. I couldn't tell if it was revulsion or attraction. I could smell his cologne—something dark and sensual and expensive. Like him.

"You didn't appear to be drinking, either. I suppose you were too busy with your guests. I was hoping to invite you to have a drink with me. And Sam, too, of course."

"You drove all the way back here from Hilda's to offer me a drink?" I didn't try to hide my sarcasm.

"Not entirely, and it really wasn't very far out of my way." His voice was hypnotic. "The Arches has a fine selection of cognacs. Won't you consider joining me for one?"

I'm not sure why I didn't refuse instantly. Maybe it was because I felt I had unfinished business with this man. Not the Rocko thing, or at least not entirely. But I had pressed him the other night, and nothing had happened. Admittedly, it had been a very light press, nothing like the slam I had given Rocko. But there should have been *some* response.

Or it could have been that I loved the Arches, a restaurant where famous people had been going for privacy since it opened in 1922. From the outside, it looked singularly uninviting. Inside, the ancient tuxedoed waiters served melt-in-your-mouth steaks and classic Caesar salads with the practiced ease acquired by decades of repetition. Not that I often sat in the dining room—I couldn't justify the exorbitant prices to dine alone—but I occasionally stopped in to have a quiet drink in the old-fashioned bar and watched the elegant dance of perfect service, provided without fanfare.

Still, I hesitated. "I have to get Sukey home. She's still recovering from the heroin overdose your cousin gave her." No point beating around the bush.

"She seems in remarkably good spirits to me." Dominic looked out to the curb, where Sukey was laughing with the caterers as they loaded the last of their chafing dishes and trays into the van. "I have to admit, I was a little taken aback when I met her. From what Rocko had told me, I expected her to be less…well, more concerned about not having heard from him."

"She was. Then she realized that someone who really cared about her wouldn't treat her that way." I saw him wince and liked him a little more for having the decency to be embarrassed over his cousin's behavior.

"I had no idea Rocko had degenerated so far. If it wasn't for Aunt Celeste, I would probably have given up on him years ago." He stood. "In fact, I think that I owe your friend an apology. For the family's sake."

The caterer's van had driven off, and Sukey was walking back toward us, yawning.

"I'm pooped," she said, then checked herself when she saw Dominic. "Oh! I thought you were alone."

"I came back to speak with you…both of you." He took Sukey's hand, and her eyes grew wide but showed no apprehension. "When I asked you about Rocko earlier, I didn't tell you that he was my cousin. When I learned what he had done…" He shook his head sadly. "I am so very, very sorry about what my cousin did to you. It was inexcusable, and on behalf of my family, I must offer you our most heartfelt apologies."

"Uh…okay." Sukey withdrew her hand, looking confused. "It wasn't your fault. I never should have trusted him in the first place. I know that now."

Dominic nodded solemnly. "You are absolutely right. When Rocko was a kid, he used to follow me around. I mostly ignored him and usually managed to get away from him. He wasn't the brightest bulb on the Christmas tree."

The silly expression sounded incongruous in his cultured tones, but Sukey smiled in response. I realized he was playing to his audience—using less sophisticated terms when talking to a less sophisticated listener. Very, very smooth.

"Maybe if I had taken him in hand, taught him how to get along, how to respect people…" He trailed off. "In any case, I feel responsible. I promise you, I will find some way to make it up to you."

"You don't have to do that," she said, but I could see she was pleased. "I'm fine now." She yawned hugely. "But when I get home, I'm going to sleep for about twenty hours."

"I have just invited Mercy for a drink at the Arches. Perhaps you would like to join us?" He spoke as if I had already accepted his invitation, which I most assuredly had not.

"God, no. I would fall asleep on the bar." She looked at me. "You go, though. I'll lock up and drop your car at your place."

I started to protest, and she said, "No, I know you love the Arches. Just don't stay out too late. With all the people that wanted appointments, I have your calendar one hundred percent booked for tomorrow."

I looked at Dominic, who was smiling like the cat

who had just licked up the last of the cream. Or maybe the leopard who had snarfed down the tastiest bits of the gazelle. "Let me get my jacket," I said. It had my keys and my cell phone. I refused to carry a purse, which Sukey considered aberrant behavior. Where would I keep my lipstick, for God's sake?

Which reminded me to check my appearance in the office mirror. I found the red tube that François had used on my lips in the desk drawer and cautiously re-applied it. I've never been good at coloring inside the lines, but I managed to get it where it was supposed to be. I stuck the lipstick in a jacket pocket, locked the office door, removed the car keys from the ring and gave them to Sukey. She yawned and headed down the back stairs, and I went on to meet Dominic.

He drove a black Jaguar. Of course. What else?

7

"I want to be young again," said Hilda in the mellow tones of a trance. I sighed. She had come in saying she wanted help sticking to her diet, but we had been in the interview portion of the session for almost twenty minutes, and every question just revealed another layer in a writhing mess of resentments, insecurities and self-indulgence. I didn't know where to start, and technically I only had permission to address the diet-and-cheating issue. Well, one thing at a time. She could afford as many appointments as it took. I switched subjects.

"When do you cheat on your diet?" I asked.

"When I drink," she replied. Ah, here was something I could work with.

"Are you allowed to have alcohol on your diet?"

"Yes."

"How much?"

"One drink per day." I nodded. I figured she had already violated that rule by halfway through brunch.

"Do you eat foods that aren't on your diet when you have been drinking?" I probed.

"Yes." Okay, I had somewhere to start.

"Hilda, you no longer feel like drinking alcoholic beverages. They do not appeal to you. You would rather have a club soda or water. When you know you have been eating in a healthy way, you feel good about yourself. You look in the mirror and like what you see. You love your body and only want to give it healthy things. Do you love your body?"

"Yes."

I sighed with relief. If I had started this a few years earlier, I could have saved her a few hundred grand in tucks, lifts and implants, but it was better late than never.

"You feel very relaxed and happy now, and you are glad we had this session. Do you feel good?"

"Yes."

I removed an index card from my jacket pocket and read aloud the closing line I had not yet memorized, automatically reducing the level of the press to what I thought of as the extra-light setting.

"If you are happy with the results of this session, and you feel comfortable discussing it with others, you will recommend my services to others when it seems appropriate. Will you do that for me?"

"Yes."

"Okay, Hilda, that's all for today. We're done."

She blinked. "Already? I paid for a half hour." To be accurate, she hadn't paid for anything yet, but it was nice to see I hadn't altered her personality with my suggestion.

"My sessions are twenty-five minutes long, in order to give me time to prepare for the next customer." I peeked out into the office, where Sukey sat at the desk, typing busily on my computer. I wondered what she was working on.

"Actually, if you have a moment, Hilda, there is something I wanted to ask you about." She looked at me curiously, and I went on. "It's about Dominic. How do you know him?"

"Dom?" She shrugged. "Oh, just from around, you know."

I didn't know. "Around where?"

She shrugged again. "The Bay Club, the Villa Nova. The John Wayne Tennis Club. You know. Around."

This wasn't helpful. She had just named three places where Newport Beach's more affluent citizens—and there were plenty—hung out. Two were private clubs, and I had never been inside. The Villa Nova was an Italian restaurant across from the Arches, famous for its bay view and piano bar. While the food was good, I had never joined the boisterous crowd at the piano bar, singing old show tunes and the occasional aria.

"Why do you want to know?" She looked at me suspiciously. Despite the fact that Dom was young enough to be her son, she obviously still harbored hopes.

"Just curious."

My next appointment walked in the door, out of breath from the stairs. I pegged him, correctly as it turned out, as a quit-smoking case. I really needed to write a nice thank-you letter to William Morris—they were going to pay my rent this month.

At Sukey's gesture, Hilda took the seat next to Sukey's desk and took out her checkbook, then turned back to me. "I saw him at the Villa Nova Sunday night, and I mentioned I was going to your opening. He said he was very interested in hypnotherapy, so I invited him. Did he make an appointment?"

"No," I answered truthfully, although I would have considered it confidential if he had.

Hilda's cell phone rang—"Fly Me to the Moon," I noticed—and she answered it. "Yes, Gloria? Lunch? Certainly, but not there… No, we always just end up drinking all afternoon… I know, but I'm not in the mood. Why don't we go shopping instead?… What?… Yes, that would be perfect. See you there. Twenty minutes." She hung up.

Smiling to myself, I gestured my waiting customer into the other room.

After Hilda's complexities, the middle-aged family man with little to trouble him other than tobacco was a slam dunk. We finished in well under the appointed half hour, and I had a few minutes to reflect on last night's strange interlude with Dominic.

I had wanted to dislike him, but he made it difficult. He was charming, handsome, considerate and had impeccable timing. Every time the conversation veered into uncomfortable waters, he changed directions.

"I should have guessed you were a hypnotherapist when I met you," he had said, as we savored the aroma of Martell Classique in the Arches' beautiful balloon snifters.

"Why is that?" Had he sensed something when I tried to press him?

"You seem very self-contained. When you do not

reveal a lot about yourself, it encourages others to do so. Mother Nature abhors a vacuum, and so does human nature."

A sensation of relief flooded me, and I realized this was a normal pattern when I was around Dominic. Discomfort followed by relief. It kept me off balance but interested. I sensed this was a dance at which he was a master.

"You knew where Sukey was when we spoke last Friday, did you not?"

Yep, back to discomfort. Although the dance wasn't so bad, now that I was starting to recognize the steps.

"I never said otherwise."

"No, you did not." He smiled. "I suppose discretion with other people's business is also an essential trait in your profession."

Ah, yes, relief. I sipped my cognac, trying to discern the elegant hints of old wood and spice the bartender had promised. It was good, whatever it was.

"Why did you invite me here tonight, Dominic?" Let's see how he felt about someone else leading the dance.

"You are an attractive woman. And that dress…" He let his eyes trail down to my cleavage and back up, lingering on my lips before returning to my eyes. "Have you considered I might just be hitting on you?"

"No."

This time his laugh was genuine. "Remind me not to play poker with you." He raised his glass to me before sipping, as if conceding a point. "All right, the reason I invited you is, inasmuch as you did not tell me you knew where to find the charming Ms. Keystone, I thought you may also have held back something about Rocko."

"I've already told you, I don't know where he is."

"And I believe you." His gaze grew more pointed. "But you know *something,* and for reasons of your own you are choosing not to tell me."

This was so undeniably true that I decided to take drastic measures. After all, I had been doing it all day and was starting to feel confident about my control again.

"Tell me why you're *really* looking for Rocko." This time, I used a much firmer press.

Instead of giving the instantaneous answer I had come to expect when using my ability, Dominic stared at me for a long moment before replying. "What makes you think the reasons I have given you are not the truth?"

I put my brandy snifter down abruptly, making a loud sound on the polished bar top. The bartender glanced our way but subsided when he saw nearly full drinks and no signals for service.

Nothing. Dominic had no reaction to my press whatsoever. If he was even aware I was doing something to him, there was no sign, but how could I be sure with a man so perfectly controlled?

"Is something wrong?" he asked, as if we had not both just been accusing the other of being a liar, if not in so many words.

"No, I'm fine. It's just I have to get up early in the morning, and I'm suddenly very tired. If you don't mind…?"

"Of course." He signaled the bartender and paid for

the drinks, and within moments his big, sleek car was purring down Balboa Boulevard. The obvious flaw in my agreement to have a drink with him belatedly hit me—Dominic was about to find out where I lived. I didn't suppose he would go for the "just drop me at the corner" routine. Oh well, it wouldn't have been hard for him to find out if he really wanted to.

When we pulled up in the alley next to my side door, I was relieved when Dominic did not turn off the engine.

"I hope to see you again, Mercy. I think we still have a lot to discuss."

I made a noncommittal noise and got out of the car before he could…what? Kiss me?

Now, in the quiet of my therapy room, I reflected that I had felt an attraction to him last night, but it wasn't sexual. Well, not exactly. He had waited until I had my door open, then driven away. The perfect gentleman. Sort of like Dracula just before he drank your blood.

The rest of my working day was relatively stress-free, other than a woman who wanted me to "fix" her rebellious teen. I explained that in order for me to take the case, the daughter would have to give her willing consent. It wasn't a legal matter but a personal policy. Mom wasn't happy, but agreed to try to persuade the daughter to come in voluntarily. At six o'clock, I locked my door and headed home, where I donned my oldest, baggiest jeans and an enormous sweatshirt before stepping outside for an evening stroll.

Even in September, Balboa's evenings are cool. I

took a circuitous route toward Jimbo's. After a night of designer clothes, champagne and fine cognac, I wanted to smell the stale-yeast-and-ancient-nicotine ambiance and have a draft Bud. When I rounded the corner near the Newport Landing, I saw Sam's unmistakable outline as he stood near the boardwalk with a bald man dressed in polo shirt and khakis. The man was shaking his head, and Sam seemed to be trying to convince him of something. I started to alter my direction, but Sam had seen me and motioned me to come over.

"Mercy, I'd like you to meet Jeff Sorvine."

The bald man held out his hand, and I shook it.

"He's giving me an estimate on the repairs to the pump and the gas storage tank."

From the look on Sam's face, the news had not been good.

"Nice to meet you, Mercy. Sam has been telling me about your new business. Do you have a card?"

"Sure." Sukey had reminded me to put a couple in my wallet, and I took one out and handed it to him. "Are you in the market for a hypnotherapist?"

"Doc says I have to quit smoking. I've tried to go cold turkey a few times, but I don't make it more than a few hours."

I nodded my understanding—his story was typical.

"You any good with this smoking stuff?"

"It's my bread and butter," I replied.

"You got anything tomorrow? I gotta go back out to Riverside on Thursday."

"You'll have to call, but I think I overheard Sukey rescheduling someone from tomorrow morning."

He nodded, then returned his attention to Sam. "Call me when you're ready, Sam. I wish I could do more for you now, but with the economy the way it is…"

"Yeah." Sam shook Jeff's hand, and the latter headed toward the Landing's parking garage.

"I'm going to get a beer at Jimbo's. Join me?" I asked.

"Sure."

He walked alongside me with his hands in his pockets, his shoulders slumped. I decided not to pry—he would tell me about it if he wanted to.

We got our beers and sat at one of the worn booths that ran between the bar and the pool table. I waited.

"It's going to cost more than I thought," he said glumly.

"With or without the insurance?" I asked.

"Either way." He sipped his beer. "The problem is, I don't know how much I'm going to get from the ferry company's insurance and they're going to do some big investigation before paying off. If I could get the repairs started in the meantime, I could get a head start on all the inspections and licenses. But without the insurance money…" He stared into his beer.

"I take it Jeff won't do it without cash up front."

"Yeah, I guess he's had one too many customers declare bankruptcy and he's ended up eating the bill. He doesn't do credit anymore."

"Are there other contractors who might do the work on credit?"

He shook his head. "None as highly recommended as Jeff, or with as reasonable a price." He sighed. "If it was just me, I wouldn't be all that worried about it. I could just lock the door, get on my boat and sail away. But I can't leave Dad right now."

I let that sink in. "Sukey told me he has Alzheimer's. Doesn't Medicare pay his doctor bills?"

He nodded. "Yes, and the Veterans Administration does what it can, too. But the only way to get everything covered is to put him in a VA or state-run facility full-time, and I'm just not willing to do that." He shrugged, maybe embarrassed by being so vulnerable—I didn't know him well enough to tell.

"Most days, he knows who I am and where I is. He still enjoys movies and visiting with his friends, and giving me advice about the business. I'm afraid if he was shut away in some…warehouse, he would just start a downward slide."

Great. Not only had I destroyed a good man's business, now I might end up being responsible for putting his father in a nursing home.

"I'm sorry, Sam. I wish there was something I could do."

To my surprise, he reached across the table and gripped my hand. I felt tears well in my eyes. *What the hell is going on here?*

I withdrew my hand and swallowed the last of my beer. "Would you like another?" I asked.

"No, I need to get back to Dad's." He stood up, and I did the same. "Maybe I could take you to meet him one of these days. He still likes meeting new people, although he usually doesn't remember them the next day."

"Maybe. I'm pretty busy right now." I recognized the reluctance in my own voice and saw from Sam's face that he heard it, too.

"Yeah, well, I'll see you around." His eyes were no longer on me, and a fresh wave of guilt washed over me.

"Um, Sam?" He turned. "Maybe we could go next Sunday night, if you don't have to work too late."

He brightened visibly. "Yeah, that might work. I'm sure I'll see you before then." He walked out with a lighter step, and I moved to the bar.

"So, kid, something going on between you and the Egghead?" Jimbo would never have asked this in earshot of other customers. That is, if he had a normal voice, he wouldn't have. On a quiet Tuesday night, his voice probably carried into the last stall in the men's bathroom.

"He's a friend," I said, and Jimbo grunted. He managed to convey a lot of information in that single grunt—skepticism, approval and amusement. He wouldn't pry further, I knew. He was just keeping track of his customers, which was good business.

"How's the hypnotist business going?"

"I'm a hypnotherapist, not a hypnotist."

"Same difference."

"No, a hypnotist is an entertainer. A hypnotherapist is…well, a therapist." I was used to the misunderstanding and knew Jimbo meant no insult.

"So you can't make people cluck like a chicken or anything."

"Well, I could if they asked me to, I suppose. But

I haven't seen a lot of call for animal noises yet. Of course, it's still my first week." I looked at him solemnly, and he laughed uproariously.

"Well, I've given out a few of your cards, kid. If I send you enough referrals, will you give me a freebie?"

I couldn't tell if he was joking or not.

"Sure, Jimbo. But what do you need me for? It's well-known you're already perfect." I decided to keep it light.

"True," he nodded. "But perfect could be a good place to start. Who knows?"

I was about to leave when he stopped me. "Hey, kid, I forgot to tell you. That dude was in here again, asking about you."

"Which dude?" I had a sinking feeling I knew.

"That big guy, wears the fancy suits. Sells antiques or something."

"What did he want to know?" I asked, sitting back down.

"I don't know. How long you been around here, where else you hang out, where you're from originally. That sorta thing." He eyed me. "He giving you trouble?"

"No, no trouble."

I pondered this new information. *So Dominic's been checking me out. Maybe I had better do the same about him.*

"Before he came in here Friday night, you ever see him before?"

Jimbo shook his head. "No, he ain't a local. At least, not a Balboa local. I woulda remembered if I'd seen that car before." He stopped polishing the whiskey bottles and thought for a moment. "Come to think of it, Lawyer Bob was talking to him like he already knew him. And Taylor what-his-name, the car salesman."

I vaguely knew both guys, who were fringe-regulars. There were a number of local business types who probably frequented the higher-end restaurant bars along the Pacific Coast Highway but sought more anonymous environs when they got down to serious drinking. Both men Jimbo had mentioned fell into this category. Since both were usually well into their cups by the time they arrived, I had had little interaction with either one.

"How about Rocko? How long has he been coming around?"

Jimbo grimaced. "Coupla months, but real steady. You would have met him, you hadn't been working nights and weekends getting your new place ready."

"He ever cause trouble?" Jimbo's tone had already told me he hadn't liked the man.

"Nothing I could throw him out for. But it's only a matter of time, guy like that. Ain't been around since last weekend, though. I say good riddance."

I resisted the impulse to tell him he didn't need to worry about Rocko's reappearance and stood up to leave.

"Thanks for the heads-up, Jimbo." As I headed out the door, he stopped me a second time.

"Oh, yeah, one more thing. That guy, he asked me if I knew who your parents are."

"My *parents?*" Alarm must have made my voice sharper than I intended, because several other patrons turned to look at me.

"Yeah. I told him I had no idea."

Neither have I, came my unspoken response. *But I wonder if Dominic does.*

8

It was my third day in business, and I had already discovered some major pitfalls in my chosen career. One was that there was no way to goof off. Not that waiting on tables had involved a lot of downtime, but the worst thing that had ever happened as a result of my mind wandering during a dinner shift was a messed-up order and resultant tip reduction.

The disturbing news—that Dominic had been asking questions about me and, even more alarming, my parentage—kept insinuating itself into my sessions. I had to ask people to repeat themselves several times and, on two occasions, I discovered I would have missed something significant if I hadn't done so. Between sessions, I asked Sukey to run across the street to Alta Coffee and get me an extra-large caramel mocha, in the hope that sugar and caffeine would help restore my concentration.

While waiting for her to return, I went out to get a breath of the ocean air and wait for my next appointment. A familiar bald head was coming up the staircase, and I recognized Jeff Sorvine, the contractor who had done the estimate for Sam's repairs.

"Mr. Sorvine, please come in. My office manager just went for coffee, and I'd like to wait for her to come back before we start, so we won't be interrupted."

"Sure." He seemed a little winded from the steps and happy enough to take a seat in one of the comfortable chairs. "How's business?" he asked me as soon as he had gotten his breath.

"Good. Too good." I took a seat opposite him. "I had a reception Monday, and a lot of people made appointments. Then pictures from the reception ran in the paper on Tuesday, and the phone has been ringing continuously. It may not last, but right now I barely have time to take a lunch break."

I heard Sukey on the stairs, exchanging greetings with the boat designer downstairs.

"How about you? Is your business going well?"

"Well enough. I have a couple of big jobs starting next month, but this month I have a little time to breathe."

Which means you would have time to fix Sam's pumps if you were willing to let him pay you for it later. The thought came unbidden, and I tried to drive it from my mind. I mentally recited rule number two. *Never use the press to get an unfair advantage for personal gain.* But this wasn't for me—it was for a friend. When I had formulated the rules, I hadn't taken friends into consideration. Because I hadn't really had any friends, or so I thought. But I did now. Maybe I had been making friends for some time now and just hadn't been paying attention.

There was Sukey, of course. And Sam. But what about Jimbo? I would have said he liked me as well as he liked any of his customers, but hadn't yesterday's conversation showed a dash of personal concern? François had come over and done a makeover that would have cost hundreds of dollars in his shop and he hadn't even felt thanks were necessary. Hell, I even liked Hilda, most days. When had *that* happened?

My reverie was interrupted when Sukey appeared carrying a cup from which wafted the delicious aromas of dark-roasted coffee and chocolate. Belatedly, I realized Jeff was empty-handed. "I don't have a coffeemaker yet, but would you like me to pour some of this into a cup for you?"

"Nah, I don't drink it after lunch. Keeps me up."

Wasn't that the whole point?

When Sukey closed the door, I got the session started. Between sips, I told Jeff what to expect, and then started asking him some general questions about what he wanted. A three-plus-pack-per-day man, he said smoking was easily his biggest issue, but I poked around to make sure there wasn't some underlying stress exacerbating the habit. Like financial problems with his business, for instance.

I found nothing exceptional—a few hassles with an ex-wife, but nothing out of the ordinary. *He could easily afford to do the job on credit,* said the annoying voice in my head. I shushed it and concentrated on my well-practiced suggestions regarding the repugnance of the taste and smell of cigarettes and the pride Jeff would feel in thinking of himself as a nonsmoker. He was an easy subject, and I knew he would be down at the car wash trying to get the cigarette smell out of his truck by the end of the day.

"Do you feel good about yourself, Jeff?" I said automatically.

"Yeah, I feel great."

"Good." I picked up the now-mostly-unnecessary index card with the tell-your-friends speech on it, then hesitated. What harm would it do? Sam would pay him back, and even if he didn't, a job on the scale of Sam's requirements was peanuts to this man.

Before I could change my mind, I said, "You want to help Sam Falls with his gas-dock repairs, because he's a nice guy, and you like and trust him. You do like and trust him, don't you, Jeff?"

"Yeah, he's a great guy."

"You'll feel good if you tell him you'll do the job now and let him pay you when he gets his insurance money. Won't that make you feel good?"

"Yes."

I paused for a much longer interval. My heart was already racing in agitation at what I had just done. I could argue I was benefiting my customer with the suggestion he do a job that would ultimately make him money. But the next thing I was going to press him about was purely self-serving. But it was too late to go back, so I went on.

"After this session, you will not remember that we discussed Sam or his gas dock. You will just come to the conclusion that you want to do business with him and that he's a good risk to pay you later. You will remember the rest of the session, but not talking about Sam. Do you understand what I have just told you?"

"Yes."

I let out a breath that I hadn't realized I was holding, but the pressure in my chest did not abate. Without thinking, I picked up the index card and read off the spiel. When he stood up and shook my hand, my smile felt like it had been welded on my face with hot metal. I glanced around the empty waiting room and sighed with relief.

"Your next customer had to cancel," said Sukey. "We probably need to come up with a policy that says they have to give twenty-four hours' notice or pay anyway. I could have filled the slot five times if I had known about it."

"That's okay—I could use a break. I think we're going to have to rework the schedule a little so I don't see more than about ten people a day. My brain is starting to hurt." I was just babbling, but Sukey's brow furrowed with concern.

"Do you need an aspirin? I think I have some."

"No, I think I'll just lie down on the sofa and rest for a minute. We only have one more today, right?"

"Yes. A Mr. Jordan. Didn't say what he needs."

"Why don't you go on home, then? Close the door, and when he rings the buzzer, I'll get up and let him in."

Sukey looked dubious. "Do you know how to use the credit card authorization thingie?"

"I think so. It's like the one where I used to work. Go on, I'll be fine. If I can't figure it out, we'll send him a bill."

I knew her reluctance was just for show and that she would be on a bar stool at Jimbo's within ten minutes. She had already quit her waitress job, although she'd agreed to help out on special occasions and if they were shorthanded. She took off, and I locked the door and headed for my couch.

I was beginning to regret what I had done to Jeff Sorvine. Actually, I had regretted it the moment the first suggestion was out of my mouth. I seemed to be saying *just this once* to myself too often lately. With Rocko. With Dominic. And the *what harm would this do?* thing had popped up a time or two, as well. It was like cheating on a diet—*one* cookie won't matter. The next thing you know, the whole bag is empty.

Of course, I hadn't violated rule number four, yet. Well, not since Rocko. It was the most straightforward. Simply stated, it was like the most basic tenet of the old Hippocratic oath. *Do no harm.* In my adolescence and early teens, I had done some serious harm until I came to at least a partial understanding of the press. Usually it had been an accident. But not always.

Why don't you do the world a favor and go take a flying leap! Nearly eighteen years later, my own angry words still echoed in my head. Joel hadn't been a bad kid, not really. He was just at an age where anyone or anything different made a convenient target. After a variety of other insults had found no mark, he had made the mistake of calling me a freak. He had no way of knowing what a sore spot he was hitting, and I was still too young to understand that one of the reasons he was always harassing me was that he liked me. I just wanted him to leave me alone.

No sooner had the words left my mouth than Joel had walked to the edge of the library entrance and jumped— right in front of a van full of special-education kids coming up the parking ramp after a field trip.

It was three months before Joel recovered enough from the head injury to answer the question: Why did you jump? But he didn't even know—would never know. Except, there had been witnesses. Witnesses who had seen the smug look of satisfaction on my face as Joel headed for the eight-foot drop that should have left him bruised and scraped but otherwise unhurt. Witnesses who had seen that expression change to horror when I heard the squeal of tires, and who had heard me shout *No, Joel, I didn't mean in front of a car!* when it was already too late.

There hadn't been any charges, of course. The witnesses had been clear that Joel had not been pushed, and the police only shook their heads when a bunch of sixth-graders insisted I had somehow *made* him jump. They didn't believe them, and I was careful to do nothing to arouse suspicion.

But my adoptive parents had believed them. They had already seen enough—felt enough—to suspect what I was capable of. When they had decided to adopt a child, they had not signed up for a journey into the metaphysical. I had deeply resented that they didn't care enough about me to love me in spite of—

what? In spite of not being human? I had already started to wonder, even then.

I could have used my abilities to make them keep me, but I didn't do it. Even at twelve, I knew that if I used the press to make someone care for me, it wouldn't be the real thing. It wouldn't be *normal*. And God, how I had longed to be normal.

Still did, truth be told.

My headache hadn't improved a half hour later when the buzzer rang and I went out to unlock the door for Mr. Jordan. I started to explain. "I let my office manager go home for the day…" Then I stopped. Dominic was standing in front of the door, a sheepish expression on his face. "I was expecting—"

"A Mr. Jordan," he finished for me. "I know. I gave Sukey that name when I called for an appointment."

"Why did you do that?" My heart was hammering. I most decidedly did *not* want to be alone in my office with him, although I couldn't have said why.

"Because I was in need of your professional services, and I was afraid you would refuse to see me." He smiled. "I thought you might have a policy about hypnotizing personal friends."

"You're not—" I swallowed. I had been about to point out that he was not a personal friend, but something stopped me. I had the feeling he wouldn't take it well, and for some reason, I didn't want to antagonize him.

"I'm not what?"

"You're not…a typical customer," I said, recovering reasonably quickly. "You strike me as someone who doesn't usually ask anyone for help."

During our conversation, he had somehow eased me away from the door, and we were now standing in the middle of my office.

"On the contrary," he said, turning and walking into the adjoining room. "In matters where I am not an expert, I find it makes more sense to seek the help of those with more experience. It saves time." He sat on the sofa and put one arm along the back, as if he expected me to sit next to him. I sat as far away as was possible.

"I see." I didn't really. "And in what area do you believe me to be an expert?"

He raised his eyebrows as if in surprise. "Why, in the area of hypnosis, of course. The topic fascinates me."

This wasn't going well. I had already tried to press Dominic—twice—with no results. Just what kind of session was he expecting?

"And why do you want to be hypnotized?" I stalled for time.

He shook his head. "I don't. Not yet, anyway. I just have some questions about the process. I will pay your normal fee, of course."

"Okay," I said cautiously. *What was he after here?*

"Well, to begin with, do you believe anyone can learn to be a hypnotist? Or does one have to be...born with the talent?" His expression didn't indicate that he meant anything unusual by this question.

"Anyone can learn the techniques," I replied, "but it takes a certain amount of aptitude to use them effectively."

"And you have that aptitude?"

"Yes." *In spades.* He nodded, as if this was the answer he was expecting.

"I see in your brochures that you went to school to learn hypnotherapy. Did you know you had the talent before you went there? Or was it just a shot in the dark?"

I didn't like where this was going, but I had no reason to stop him. Yet.

"I had done a little research. I had a pretty good idea I would...take to the training."

"What kind of research?"

I shrugged. "Reading. Internet. That sort of thing."

"Were you ever hypnotized yourself?"

"Yes, at the school." I did not add that I had been terrified, and my nervousness had impaired the instructor's ability to succeed in getting me into a trance.

"You're adopted, aren't you?"

This abrupt change of tack took me by complete surprise. "What makes you say that?" The out-of-left-field comment had left me almost short of breath.

Dominic merely shrugged. "Just a hunch. I am, too, you know. Maybe the orphans of the world just recognize each other." He leaned forward and gave me his Casanova-cum-carnivore smile. "I would lay odds we have a great deal more in common than not knowing our birth parents."

I was too stunned by the implications of this statement to react for a few moments. He had gone on as if I hadn't avoided his adoption question. *Like what?* was the obvious response, and I refused to give him the opening. I shook my head.

"I doubt it," I said instead. "Look, Dominic, if you don't want a hypnotherapy session, that's fine." I stood, and overrode him when he would have stopped me. "I have a terrible headache and would have called to cancel the appointment—if the fictitious Mr. Jordan had left a phone number."

I hadn't closed the hypnotherapy room door, and I swiftly went out to the office and sat behind the desk. He got up and followed me, but I opened my desk drawer and took out the first available handful of papers.

"I still have a few things to do before I leave, so I hope you won't mind letting yourself out." I smiled brilliantly and falsely, and he held up both hands in a gesture of surrender.

"All right, you win. I'll go."

I tried unsuccessfully to avoid his eyes, and he gazed at me with his predator's stare. "But we are going to have this conversation sometime, Mercy. I promise you that."

He turned and walked out, and I waited until I heard his faint footfalls on the stairs before running over to the door and turning the deadbolt.

I really didn't have any paperwork to complete— Sukey was keeping up with everything, and I only added a few notes to the files at the end of each session. I waited a good fifteen minutes before turning off the light, in case the black Jaguar was still sitting at the curb. The moment the room went dark, the phone rang, nearly sending me through the ceiling.

Had Dominic seen the lights go out? Was he calling

to taunt me? I stood in the darkened room and felt a trickle of sweat move down my spine as I waited for the next ring. Even though I expected it, I jumped. Each subsequent ring caused a similar reaction, until after five repetitions, Sukey's cheery voice on the return message filled the air.

"You have reached the office of Ms. Mercedes Hollings, hypnotherapist. We're either out of the office or helping another client. Please leave a detailed message, and we'll call you right back." Dread filled my stomach as I waited for the beep.

"Mercy?"

To my immense relief, Sam's voice came over the tinny speaker.

"This is Sam. I was wondering if—"

"This is Mercy." I grabbed for the receiver as if it were a lifeline. "I was just on my way out."

"Oh, hi. I didn't have your cell number, but Sukey dropped off some of your brochures."

"Yeah." I sat down on the desk, my knees suddenly too wobbly to support my weight. If Sam thought my one-syllable answer odd, his voice didn't show it.

"Listen, Mercy, I just got some terrific news, and I feel like celebrating. Your brochure says you're closed on Fridays, and I was wondering if you'd like to do something."

"Sure," I replied without thinking, then realized I had just agreed to some sort of date. "Like what?"

"Oh, let me worry about that. Just wear something comfortable and come by the store around noon."

"Who's going to watch the shop?" I asked, starting to regain my bearings. *Just keep breathing*.

"Lifeguard Skip. It doesn't take two people, with the gas dock closed, and it turns out he knows a lot about boat engines and rigging sails."

"Okay, sounds good. I'll see you then."

He said goodbye and I hung up. My heart rate was returning to normal. That lasted for about thirty seconds as I reviewed the conversation. *I just got some terrific news….* As if I didn't know what it was.

I went to the front door, took a deep breath and opened it. No one was lurking in the courtyard, and the curb in front of building was empty. Nor was anyone hiding in the bushes on the way to the shipyard parking lot, where I had rented a space. I drove home on autopilot, changed into sweats, then sat on my front porch and listened to the waves I could not quite see. As I sipped the red wine that failed to sooth my tattered nerves, the full moon almost annoyed me with its serenity.

We have a great deal more in common than not knowing our birth parents. I sincerely hoped not. But I had a sinking feeling that Dominic was right.

9

"How could you live in Balboa for five years and not know how to sail?" Sam's incredulity was tempered by a smile. He had just asked me to "grab the mainsheet" and my resulting blank expression had prompted him to explain that he wasn't asking me to make up a bunk in the tiny cabin below. He was still laughing over his own joke.

"No one ever invited me before," I explained. "I've been out on a few powerboats, but this is better. It feels more…real."

I looked at him as he watched the sail for a moment, then adjusted the rudder ever so slightly. He was gorgeous on land, but here, in his true element, he was breathtaking. The wind whipped his sun-streaked hair around, and his eyes reflected the color of the sea. When we crested a wave and were sprayed with foam, we both laughed in delight.

"Blue-water sailing," he agreed. "Nothing like it."

I was relaxing for the first time since Jeff Sorvine had left my office. Seeing Sam's happiness and relief at having a timeline for his repairs did a great deal to temper my guilt, both over having caused the destruction in the first place and for having pressed Jeff. Dominic's veiled references still danced at the corners of my mind, but it was impossible to be unhappy when the sun sparkled off the water and Sam Falls smiled.

We sailed a zigzag course southward, passing Laguna Beach, where the cliffs crowded the shoreline and houses seemed to hang in midair. We turned and headed out toward San Clemente Island, turning northwest before we could get too close. The island is part of the nearby Marine base, and is used as a bombing target on one side and an endangered bird habitat on the other. Only in California.

The sun was nearing the mountains on Catalina as we headed north, and the wind that had been filling our sails since early afternoon slowed and then died almost completely. "Will we have a problem getting back?" I asked, concerned.

"No, it will pick up again. Plus, the motor works fine." He came and sat next to me. "Actually, I had planned on the twilight lull when I asked you to come out here." He gave me a quick kiss, and I tasted salt water on his lips. Then he disappeared down the main hatch. "I'm going to start handing some things up. Can you grab them?"

"Sure." A small cooler came up, followed by some foil-wrapped packages, a plastic bag filled with charcoal and a tiny hibachi. He popped back up with some plastic cups in one hand and a corkscrew in the other.

"I'm sorry I can't offer you a real wineglass, but good crystal doesn't do well in a twenty-eight-footer."

He climbed the rest of the way up the ladder and took the hibachi from me. "Also, open-fire cooking isn't really recommended on any vessel, but I like my fish mesquite grilled, so I've had to rig up some customized safety measures."

He proceeded to remove some odd-looking pieces of wood from where they were stowed under a seat, and I saw that they bolted together to make a shelf that fit to the railing near the cockpit and allowed for an aluminum-covered platform to be suspended off the side of the hull. It had four square holes into which the feet of the hibachi fit snugly, and clamps attached to the handles. Within ten minutes, Sam had taken down and secured the mainsail, and had coals heating in the hibachi's interior. "By pulling on this handle," he explained, showing me the ingenious design, "I can dump the hot coals into the water."

I found a bottle of chardonnay in the cooler, along with a plastic bag of fresh mahimahi and some lemons. The foil-wrapped packages contained potatoes and vegetables, and these were settled among the coals as I uncorked and poured the wine and Sam cut the lemons into wedges. A small vial of mixed herbs, salt and pepper materialized from a pocket, and Sam let the fish marinate in its bag while we drank a glass of the cold, crisp wine and watched the sun set behind Catalina Island.

We talked, ate fish, drank wine and listened to the music of the ocean. When the night got chilly, Sam produced a thick blanket and tossed it over both of us. A second bottle of wine was retrieved from an ice-filled locker, and our easy conversation diminished as the motion of the unusually calm Pacific rocked me toward sleep.

"This has been the most wonderful meal of my life, Sam," I said drowsily.

"Really?" He sounded surprised, and I roused myself from my stupor. I wasn't usually so open with my emotions, but the wine and the evening had lulled me. The boat's running lights were off, but Sam was keeping an eye on our drift, and the almost-full moon had risen. I could make out his features in the reflected light and thought I could still discern blue in the glint of his eyes.

"Yes, really. Everything was perfect. It makes me understand why someone would want to live on their boat."

"It's not always like this," Sam conceded. "But when it is..." He trailed off, and I thought he was searching for words, when suddenly I felt his lips on mine. He tasted of wine and salt and maleness, and after only a moment's hesitation, I let myself slide fully into the sensation. No longer drowsy, I felt every nerve in my body awaken and cry *More!*

I felt his hands on my back under the sweatshirt, and I found my own fingers unbuttoning his shirt. His chest was solid and smooth, with just a light covering of hair that started below his collarbones and narrowed into a trail that snaked around his navel and ended...well, I didn't know where it ended. I ran my fingers lightly over the soft hairs and felt his answering shudder.

"Oh God, Mercy." Sam's voice was harsh as his lips moved from my mouth over my jaw and down to my throat. He leaned back and grabbed the sweatshirt and, in one smooth motion, pulled it up and over my head. My bra disappeared before I knew what was happening, and I gasped and would have covered my breasts, but he gently moved my hands away and looked at me solemnly in the moonlight.

"You are so beautiful." His voice was reverent and mingled with the music of the gentle waves and gradually rising wind.

"So are you," I replied, and he laughed quietly. "No, I mean it. Out here, you're like…" I put my hand on the side of his face. "You're like one of the dolphins we saw, gliding along beside the boat. You belong here."

He took my hand and kissed it, then put it aside as his hands reached out and cupped my breasts. I moaned as his fingers found my nipples, teasing them into hardness. I pulled his head toward them, and soon his tongue circled first one nipple, then the other, stopping to gently nip and suck. I felt moisture erupt between my legs, and my body thrummed with a rhythm it hadn't felt in years.

I wasn't a virgin. I had been with men before, from the foster brothers with whom I had clung in mutual desperation to the casual encounters I had thought would keep me safe from the inherent dangers of getting too close. But a few years ago, I had stopped all that. Not because I thought casual sex was immoral—I didn't. But I no longer found it satisfying—never had, really. I didn't want sex without intimacy, and intimacy terrified me.

Now the pulsing waves of desire that coursed through my body threatened to engulf me…drown me. I wanted that oblivion—craved it, needed it. But…but….

Sam reached for the fastening of my jeans, and I caught his hands in mine.

"Sam." His name came out hoarsely, and he struggled to get his hands away from mine. *"Sam."* This time something in my tone got through, and he stilled and looked at me.

"I can't do this…not yet. I'm sorry." I cringed inwardly, afraid he would be angry. Instead, he smiled.

"I understand. I didn't plan for this to happen tonight. It was just that you felt so good and it seemed so…so right." He sat up and adjusted his unbuttoned shirt. I crossed my arms in front of my breasts, and he retrieved my sweatshirt for me.

"It's been a very long time for me, Mercy. I got carried away, and I hope I haven't offended you."

A long time? He had no idea. "Of course not, Sam. I wanted it as much as you did, I think. But I can't just…I need more time." I suddenly felt very awkward. "Can I help you get this stuff—" I indicated the hibachi and the empty wine bottles "—cleaned up?"

"Yes, that would be great."

We worked as a team to disassemble and restow all evidence of the meal; then Sam hoisted the sail, and we headed back toward Newport Harbor, albeit at a much more leisurely pace in the light wind. I still felt a little discomfited, but at least the silence didn't seem strained.

"You said it had been a long time," I began tentatively, once we were comfortably underway. "Were you…involved with someone?"

"Yes," he said shortly. "We were engaged."

"But you never married?"

"No." I felt him tense, then relax. "She—Sylvia was her name—she ran the office at the marina in Key West where I kept my sailboat. I'd known her for years, or at least I thought I did." He was silent, and I coaxed him to continue.

"What happened?"

Sam sighed. "She got pregnant. I hadn't thought about getting married before that, but I thought we were in love, and it seemed like the right thing to do. She seemed overjoyed when I proposed. She was making plans, calling out-of-town friends, picking out invitations. We didn't have a lot of money—her parents were dead—but she had a little house and my salvage business was holding its own." There was a long silence, and I thought he had decided not to continue.

"Then one day, I was staying at her house. I had the flu, and the weather was too hot to be sweating through a fever on the boat. So she went to work, and then the phone rang. I thought it was her, telling me something she had forgotten. So I picked it up."

There was another long pause; then he continued. "I've always wondered what would have happened if I hadn't answered that call."

"Who was it?" I was afraid I knew, but I was wrong.

"It was the baby's father." My eyes widened, but he went on. "No, not someone she was sleeping with. It was the guy who was paying her to be a surrogate mother. He and his wife couldn't have a child, so she had undergone artificial insemination and was supposed to turn the baby over as soon as it was born."

"And she let you think it was yours?" Sam nodded, and I asked another question. "What was she planning to do when the baby was born? Tell you it had been stolen from the hospital?"

"I never really got a straight answer. I think she had already gotten most of the money and thought she could keep the baby and that we could run away together. She would have the money *and* the baby. And me." He shook his head. "I thought I knew her. But all the time she had this big secret." After another pause, he went on. "I really hate secrets."

Houston, we have a problem.

When we got back to the dock, it was easy to say I was tired and had a full schedule of appointments the next day, because it was absolutely true. Sam walked me back to my apartment.

"I'm sorry I laid my big sad story on you, Mercy. I didn't mean to bring down such a great day."

"You didn't," I said. We were lingering in the alley, both reluctant to let the evening end, yet knowing it would be a mistake for him to come inside tonight. Our hormones and our feelings were both just too raw. "I'm glad you told me. And I loved our day together. And the evening, too." I leaned forward and kissed him with tenderness, but broke away before it could turn to heat. "Call me, okay?"

He nodded, and I went into the house. Fred ran to greet me, and I picked him up and went to sit on the sofa without turning on the lights.

I really hate secrets. I wondered what he would think of mine. Could I tell him? I had always thought I could never tell anyone. But maybe, just maybe, Sam would understand.

A movement in the dark caught my attention, and I was instantly on full alert. Something had been different since I walked in, and I realized what it was. *Cigarette smoke.* A glowing tip moved in the corner near the fireplace, and I discerned the vague outline of someone sitting in the chair there.

"Who is it?" I was surprised to hear the steadiness in my voice.

"I've been waiting a long time for you to get home, Mercy," said an all-too-familiar voice. "I was afraid Sam was going to keep you out all night."

I reached over and switched on the lamp. There, wearing a black long-sleeved T-shirt and matching jeans, sat Dominic. An ashtray was on the small table to his right, and when he casually flicked ashes into it, I saw that a number of discarded butts were already filling it.

"How did you get in here?" I was stalling for time. I knew the old windows were easy to open—I had come in that way myself when I misplaced my keys.

"Come now, Mercy. Isn't the more pertinent question *why* I'm here? You're usually so perceptive. You disappoint me."

"I don't really give a shit why you're here, Dominic. Because you're leaving. Right now." I stomped to the door and flung it open.

Dominic didn't move.

"But we have so much to talk about, Mercy. About your special…talents. And how you used them to do something to convince that moron, Rocko, to do something stupid. But, more important—" He stood, and I was reminded that he was at least a half a head taller than me "—about what the hell Rocko did with my half-million dollars' worth of heroin, and where it is now."

10

"*Your* heroin?" I was interrupted by an annoyed squawk from Fred, whom I was still holding. At Dominic's last words, I had inadvertently tightened my grip and squeezed him too tightly. I released him, and he disappeared out the cat door with alacrity. "Y-your cousin had a half-million dollars' worth of…" I trailed off. What had I told Rocko about the heroin? My brain refused to function.

Dominic made a disparaging noise, and I stepped backward. "Cousin? Do you really think Rocko and I could share the same blood?" He stepped forward and put a finger under my chin, looking at me as if he were examining one of his precious antiques. "No, Rocko and I were once foster brothers. Though not for long." He circled around me, letting the finger trail over my jawline and around my ear. "We both did things that made our foster parents very…nervous."

"Don't touch me!" I snapped and pressed simultaneously, without planning.

Dominic drew back in mock horror. "Ouch! Quite a strong ability you have there, Mercy. Stronger than mine, I fear. I can be…persuasive, but nothing like that." He sighed dramatically. "Too bad. I would find it quite useful. But I can block *your* efforts, as you have no doubt already discovered. So I wouldn't bother trying to sway me, or whatever you call it."

"Press," I said automatically. Perversely, it felt good to say it aloud. "I call it the press."

"The press." He repeated the words, tilting his head as if trying them out. He nodded. "Yes, that's a perfect name for it. Tell me, does it only happen when you want it to? Or does it pop up uninvited from time to time?"

"I can control it." I could feel the tight-lipped expression on my face and willed myself to relax. I didn't want him to see how afraid I was of him. I knew it would give him satisfaction.

"So you say." Abruptly, he stopped his circling and returned to the chair. "Why don't you pour us each a glass of that vodka in your freezer? I didn't check to see if you have olives."

"I'm not thirsty." I moved to the sofa and sat down. "But help yourself." We stared at each other for a moment, and I had to force myself not to look away.

He laughed. "I wouldn't try to match wits with me, Mercy. Or wills." He got to his feet and walked into the kitchen.

Briefly, I looked around to see if there was something I could hit him over the head with. I considered an oriental vase borrowed from the landlord, when his voice came again.

"I also wouldn't recommend trying to sneak up behind me with some kind of blunt object."

I heard the freezer door close and the refrigerator open.

"Ah, vermouth and blue-cheese-stuffed olives. Excellent."

I heard the sound of glass on the tile counter, and he returned with two filled martini glasses. Handing one to me, he said, "There wasn't much vermouth." I put my drink down on the coffee table without tasting it.

He shrugged. "Suit yourself." He returned to the fireside chair and sipped, savoring the flavor. "Hangar One. Not an expensive vodka, but an excellent one. I commend your taste."

"This sophisticated scoundrel act is starting to get boring, Dominic. Say what you have to say and get the fuck out of my apartment."

His eyebrows rose. "But it's not an act, Mercy. I really am sophisticated. And I am most assuredly a scoundrel." He smiled unpleasantly. "I acquired sophistication by choice, Mercy, just as you acquired your brooding loner persona. Not very original, I might add. But I was born a scoundrel. Just as you were."

"You don't know anything about me, Dominic." My words sounded hollow, even to me.

"On the contrary. I know you like no one else you've ever met. You see, Mercy, I *am* you. Or at least, I am what you are."

"Which is?" I tried to sound sarcastic, but I didn't think he was buying. *Does he really know what I am? If I'm human?*

He eyed me over the rim of his glass. "You really

don't know, do you?" He put down his drink abruptly, then rested his elbow on the arm of the chair, supporting his chin with his hand. His veneer seemed to slip for a few moments, and his expression turned thoughtful as he appraised me.

"Most of them say you don't really exist, you know. That you're some kind of…urban legend. I wonder what they would give to know where you are. To know *what* you are."

"Who the hell are you talking about, Dominic? Who says I don't exist?" He might have been trying to play me, but the speculation in his eyes seemed real. "Don't try to feed me some line of bullshit. I know exactly what I am." It was a huge bluff, but he didn't know that for sure.

"So you say." The sharpness left his gaze, and the languid elegance returned. It was really starting to creep me out, the way he changed personas in the space of a heartbeat. He continued. "But back to the matter at hand. It took me a little while to be sure. It seems you can shield yourself from me as effectively as I can from you. But after I saw the police report about Rocko's little boat accident…"

I must have looked surprised, so he explained. "Oh, yes, I know about that. Rocko's fingerprints, as you can imagine, were on file. The police figured out it was him. I had already searched his apartment before they arrived, but I didn't find any heroin—or any money, for that matter. But a few of his things were gone, as if he had packed a bag or two. It looked as if he left in a hurry."

He took another sip of the martini, then plucked out the olive and chewed it thoughtfully. "I can just imagine the scene. 'Get out of town and never darken poor sweet Sukey's door again.' Something like that?"

I stared stonily, refusing to react, but he went on as if I had confirmed his suspicions.

"The problem is, he seems to have taken my drugs, along with a not-inconsiderable amount of money, with him. So, you see, Mercy, I am going to have to ask you to tell me where he has gone."

"I don't know where Rocko is," I said, keeping my voice as neutral as possible. "And I don't know what you are talking about."

He laughed unpleasantly. "Of course you do."

I did a double-take. He hadn't moved his lips.

"Oh, you didn't know about the telepathy?" he said aloud. "Well, well, well. I guess you aren't as far along in your development as I had assumed."

"You can read my mind?" Every secret I had ever wanted to keep to myself threatened to rush to the front of my consciousness.

"Sadly, no." He shook his head, as if this really did make him sad. "If I could, I would not have to ask you these tiresome questions. But I can send you a message, if you don't block me out. And I can sense when you are…being cautious about what you say. Which is pretty much all the time, from what I can tell."

I relaxed a little. I wondered if I could send *him* a message. *Fuck you and the horse you rode in on.* He actually grinned.

"Nice first effort. I didn't catch the actual words, but

the intent was crystal clear." He chuckled, and I had to suppress a shudder. This time it was definitely revulsion. He stood. "All right, Mercy, since you are not going to cooperate and you do not appear to be particularly afraid of me, I am going to leave you. But I do have one final thing to say."

His whole demeanor changed. The relaxed elegance, the savoir faire—all of it vanished in an instant. He no longer even appeared to be handsome, just deadly. When he spoke, his voice bore no resemblance to the honeyed rumbling purr he usually affected.

"I will give you three days to find Rocko and my property. Actually, I don't care what happens to Rocko—kill him, if you want to. But the heroin will be returned to me."

He stepped closer to the sofa and leaned forward. I scrambled backward, but he put his hand out and trapped me. I gulped.

"If I don't have my property by the end of the day Monday, someone you care about is going to be hurt. Badly. Then another one on Tuesday. And so on, until the heroin is in my hands." He straightened, and sort of shook himself. The polished veneer returned as effortlessly as it had disappeared.

"Don't even think about going to the police. You have no idea which of them I have in my pocket. And what are you going to tell them? I assure you, there is no evidence that can be tied back to me. I have been much too careful for that."

He picked up my untouched martini and drained it in one swallow, then picked up the olive. "Shame to waste it," he said, and actually *winked* at me as he popped it into his mouth. "I'll just let myself out. You might want to take a look at the lock on the window in the spare bedroom—I think it may need some repair. Good night, Mercy."

When the alarm clock finally saved me from a seemingly endless stream of nightmares, I was more than happy to get out of bed, no matter how fitfully I had slept. I tried to wash away the last evening's horror, but I ran out of hot water before achieving oblivion. I continued to rinse myself, first with lukewarm and finally with cold water. By the time I stepped, shivering, onto my bathroom rug, Fred was complaining about the lateness of his breakfast.

Someone you care about will be hurt. Badly. I looked at Fred. Did he qualify? Sukey was an obvious first choice. And Sam. What could I tell them? How could I protect them? The answers were no more obvious this morning than they had been during my tempestuous night.

Somewhere about four in the morning, the exact words I had spoken to Rocko had found their way back through the fog of terror and into my brain. *Flush all your heroin and any other drugs you have hanging around down the toilet.* Of course, I had said *your* heroin…was Rocko smart enough to have differentiated between his own property and Dominic's? Not likely, especially with my now regretted caveat about any other drugs that might have been *hanging around.* Shit.

Too jittery to dawdle, I arrived at the office well

before Sukey. "What's Fred doing here?" she asked, bending to scratch behind his ears.

"I heard someone in my neighborhood might be... messing with cats." Almost true. "I didn't want to trap him inside alone all day, so I brought him."

"That's terrible!" She sat down at her desk and scooped Fred into her lap. "Who would want to hurt a handsome guy like my lover boy?" Fred writhed in ecstasy and purred like a jackhammer. "You can hang out with Auntie Sukey today, can't you, Fred?"

Fred had no objections, and I went into the other room.

The phone rang, and Sukey picked it up. "Mercy Hollings's office. Oh, hi, Sam... Sure, she just got here... No, she's not busy yet. Hang on." She hit the hold button and sang in the tones of an excited eighth-grader, "It's Mr. Wonderful."

My heart temporarily leapt, then fell back to my ankles. *Someone you care about...someone you care about...* The echo thundered in my brain, and I had a sudden vivid mental picture of Sam's boat going up in flames. Sam's outline, wreathed in fire, was visible through a cloud of...

I froze with my hand on the receiver. That hadn't been my imagination—it had been a deliberate message, courtesy of Dominic.

"Get *out*," I growled aloud, and I actually heard his evil chuckle before a door in my mind shut with something that felt like a snap.

"What did you say?" Sukey called from the front office.

"Nothing," I shouted back. "Look, Sukey, could you tell Sam I can't talk right now?"

"Why? Is there a problem?" Concern was plain in her voice.

"No problem. I just don't know… I just can't talk to him right now, okay? Can you take a message?"

I saw her shrug as if it was my life, so there was nothing she could do if I wanted to ruin it, and she hit the telephone button.

"Hi, Sam? I was wrong—she's already busy. Can I take a message? Sure, okay."

I closed the office door to postpone the inevitable questions.

It had been easy to shove Dominic out of my head once I knew he was in there, and I was pretty sure I would be able to keep him out, now that I recognized the sensation. I wondered about this telepathy thing. Could I read other people's thoughts? I had always been pretty intuitive, but I had assumed my customary caution with people had made me especially observant. Was there more to it than that?

But I had no time to explore this new idea right now. I had to figure out how to protect my friends. That's right, *my damned friends. Mine.* I felt a huge welling up of outrage that Dominic had the—the nerve to think he could hurt people I cared about. It had taken me twenty-nine years to learn how to let myself give a damn about others, and if he thought he could just waltz into my life and start screwing with that, he had another think coming.

I needed a plan, and I needed it fast. I walked back out into the office. "Sukey, how many appointments do I have today?"

"Six. The last one is at three-thirty." She spun the appointment book around on the desk to show me. My Saturday hours only went until four, and the three o'clock slot was empty.

"Call the three-thirty and reschedule for next week. I'm going to need to be out of here as soon as I'm done with the two-thirty." I wasn't sure how much difference an hour would make, but I'd take it.

"Okay." She made a note. "Are you going to tell me what's going on?" She raised her eyebrows.

"Nothing. Just something I have to take care of." I looked at her speculatively. "What are you doing after work?"

"I'm driving out to Palm Springs to see Jeannette."

I nodded—this was perfect. Sukey always spent the night when she went to visit her cousin, and I doubted Dominic would be staking out her place. He had given me three days, but I didn't trust him one whit. He might get itchy and decide a demonstration was in order.

"Good. Have a good time. You could even stay over Sunday night, if you're too tired to drive back. I can handle it here Monday morning."

"Thanks. Jeannette and I get a little carried away sometimes."

My nine-o'clock appointment arrived and postponed any further questions about Sam. How was I going to get him to lie low?

Press him, of course. I recoiled from my thought.

This was getting too damned familiar. I was violating my own rules left and right, and each time it got a little easier to justify. And to do. No, I would not press Sam. Or at least not unless I had to as a last resort.

At three o'clock I tucked Fred under one arm and locked the front door. He enjoyed riding in the car, although he was a little confused about why the people in passing cars didn't stop and pet him, even when he meowed nicely. I hurried home to change, so I could get to work on the first step in my plan. The only step so far, really. I put on a pair of jeans and a T-shirt, then reevaluated. Would it be better to fade into the background or to stand out a little? I wanted to get these guys to talk to me but not to drool down my shirt. Well, not too much, anyway. I exchanged the T-shirt for a lower-cut, clingier model and checked the mirror. Not bad.

I was a little worried about leaving Fred home alone, but I could hardly have suggested that Sukey take him to Palm Springs. I walked out to my patio and hollered toward the balcony above.

"Hey, T.J.! You up there?"

I heard the screen slide open, and a perfectly coiffed blond head popped over the rail.

"Sure, honey. You need something?"

I saw that T.J. was wearing an orange kimono—one of his large collection of the silky garments.

"Can Fred come up and hang out with you tonight? He hasn't been feeling too well, and I don't want to leave him home alone."

"Freddy boy is always welcome up here. We're

having fish for dinner. Does he like sea bass?" T.J.'s partner, Otis, had been to an exclusive cooking school, and the couple usually dined well.

"He'll never want to come home," I replied. "Thanks a million."

On my way out, I took Fred upstairs and turned him over to the ministrations of a doting T.J. I had little doubt they'd be feeding him caviar before the night was out.

I headed off the peninsula and into Costa Mesa. Every town has a few bars that do almost as much business in the daylight hours as at night. They don't cater to the nine-to-five crowd, and their customers don't pay much attention to the clock, except for those annoying few early morning hours—between two and six—when California bars are obliged to close.

The Keg was one of these, although it had lately gained some popularity with the college crowd. Since Sukey had been there with Rocko, it seemed as good a place to start as any. I pulled into the parking lot and turned off the engine. Was I really going to do this? I lifted my hands from the steering wheel and saw that they were shaking. I willed them to be still. They obeyed. I caught a glimpse of my eyes in the rearview mirror. They looked like stones. I glanced away and got out of the car.

I had always thought of Jimbo's as a dive, but it had a certain hominess about it. This place was just plain scary. The bartender looked like he had come from central casting. He had a shaved head with a tattoo on it, and a ring through his nose. Not the side of his nose, either. It looked like the kind of thing used to lead an ox, which I decided was appropriate when I considered his size.

I sat down at the bar, and he looked me over. He made no secret of the fact that he was including a careful appraisal of my cleavage in his scrutiny. Then he came and stood in front of me and cocked his head. Apparently, this was his version of "May I help you?"

"Draft." Silently, he picked up a glass from a row behind the bar, filled it and put it in front of me. "Buck seventy-five."

I laid a ten on the bar, and he made change. I turned and looked around. There were other patrons at the bar, mostly drinking beer, but I saw some whiskey drinkers, as well. A couple of ancient Hispanic men were playing pool with solemn concentration. I was the only woman, but I was pretty sure it wasn't a gay bar.

Since none of the faces I had been looking for were present, I swiveled back around to face Mr. Congeniality.

"Let me ask you a question."

He walked over to stand opposite me, then leaned against the bar and lit a cigarette, taking his time.

"You got another one of those?" I asked, and he gestured toward the machine in the corner.

"Give you one, everybody wants one."

I picked up my change from the bar and went over and bought a pack of Marlboro Reds. It didn't seem like a low-tar kind of place. When I returned to my seat, Baldy hadn't moved. I broke open the pack and removed a cigarette, and he shocked me by leaning forward to light it. Probably just another excuse to look down my shirt, but it was progress.

"You know a guy named Dominic?" I asked, exhaling smoke.

"Who's askin'?"

Here it was, the point of no return. I had done this before, but this time it was premeditated. I took a deep breath and pressed. "Tell me what you know about Dominic."

"Came in here the other night, lookin' for Rocko. Seen him a few times before. Think Rocko works for him, maybe."

"Tell me why you think Rocko works for him."

"Rocko thinks he's the cock of the walk, always talkin' big, always fulla shit. When Dominic comes in, Rocko gets real quiet. Acts like he's afraid or somethin'."

"Why?"

"Dominic's a scary guy."

I could definitely concur on that point. I went on. "What does Rocko do for Dominic?"

"Dunno."

"Could you guess?" So far, I hadn't learned anything new, so I kept pressing.

"Rocko's not too smart, so it can't be nothin' too complicated. Rocko sells some dope sometimes, but I don't know if he's doin' it for Dominic."

"What about heroin? You ever hear about Rocko selling heroin?"

"Not in here." I was getting nowhere, so I changed directions.

"If you were trying to find Dominic, where would you look?"

The bartender paused, thinking about it. "Maybe that tittie bar on Seventeenth. Rocko goes in there a lot."

I figured this loser had told me all he knew, so I said, "You can forget everything about this conversation, everything after you lit my cigarette." Then I let go of him and saw the familiar blinking that was a grotesque parody of my customers when I finished their hypnotherapy.

"You want another beer?" he asked, noticing my empty glass. I didn't remember drinking it. I'd better be careful. I wouldn't be able to keep that up all day—and night, probably.

"No, thanks." I left the rest of my change on the bar and went outside, savoring the cool air on the way to my car. *One dump down, forty or so to go.*

My plan wasn't very well-formed, but it was all I had. I remembered Dominic's words.

Don't even think about going to the police. You have no idea which of them I have in my pocket. And what are you going to tell them? I assure you, there is no evidence that can be tied back to me.

Maybe he was telling the truth, and maybe he wasn't. Certainly someone had told him about Rocko's fingerprints—someone with access to police reports—but he couldn't have the entire staff of both the Costa Mesa and the Newport Beach police departments under his control. He'd already admitted his press wasn't as strong as mine. And as for evidence, why bother to tell me there wasn't any if he wasn't trying to discourage me from finding out?

No, I couldn't go to the police with what I had, which was basically nothing. But if the very first lowlife I had talked to had guessed Rocko was working for Dominic, I'd bet there was more to be found. And I was going to find it. Somehow, before Monday, I had to find out enough about Dominic's drug operation so that a few anonymous phone calls would ensure that he would be too busy covering his own ass to worry about hurting my friends.

I got back in my car and flipped my rearview mirror to an angle that prevented me from seeing my face again. I was afraid that when I looked into my eyes, I would see Dominic staring back out at me. *I may have to become him to defeat him,* a voice in my head said, *but I don't have to like it.* I put my car into gear and drove out of the parking lot.

11

I hadn't set the alarm for Sunday morning, so was instead awakened by a combination of ringing telephone and sandpaper cat tongue. I picked up the phone without checking the caller ID and said, "Hello?"

"Hi, Mercy, it's Sam."

"Sam." A pleasant sensation spread through me, to be immediately displaced by panic. "Are you okay?"

"I'm fine? Why wouldn't I be?"

I could tell my odd question had puzzled him, so I hurried to explain. "I'm sorry, I'm still half asleep. What time is it?"

"Eight-thirty. Sorry, I had you pegged for an early riser."

"Usually I am. I had some…business to take care of last night, and it kept me out late." I removed Fred from my chest and struggled to sit up. "What's up?"

There was a pause. "I was calling to see if you were still up to visiting Dad this evening. Skip's going to close up for me, so I thought we'd leave around four."

Shit, I had completely forgotten. "God, Sam, I'm

sorry. I completely forgot, and there's something I really have to do."

Another of those pauses, this one longer. "I take it these aren't plans you can change." He didn't sound happy. *I really hate secrets.* Well, this particular secret was for his own good.

"Not really, no." I winced at the curtness in my voice and hastened to add, "But I really do want to meet your dad sometime. Maybe next weekend." *If we're all still alive.*

"Yeah, sure. Look, I gotta go—someone's checking out one of the powerboats."

"Okay. Bye, Sam." I was about to say something about calling him soon, but the call disconnected. *Damn.* Well, I could repair the damage later. I hoped. Today I had people to see.

I picked up my clothes from where I'd flung them last night before finally falling into bed. They stank of stale cigarettes and beer, which meant I did, too. California has a law against smoking in bars and restaurants, but the establishments I'd visited last night openly ignored it.

As I measured coffee and assessed the age of the few slices of bread still in the bag—not moldy yet—I mentally reviewed what I had learned so far. Not as much as I had hoped, but a lot more than I had expected.

Rocko had been hanging around town for a couple of years, mostly sticking to a circle of blue-collar bars in Costa Mesa and Fountain Valley. He wasn't known to have had a regular job, but he sold a little marijuana and crank—low-quality powdered speed, usually snorted—and was considered to be a pretty decent auto mechanic, if somewhat unreliable. He liked to fight and had been picked up by the police once or twice, but most of the places he frequented leaned toward self-policing, with fights broken up and minor injuries tended by patrons.

Then, about six months ago, Rocko had stopped hustling cash-paying engine-repair jobs, yet he seemed to have more money in his pocket. About the same time, Dominic had begun making his occasional appearances, although he never stayed longer than it took to order a drink and have a chat with Rocko. Bartenders notice things—it's essential for survival in an environment where inhibitions are often left behind with the second drink. Dominic was remembered for his lavish tips and the way people reacted to him.

I had finally found the two men who had accompanied Rocko to Jimbo's on the one and only night I had seen him there. I'd been afraid that I wouldn't recognize them, but I needn't have worried. I had been at the Pierce Street Annex, a reasonably respectable rock-and-roll bar with an ear-splitting band, where the two were unsuccessfully trying to pick up the college girls gyrating on the dance floor. They stuck out like sore thumbs among the smooth-skinned scions of the Newport Heights set, most of whom were dressed in sloppy cargo shorts and eighty-dollar polo shirts.

The two Rocko wannabes—the very thought made me shudder—were standing at a corner of the bar and adopting macho poses, flexing their biceps whenever a girl walked by. It wasn't working, though it might have been amusing to watch for a while, but I had an agenda.

"Hi, boys. Didn't I meet you two last weekend at Jimbo's? You're Rocko's friends, right?"

"Yeah," said one, and they both tried to pretend that women approached them all the time. It would have been more effective if both sets of eyes weren't glued to my boobs.

"Why don't we go out to the patio? It's too loud to talk in here." I didn't press, but I didn't have to. As Sukey had pointed out, they're really good boobs.

Once in the relative quiet of the patio, however, I didn't have time to fuck around. I had never tried to press two people at one time before, but it was a night for firsts. "Tell me what you know about Dominic."

"Rocko's boss?" asked one, and I nodded. "Rocko was moving drugs for him."

"What kind of drugs?"

The speaker shrugged, and the other chimed in. "Cocaine and crack."

I nodded, and the original guy spoke up again. "But he was going to get some heroin. A lot of heroin."

This was apparently news to bachelor number two, so I ignored him and concentrated on the first guy.

"Tell me about the drugs."

"Rocko was just small-time. He would get a little product from Dominic, push it out to the guys that dealt in the bars and stuff. He made a cut and could keep a little of the stuff for himself and to share with his friends."

"Like you guys."

"Yeah, like us. And for chicks. You know."

Yeah, I knew. "Are you talking about the cocaine or the heroin?"

"The coke. But Rocko was bragging that he had done such a good job that he was moving up. He was going with Dominic on a pickup, then taking the stuff back to his place. Dominic was gonna let him cut it and, you know, repackage it."

"For sale on the street?"

"No, to pass on to some guy in Santa Ana. For his people to sell."

The conversation had gone on for some time, but I had learned no more. After wrapping up with my now usual instruction to forget all about our little chat, I called it a night.

So Dominic had thought he was covering his tracks. He had apparently not thought it necessary to tell Rocko not to brag to his fan club. And if Dominic had made one mistake, he could make more.

So today I had a couple of choices. If someone in Santa Ana had been expecting a big delivery of heroin, there were probably some unhappy customers on the street and some very nervous dealers on the street corners. But I didn't think I could face a crawl through the Santa Ana streets so soon after last night, and I had another lead.

Jimbo had said that Lawyer Bob and Taylor the Mercedes salesman had both recognized Dominic, and Hilda had given me the name of three places where she had seen him. It was time for a whole different kind of bar crawl. I picked up my cell phone and punched in a number that I had never actually called before.

"Hello, Hilda? It's Mercy." I was expecting her to sound fuzzy, figuring I was probably waking her up.

"Mercy! I was going to call you. I've lost six pounds, and I've told simply everyone that they *must* go see you." She sounded as if she had been up for hours.

"I'm not calling too early, am I?" I didn't really care, but I was surprised by her perkiness.

"Heavens, no, I've been up for ages. I haven't been drinking, you know. I think you pegged it when you pointed out that's why I wasn't losing weight. And the clubs are kind of boring when everyone's drunk and I'm not, so I've been getting home kind of early."

"I'm really happy to hear that, Hilda." And I was. If ever I needed a reminder that my abilities could actually be used for something other than to coerce assholes to talk, it was this morning. "Actually, I was calling to ask a favor."

"Name it."

Who was this woman? And what had she done with Hilda?

"I was calling to ask if anything interesting was going on at the Bay Club or the Wayne Club today and if you would be willing to take me with you."

"Really?" Hilda had invited me to these establishments a dozen times, then given up. "Wait a minute, I should have the monthly calendars here somewhere. Hold on."

I heard a clunk as the phone hit a hard surface, then some drawers opening and closing.

"Here they are. Let's see…Sunday. You're in luck. There's a friendship regatta at the Bay Club—racing small boats against some of the other clubs, you know—and those are always fun. After the race, all the single boat owners usually hang out at the bar. You can come, but I get first shot at any likely prospects." Good old Hilda. It was nice to know that alcohol wasn't responsible for all her personality flaws.

"Sounds perfect, Hilda. Should I meet you?"

"God, no, I'd never live it down if you were to valet park that tin can you call a car at the Balboa Bay Club. I'll pick you up at eleven, or better yet, come to my house and we'll ride over together."

"Sounds good. Oh, and Hilda? One other thing." I took a deep breath. "Can I borrow something to wear?"

The Balboa Bay Club is not the oldest nor the most exclusive of Newport Beach's private yacht clubs, but it *is* the most expensive. If you look up nouveau riche in the dictionary, you will see pictures of a number of its members, as well as a few shots of the seldom-away-from-the-dock trophy yachts that line its piers. But for every pretender, there was at least one or two legitimate sailors in the club, and the competition in the semi-annual Newport Harbor Friendship Regatta, which the clubs took turns hosting, was fierce.

I had shown up at Hilda's door with an assortment of pants, some battered deck shoes and my one good pair of sandals, which showed little wear and tear, because they were horribly uncomfortable—but were too expensive to throw out. Hilda and I are about the same number of inches in circumference, but I'm a good six inches taller and couldn't possibly borrow her slacks, nor squeeze into her tiny shoes.

After a careful perusal of my pants, she decided the khaki slacks were the least offensive, and she actually clucked with approval over the torturous sandals. One of her guest bedrooms was essentially a giant walk-in closet, and I stared in amazement at the racks of clothes, many of which still had tags.

She started sorting through a selection of sweaters that seemed to be on a nautical theme. The sailors I knew never wore anything with gold braid or appliqués of sailboats, but Hilda assured me that the Bay Club was different. Her own culotte set had enough gold braid on it to make an admiral jealous, and the matching gold sandals had spiked heels that would never be allowed on a boat deck.

We finally agreed on a relatively simple twinset with only a little red-and-gold braid on the neck and sleeves, and some kind of coat of arms on the cardigan pocket. *St. John,* the label read. The price tag, which she removed without a second glance, said $885.00, and that didn't include the matching shell. I decided to avoid red wine and anything with tomato sauce.

An hour and a half later we were seated on the much-coveted balcony rail seats, drinking club sodas with lime and checking out the few men who had arrived. Hilda had been torn between making an entrance and arriving early to stake out the best seats in the house, and I had voted for the latter. If I had to stand for hours in these shoes, I was probably going to kill someone.

"Isn't this where you met Dominic?" I asked when I thought we had been there long enough so the question would not seem suspicious. I would *not* press Hilda, at least not outside the hypnotherapy room. She was my client and, strange as it seemed, my friend. It shouldn't be necessary, anyway. She loved to gossip.

"Yes, but he's not a member." Hilda had been happy to tell me that her initial enrollment fee had been fifty thousand dollars, and that was fifteen years ago. She hadn't told me the annual dues. I knew she eagerly scanned the lists of new candidates being sponsored for membership, looking for celebrities and potential boyfriends. She would have known if someone was trying to sponsor Dominic.

"Do you know who invited him?"

"Why do you want to know?" she asked, her tone mildly suspicious.

"I don't see anyone else I recognize. I just thought it might be nice to see a familiar face."

This was apparently an acceptable answer, as she continued. "I'm not sure who invited him, to be honest. It might even have been at one of the Thursday Opens."

I nodded. Even I had heard of the night when the club opened its doors to nonmembers. Young girls looking for sugar daddies and unscrupulous men looking for rich widows prowled the bar. From what I'd heard, the members were on to them, and they mostly ended up with each other.

"But I'm sure you would recognize some of the other members, Mercy. I see people from here around town all the time."

I was about to argue that I didn't go to the same places she did and so was less likely to recognize anyone, when a voice to my left interrupted.

"Mercy Hollings, is that you?"

I turned. An elderly couple, carefully dressed as if coming from church, were standing at the door to the dining room.

"Edna?" I stood, managing not to wobble on the ridiculous heels, and bent to kiss a powdered cheek. "And Ralph, isn't it? How have you been?"

I knew the couple from the library, where Edna volunteered a couple of days a week. I'd had no idea they were part of the Bay Club set.

"We've been fine, Mercy. We read about your new business in the paper."

"Yes, it's going very well, and—Butchie!" The former owner of Sam's business came through the door and joined them. "Don't tell me you're a member here."

"Hell, no!" Butchie was dressed just as I had always seen him—ancient khakis, a ball cap and a gimme T-shirt advertising something nautical. "But half my old customers are. Edna and Ralphie here invited me to have a snort and watch the races. Even though I've never forgiven Ralphie for proposing to Edna first."

"Oh, behave, would you?" Edna said, looking vastly pleased as Ralph gave Butchie a mock-threatening growl. "Stop by and say hello, dear, before you leave," she said to me.

Just then the hostess appeared, and the three were escorted to a table at the opposite end of the deck.

"See what I mean?" said Hilda when I returned. "You'll see a lot of familiar faces before the afternoon is out. Oooh, fresh meat, three o'clock. Don't look at them!"

I obediently kept my back turned to whomever Hilda was surreptitiously scoping out, but she soon turned away dismissively. "Fake Rolexes," she said in disgust. "You can tell by the second hand."

I filed this little piece of information in my who-gives-a-shit folder and turned to begin my own perusal of the crowd.

The number and density of people steadily increased as the afternoon wore on and, by the time the first finishers from the race started to arrive, the upper and lower decks were both crowded. By four in the afternoon a live band had started playing and the place was wall to wall.

I was about to tell Hilda that I wanted to go when I spotted a familiar face through the crush. Lawyer Bob, aka Robert Randall, attorney-at-law, was trying to negotiate the crowded deck with a beer in one hand and a cocktail in the other.

"Save my seat," I told Mr. Fake Rolex number one, who was hitting on Hilda. Apparently she had decided that timepiece authenticity wasn't all that important, because she seemed to be enjoying his blandishments.

He gratefully took the seat I had vacated, and I followed Bob. Luckily the crowd prevented me from moving too quickly, so I didn't have to worry about looking as if I knew how to walk in those damned shoes.

I caught up with him just as he handed the beer to a big-bellied man with a deep red sunburn and white hair. "Hi, Bob. Remember me?" He turned to see who was talking, and I smiled brightly.

"Oh, hey, Mercy. Haven't seen you here before."

"First time. You come here a lot?"

"Me? Yeah, I'm a member. Good for business contacts." He gestured toward the sunburned man. "This is Grant. He was in the regatta."

"How did you do?" It seemed polite to ask.

"Not bad."

He was checking me out, and I was glad I had chosen one of Hilda's more modest offerings. I turned to Bob. "Bob, do you know a guy named Dominic?"

"Dellarosa? Sure. Why? You looking for him? I don't think he's here."

"No, I'm not looking for him. I was just wondering what you could tell me about him."

Bob shrugged. "Not much. Grant here knows him better than I do." He turned to Grant, who had stopped trying to guess my age, weight and bra size, and was now eyeing me suspiciously.

"Why are you asking about Dominic?" *Here we go again.*

"It's not important why I'm asking," I said, now comfortable with the double press. "Just tell me what you know about him."

"Okay. He's supposed to be an antique dealer, but he doesn't have a shop. Claims to work on consignment only. I think he's really a drug dealer."

Bob looked surprised, so I concentrated on Grant.

"Tell me why you think that."

"Well, he gets these phone calls all the time where he seems like he's talking in some kind of code. Acts like he's talking about antiques, but it's really all about dates, amounts and locations."

"How can you tell?" I was starting to get interested. As Grant explained, I looked him over more carefully.

"Before I retired, I was an engineer for a company that built nuclear reactors for submarines. We did a lot of top-secret work, and we couldn't talk about it in public. But if you were at a restaurant with one of your coworkers and there were a bunch of other people around when an idea popped into your head, you'd say something like 'next time we decide to move ten cases of paper, we should try putting half the paper on one dolly and half on another.' Sounds like we're talking about office supplies, right?"

I nodded, and Grant went on.

"Except the other engineers at the table know we're taking about a problem we were working on in the lab that day." He shrugged. "So when Dominic starts talking about chairs and veneers and vases, no one else realizes he's talking gibberish. But I picked right up on it."

I was fascinated. This guy was obviously a lot smarter than he looked. I noticed that Bob was still standing there silently. If he had known anything about

Dominic, my instructions would have ensured that he told me.

"Bob, you can forget all about this conversation, except that I said hello to you. Why don't you go to the bar and get us some more drinks, while Grant and I talk some more? Will you do that for me, Bob?"

"Okay."

He wandered off toward the bar, and I turned back to Grant.

"Grant, do you remember anything specific that he said where you were actually able to figure out the places or times he was talking about?"

He considered. "Maybe. I'd have to think about it."

"Was there anything else that made you think you were right about Dominic?" I asked.

"I saw him in Santa Ana one time. Strange place for an antique dealer."

"How so?"

"My friend Gabriel, he owns a company that rents out those big cranes, like they use to build high-rises. You know what I'm talking about?"

"The kind you actually install on the site and leave up until the construction is done?" I'd seen them from a distance, but I knew what he meant.

"Exactly. Well, my friend and I were going over to Anaheim Hills to play golf, and he wanted to stop by and drop off some paperwork to one of his foremen— permits or something. So we were in downtown Santa Ana, near the courthouse. There was a bunch of construction, not just Gabriel's job, and a lot of one-way streets. We had to circle around two or three blocks to get back to the main road. Man, it was nasty back there."

I could picture it. I'd been downtown for jury selection last year. The area immediately around the courthouse wasn't too bad, but within a few blocks the city turned into a maze of graffiti-covered tenements and abandoned buildings.

"Anyway, there's this bar—don't know what it's called, Mexican place, I think—just a cinder-block square with a door. And some really scary-looking characters were in the parking lot, leaning on a big black Jag. We were stopped at the light, and the door opens and out walks Dominic. He didn't see me, because he stopped to talk to the scary guys. Then I remembered he had a car like that."

"What happened?" I asked, barely breathing.

"Nothing. The light changed and we drove away. But next time I saw Dominic, I decided it was better to keep my mouth shut and not ask him about it."

"That was good thinking," I said, no longer pressing.

Bob arrived with more drinks. I saw that he had brought me one of whatever he was drinking.

"Thanks, Bob. Can you think of anything else to tell me about Dominic?"

Both men shook their heads. I took out a business card and added a final press.

"Grant, I'm going to give you my business card. You are not going to tell anyone else about our conversation, but you are going to keep thinking about the things you overheard Dominic saying on his cell phone. If you figure out any times or places—or anything that would help me find out exactly what Dominic is buying or selling, and from whom—you will call me and tell me. Will you call me if you figure something out, Grant?"

"I'll call you." He looked serene.

"Thank you, Grant. You, too, Bob. You both feel very good and relaxed, and you are enjoying your day very much. Are you enjoying your day?"

"Yes," came the stereo response.

"Excellent."

I returned to the bar, looking for Hilda. Fake Rolex number two was sitting in her chair, and mine had been taken over by a woman who was too old for the shade of red her hair had been dyed.

"Where are Hilda and your friend?" Number two gestured, pointing toward the lower deck, where a squirming mass of bodies was bouncing up and down to the inevitable reggae. I spotted Hilda's shining hair in the throng.

I needed to get out of here. I had to work tomorrow, and I wanted to find that bar in Santa Ana before it got too dark. I could probably use the press to keep someone from mugging me, but I really didn't want to have to park my car anywhere in that neighborhood for more than a few minutes.

"Can you do me a favor? Can you tell Hilda I caught a ride home and I'll call her? Thanks." As I headed for the front door, I hoped the guy was sober enough to remember to tell her. I hadn't thought it necessary to press him, but his eyes had looked a little glazed to me.

I went to stand near where the valets were busily re-
trieving cars for those who were leaving and parking
cars for the still-arriving guests. I waited until I saw a
reasonably sober-looking lone man get into one of the
cars, then swiftly walked to the passenger side and got
in.

"Wha—"

I cut off his astonished question with a firm press.

"Take me to Balboa. You can drop me off at
Jimbo's."

He shut his open mouth and put the car into gear,
and I settled into the passenger seat. I couldn't wait to
get home and out of those damned shoes.

12

Of course, as soon as I got to Jimbo's, I realized my car was still at Hilda's, so I had to make my hapless chauffeur turn around and drive me to her house. The clothes I had been wearing when I arrived earlier were locked inside the house, but I had my car keys in my pocket. I was home, changed and back out the door in twenty minutes.

It was less than a half hour's drive from Newport Beach to the poorest end of Santa Ana, the capital city of Orange County, but it was more like a trip to another world. The other side of this multicultural town, while not wealthy, still had the feel of a family neighborhood, with barbecues and bicycles more common than police cars and crack dealers. I had rented a room there when I first came to California and never felt unsafe.

On this side of town, though, just having to stop at a light gave me an uneasy feeling. Pedestrians stared at me with hollow eyes. I didn't belong here. The people on the street were almost exclusively Hispanic. My dark hair might have passed at first glance, but I was different on some fundamental level, in a way that went beyond features and coloring. I was lacking despair.

The big cranes that still rose over downtown's urban renewal projects had given me a starting point, but there were any number of small one-way streets that could have been the ones Grant had talked about. I started a slow, looping route on the north side of Main Street, trying to find the bar.

In a rich neighborhood, slow circling will draw suspicion that you are casing the houses for burglary. Here, it drew crack dealers. I was trying not to retrace my own tracks, but I had to double back a couple of times when the one-way streets and dead ends defeated me, and I found myself cruising by a familiar street corner a second time. One member of the small group of young men clustered around the door of a seedy-looking bodega did a quick glance up and down the street, then approached my car, hands in his pockets.

My first instinct was to hit the gas, but I forced down my panic and lowered the window. He leaned on the frame.

"Hey, *Mami.* Do something for you?" His darting eyes scanned the interior of my car, apparently finding nothing to alarm him.

"Maybe. I'm trying to find a bar."

"Lotta bars around here." He looked over his shoulder, then up and down the street. This guy's eyes never stopped moving, which I realized was probably necessary to survive in this neighborhood. I took a moment to look around myself. Two of the other corner-dwellers were edging toward my car.

"Tell your friends to back off," I said quickly, pressing.

He turned and shouted something in Spanish, and the other men subsided. He turned back to me. "So, whatchoo want in a bar? I can hook you up, you don't even have to get out of your car." He put one of his arms on the roof of my car, lifting open his leather jacket, which was too warm for the mild evening. I could smell his sweat—and see the top of a pistol sticking out of his jeans, as was no doubt his intention.

"Tell me." I pressed again. "You ever see a guy in a black Jaguar hanging around here? Big guy, expensive clothes."

"Maybe. You be surprised how many Jags around here."

"This guy sells drugs."

He snorted. "*Mami,* they all sell drugs. How you think they got the Jags?"

He had a point.

"Who do you buy drugs from?"

"I don' buy drugs. My man drop it off, I move it, give him his money. He pay me."

I digested this. This guy was too far down the food chain to be of any help to me. Maybe his supplier knew Dominic. "Your man, who's he?"

"Jesús. Don't know his last name. He come around soon."

"You sell drugs for someone and don't even know his last name?"

"Don't gotta know. Better I don't, you know what I mean, *Mami?*"

"Yeah, I guess I do." I took a twenty out of my pocket and handed it to him—I figured it might get back to Jesús that he had been talking to someone for too long with nothing to show for it. "Tell your friends the reason you spent so long talking to me was that I'm hot and you were trying to get me to meet you later, okay?"

"Okay." He stood up and headed back toward the corner.

I continued my looping journey, more careful not to cover old ground. I saw a lot of bars, but nothing that looked like the cinder-block box Grant had described.

The shadows were getting long and I was running out of streets when I saw it. A squat, square building with a flat roof, sitting in the middle of a littered parking lot. A wooden sign said *Beer* in block letters. There was no other outside marking, other than the ubiquitous graffiti, most of which was unreadable to my uninitiated eyes. I could make out a few things. *Mad Tino,* in stylized scarlet. *Gangsta Girls.*

I parked my car directly in front of the doors. There were no windows, but maybe some customer traffic coming in and out would prevent me from having to buy new hubcaps after my visit. I beeped my alarm and went inside.

Mexican music blared from a jukebox, and the cigarette smoke was thick. It was a little sadder, a little meaner, than the Costa Mesa bars, but cut along the same lines. There were more people inside than cars in the parking lot, and I guessed a lot of the patrons traveled on foot. I went up to the battered bar and sat on a rough wooden stool. I'd have to check my ass for splinters later.

"Cerveza." I don't speak much Spanish, but I know the really important words.

A draft was poured from an unlabeled spigot and placed in front of me. The bartender had a face like a bulldog—lower jaw slung forward, heavy jowls and bloodshot eyes with too much white exposed by sagging lower lids. He flicked those eyes over me, then averted them. I put a five on the bar, and he made change. I was surprised to see that beer was only a buck.

"You speak English?" He nodded, still not looking directly at me. Well, he had to understand me to be pressed, so we were halfway there. "You will want to answer some questions for me."

Now he looked up, as if eager to comply, but his gaze moved over my shoulder, and I turned to see a man leaning against the bar to my left.

"Why you bothering *Papi?* He don't know nothing."

His accent was light, but the rhythms spoke of border towns. I gave him a quick assessment. *Great. Meet Rocko, south of the border edition.*

"Is that so? You the man to talk to around here?" I couldn't resist putting a little challenge in my tone, even though I knew it was ill-advised. I hadn't been raised in foster homes without learning something about posturing.

"Depends." He reached over and picked up my untouched beer and took a sip, grimaced, then put it back down again. "Why you give her that shit, *Papi?* If she wanted piss, she woulda asked for it."

It was supposed to make me smile, but I didn't figure it mattered whether he liked me or not, since I had no intention of using my personal charm to get him to talk.

"Depends on what?" The bartender looked confused, not knowing whether my comment was directed toward him.

I decided to have pity on him. "What other kind of beer do you have?"

Relieved, he began a recitation. "Corona, Chihuahua, Modelo—"

I interrupted. "I'll have a Modelo."

"And pour this shit out," added my new friend. The bartender picked up my glass and walked gratefully away.

"Depends on what?" I repeated.

"On whether you're a cop." He took a long, lingering look at me, and I was glad I had decided against the clingy shirt from last night. It was dirty, anyway.

"I'm not a cop," I said, adding with a press, "You can believe me."

"Okay, then I'm the man to talk to." He sat down.

When my Modelo came, I moved it out of his reach, and he laughed.

"Bring me one, too, *Papi.* And put hers on my tab."

"Thanks, *Papi.* That will be all." Released from my instructions, the bartender silently departed.

"So whatchoo want to know?" We were friends now, apparently, and he leaned close to me. I leaned away.

"First off, who I'm talking to."

"Tino."

I remembered the graffiti from the side of the building and asked, "*Mad* Tino?"

He smiled, vastly pleased. "You heard of me?" He had a gold cap on one incisor.

"Sort of. Look, Tino…" I pressed. "Tell me if you know a guy named Dominic."

"Yeah, I know him." He looked around nervously. "You his chick?" He moved back a few inches.

"No, nothing like that. I'm trying to find out about him. Tell me what you know."

"He sells drugs." Hot news flash.

"Yeah, I know he sells drugs. What I'm trying to find out is who does he sell them to? What, when, where, how much? And who does he get them from?"

Tino shrugged. "He sells to a lot of people. Not users, though. Dealers. Me, sometimes. Or he used to—coke, mostly. Some crack. But now I hear he's into heroin. Man, I don't fuck with that shit."

I was sorry to hear it. If I could get one of his dealers and press him, get him to give Dominic up… "Who does he do business with now?"

"Guy named Manny, but he don't come around here much."

"Do you know where I could find Manny?"

"No, not for sure."

Frustrated, I tried to figure out a way to phrase my question to get the most information. "If you wanted to find Manny, how would you go about it?"

He thought about it. "I'd go around to some places,

look for people I seen talking to him before. Ask them. This one guy, I seen him around sometimes. I think he might be Manny's cousin."

"Could you tell me how to find these people?"

He shook his head. "Mostly I don't know their names, but I recognize them if I see them."

I sighed. I already had one unknowing partner working on the problem. Maybe I could use another.

"Tino?" I made sure I had his full attention, then pressed firmly. "You are going to do something for me. I am going to give you my business card." I took one out and made sure I had already written my cell phone number on the back. "You are going to look for Manny. You are not going to tell anyone why you are looking for him and, if you find him, you are not going to talk to him or let him know what's going on. Do you understand?"

"Yeah. I'm going to look for Manny, but it's like…like a secret undercover mission." This guy watched too much TV, but I nodded.

"When you find him, you are going to call me at the number on the back of this card and tell me where he is. Then you are going to stay with him until I show up. If he goes somewhere new, you are going to follow him and call me with an update. You got all this?"

He nodded.

"Repeat it back to me."

He was able to repeat my instructions with enough accuracy that I was confident he understood them. I released him with the usual caveats, left my nearly untouched beer on the bar and went back to my car, taking a quick walk around it to make sure it was graffiti-free and still had all its hubcaps. It did.

Driving south on the Costa Mesa Freeway, I had a vision of an army of minions, running all over Southern California doing my bidding. I grinned at the thought. Then I remembered that in the movies, only the villains have minions. That sobered me.

I pulled into my parking space and got out of my car, thinking how tired I was, even though it wasn't even nine o'clock. The light over the side door was either burned out or I had forgotten to turn it on, and I stopped where I could still catch the glow from a streetlight to make sure I had the right key in my fingers.

A flicker of movement caught my eye and I froze. My heart leapt into my throat as a tall figure came around the dark side of the alley. "Who is it?" I said, my voice shrill. Panicked, I looked around for something to use as a weapon and settled for bunching my keys in my fist.

Then I saw who it was.

"Sam?" I sagged as my knees turned to jelly with relief. "Jesus, Sam, you scared the shit out of me."

"Sorry." Something about the tone of his voice bothered me.

"Is something wrong?" I asked.

"You tell me."

Yep, I'd been right about the tone. He was furious. He was also the kind of guy who got quiet when he was mad. Too bad. I could have used a good knock-down, drag-out fight right about now.

"Aren't you supposed to be spending the night at your father's house?" I asked, stalling for time. I found the right key again and tried to fit it into the lock, which was difficult in the dark.

"Butchie came by."

"Ah. I see." And, unfortunately, I did. I sighed. I had been hoping I would have a little more time before I had to face the I-really-hate-secrets issue with Sam. It didn't look as if that was going to happen.

"Fuck these stupid keys," I said, failing again to get the right one into the lock.

"Here, let me try."

Before I could protest, Sam had the keys out of my hand and was smoothly inserting the correct one into the lock. I really hate it when people do that. Like when I've been trying to open a jar for ten minutes and someone else does it with no effort. It pisses me off, and it was easier to be pissed off at Sam than admit that it was reasonable for him to be mad at me. At least, it was easier in my current mood.

I went inside, and he followed me, closing the door behind him.

"So?" he said.

"So what?"

"So are you going to tell me why you blew me off to hang out with a bunch of drunk socialites at the damned Balboa Bay Club?"

"I didn't blow you off, Sam. There was something I had to take care of." I went into the kitchen and opened the refrigerator, looking for something cold to drink. I opened a bottle of water and gulped. I turned around and gasped—Sam had followed me into the kitchen and was standing practically on my heels.

"From what I heard, it had to be something you could take care of from a bar stool on the upper deck." He folded his arms, waiting for a response.

I pushed past him and went back into the living room, where I plopped down on the sofa.

"I left the Bay Club a long time ago," I said.

"Yeah, I know. And judging from the smell of you, you went straight to another bar."

"Actually," I said, starting to get annoyed, "I came home and changed first."

Where did he get off questioning me about my whereabouts? I had only known him for a little over a week, for chrissake.

My eyes and tone must have conveyed my irritation, because he didn't immediately respond. I looked up to see him watching me from the kitchen door, the muscles in his jaw working. He didn't look menacing—he was way too controlled for that. But there was an unmistakable aura of power just below the surface, tightly reined.

"Look, Sam, I had some important business to take care of. It had nothing to do with you, or us, but it was really important, okay? And it had to be done. I wasn't out partying and having a good time."

"That's not what Butchie said."

"Butchie doesn't know anything about it."

Sam had left the kitchen and was standing in front of me. I didn't remember getting back to my feet, but I was looking right at him.

"I know you hate secrets. You told me, remember? And maybe—just *maybe*—I'll be able to tell you all about this someday. I don't know yet. But not now, and not with you standing there looking at me like I'm some kind of freak…"

"*Freak?* Where the hell did you come up with that?"

He was breathing faster now, and his temper and voice were both rising along with mine. T.J. and Otis could probably hear us, but I was past caring.

"All I know is that one night we practically make love, then the next day you won't take my phone call, and then you say you forgot about going to see Dad and give me some half-assed explanation about having something to do."

"Which was absolutely true!" I thundered. "Believe me, I would much rather have been visiting your dad than where I've been."

"Which is where? Just where were you that was so goddamned important?"

"I—I can't tell you. Sam, you're just going to have to trust me on this."

"Trust you?" He was incredulous. "Why the hell should I trust you? First I see you running away from my burning business, then you turn around and get a bunch of people to help me fix it. So I figure 'What the hell, Sam, she's okay,' but the same night you get all flustered when this Dominic shows up and starts asking questions. You lie to him, right in front of me."

I wanted to argue, but so far he hadn't said anything I could argue with. He went on.

"Then you invite me to your apartment, kiss me so that my head practically explodes and invite me to your party. So now I'm thinking 'Hey, something could really be going on here.'"

I had thought of Sam as a man of few words, but he was really on a roll tonight.

"So I invite you to go sailing. And that night…" He walked over and grabbed me by both upper arms. "Don't tell me it wasn't a special night for you, Mercy, because I don't believe you're that good an actress. We really connected, and it wasn't just me, Mercy. I know it wasn't."

I had been struggling to get out of his grip, but his voice almost broke on the last sentence, and I froze. His blue eyes were like laser beams, and the intensity of his gaze pierced me.

"Sam—" I started, but got no further when his mouth came down on mine.

I was dissolving. Oh my God, I was dissolving. In a few minutes I would be nothing but a puddle on my living-room floor. All I could feel were Sam's mouth and tongue and lips. It was a good thing he was holding me, or I wouldn't have been able to remain on my feet.

"Mercy," he breathed between kisses. "Oh, God, Mercy."

He plunged his tongue into my mouth, and I sucked it greedily. I felt his hands move to my back and press me against him, hard. I could feel every ridge of muscle and bone, and the hardness of his desire.

His tongue left my mouth, and his kisses moved to my throat.

"Sam," I groaned, and suddenly we were on our knees. Jolts of electricity seemed to radiate from my groin to the tips of my fingers and toes, and I was fumbling with his buttons, pulling his shirt apart and running my hands around behind his back. I felt a button bounce off my chest, and realized he was pulling my T-shirt up and over my head.

The moment the shirt was off, his hands were back on my body. "Let me—" I started, but cut off my own words with a gasp as, not bothering to reach around to unhook it, he pushed my bra up over my breasts and took a nipple between his teeth. He bit it, none too gently. Good. I didn't want gentleness, not right now.

A jolt of pleasure shot through me. I threw back my head and moaned aloud. "Aaah! Yes, please…"

I forgot about foreplay. We were in a small boat, caught in the grip of a hurricane. All the anger, desire, fear and longing crashed over us in waves. And passion—every cell in my body throbbed and strummed and begged for him. His mouth moved from my breasts back to my own mouth, and again I was enveloped in his kiss.

We clawed at one another's clothes, unwilling to pull away from the kiss, biting and sucking and inhaling one another. I devoured him and was consumed in return, as somehow his pants came undone, my zipper was lowered, our shoes came off and our underclothes tore.

There was no slow caressing, no dance of discovery. Just hard, pounding desire. The moment I was free of my jeans, I thrust my hips upward and felt him, hard as diamonds, plunging into me like a jackhammer. I was slick and wet and tight and grasping, grasping—trying to pull him farther, deeper.

"Sam! Sam!" I knew the rest of my words were unintelligible—I was screaming. Sam screamed, too, and it might have been my name or it might have been the primal howl of an animal at the moment when its deepest urges were consummated. I didn't care.

"Now, Sam! Now!" My words may have been lost, but my intention was not. I knew I was pressing, but I could no more have stopped it than the tide. "Come *now!*"

He exploded into me, filling me all the way to my womb, and I shattered into a million shards of glass that flew and cut and sliced and could never be put together again. I heard a voice screaming and couldn't tell if it was mine or his. I left my body on the floor and floated around the room with the pieces of falling glass, flung by the winds that blew through my apartment like a cyclone, finally spiraling down to deposit me back into my own form, limp and panting on the floor under Sam's sprawled figure.

I looked up at him. His eyes were closed, and his weight was on his elbows, our bodies still joined. He panted, and I could smell my own scent on his breath. "Damn," he breathed. He opened his eyes, and his gaze was still razor sharp. We stared into one another's eyes for a moment; then he rolled away, pulling his still-hard cock from me so abruptly that I gasped at its sudden absence.

His jeans were still around one knee, and his shirt

hung from his back. My bra cut into the skin above my breasts, and I rolled onto my side, reaching back to free myself. Once I was fully naked, I rose unsteadily to my feet and stumbled down the hall to the bedroom, trying to catch my breath. I heard a noise behind me and turned to find Sam, now bereft of the jeans but still wearing the remains of his shirt.

"Sam, that was—"

"I know," he said, reaching to tumble me back on the bed, my feet still on the floor. He fell to his knees and, pressing my legs apart, parted my labia with his fingers and pressed his tongue inside, running it up until it caught on the hood that sheltered the bud of my clitoris. He stopped there, catching it gently between his teeth, then sucking greedily. I collapsed fully onto my back and arched as waves of impossible pleasure drove outward to my limbs.

"Oh, God." I couldn't stand it—he was alternating between nibbling, sucking and licking in such rapid succession that I was going to orgasm again before I could even describe it. "I'm going to come again."

"Not yet," he said, suddenly standing and moving me expertly so that I was fully on the bed. He flipped himself around so that he was able to resume his ministrations, but his penis arrived conveniently in front of my lips. Well, that was one way to shut me up.

I took it in my mouth, tasting a musky flavor that I knew was a combination of my own juices and his seed. I tried to tease him gently, running my tongue along his shaft and lightly licking around the edge of the head, but every time he took my clitoris between his teeth, I involuntarily clamped down and sucked hard, causing him to groan in return. Impossibly, he was as hard as before, and I tilted my head back and let the tip of his penis slide into my throat, and was gratified when his entire body shuddered in response.

The sensitive nerves in my tongue could feel every pulse and throb, and I knew when he was growing close to another climax. I could have let him finish this way, but I was greedy for another explosion like the first, so I pulled my face away and twisted, intending to turn him over and ride him.

"Oh, no you don't." In a flash, Sam was on his knees and had pulled me around like a rag doll. In seconds he was behind me, thrusting into me like a rutting stallion. My muscles clamped down on him so hard that only our combined slickness made it possible for him to continue to move in and out, in and out, until our thundering orgasms caused us to scream anew.

This time I stayed in my body. I knew I would probably be sore in a dozen places whenever the endorphins wore off and I could feel anything other than bliss. Sam shuddered and pulled back, then collapsed on the bed beside me. I lay down and faced him, not knowing what to say.

"Water," he croaked, in the tone of a man lost in the desert. I realized I was just as parched, and was thankful the need for conversation had been put off, at least for a few more minutes.

When I stepped out of the bedroom, I saw we had left a trail of clothing and shoes from the living room to the bedroom door. In the living room, the table closest to the hallway had been overturned and a lamp was on the ground. *When did that happen?* I picked them up and then noticed the living-room blinds were wide open.

Oh, shit. I wondered if any tourists had caught the floor show. Literally. At least the lights had been dim in the living room and off in the hall. Still… I shut the blinds and got two glasses of cold water from the kitchen. Bringing them back, I caught a glimpse of myself in the mirror above the fireplace. It was pretty scary.

Sam was lying on the bed, his head turned toward the door, his face expressionless. I put down the water. "I'll be right back," I said quickly and fled to the bathroom.

I washed my face, then took a warm washcloth and made a few tentative swipes between my legs, wincing slightly but enjoying the warmth. This gave me an idea—if it felt this good to me, it would be nice for Sam, and I took a fresh washcloth, soaked it in hot water and wrung it out. Picking up a clean hand towel, I returned to the bedroom.

Sam was up on one elbow, drinking water and looking at me silently, like a big golden cat. Was that a smile? Not quite. Pulling away from his eyes, I sat on the bed and used the warm cloth to envelop his finally soft penis. He tensed, but relaxed quickly and let me finish. As I dried him, he took the warm cloth, folded it inside out and wiped his face. He handed it back to me, and this time he did smile.

I placed the cloths on the nightstand, then turned to face him. "Sam, we need to talk."

He shook his head. "Not yet." He reached up and pushed my hair away from my face. "Not until we've made love."

"Sam, not ten minutes ago…"

He cut me off. "That wasn't making love. It was *amazing*—" Again the smile. My heart did a little flip-flop. "But it wasn't making love."

"I'm not sure I can—"

"Shhh," he said, pulling me toward him. "I'm not sure I can, either. But I'm going to try."

This time, we made love. We made love like thirsty men finding an oasis, like lost children finding their mothers and being allowed to crawl back into the womb. When I came, tears sprang from my eyes and fell down on Sam's face below me. I saw that his eyes were open, and I collapsed in his arms. Then we slept, tangled together in a snarl of arms and legs and bed-sheets. We slept, and I forgot everything else, even to dream.

13

I woke up alone. I had expected to, knowing Sam had to get back to his father, but I was still disappointed. Which annoyed me. It had been great sex, right? Sure it had—mind-numbing, holy shit, call-an-ambulance sex. And if there was ever a time in my life when it was important not to let people get too close to me, this was it. But dammit, when I rolled over and saw the empty bed, I had felt…what? Relieved that we'd never had that talk, for one thing. I should have felt normal. No one other than Fred had ever shared my bed for an entire night. Ten days ago, I would have said that waking up with a man would make me feel creepy. So why did waking up without one bother me?

I made coffee and fed Fred in a daze, then sat on my patio in the foggy dawn and mostly ignored the bowl of cereal I had prepared. It was Monday. Deadline day. The last day my friends were safe, if I couldn't do something to stop Dominic.

Since that one image of Sam burning with his boat, Dominic hadn't paid any visits to my head—that I knew of. He claimed he couldn't read my mind, and I believed him. Otherwise he'd know his heroin was currently messing up the chemical composition of the sewage in the greater Newport Beach area. But since our conversation, I hadn't given much thought to his assertion that *I* might be telepathic. But if I were, did I have another tool to use against him?

Most of them say you don't really exist—that you're some kind of urban legend. I had been avoiding thinking about this part of his revelation. Who the hell had he been talking about?

Your real parents, said a voice in my head. But surely my real parents knew I existed. So who was it?

I sighed heavily. I couldn't afford to take the time to think about any of this right now. I debated putting a *Closed Due to Personal Emergency* sign on my door and taking the day off, but unless I heard back from one of my unwitting spies, I didn't know what my next step would be. At least at the office I would have the opportunity to warn Sukey when she arrived.

And what about Sam? Even though my body still ached from last night's lovemaking, we had resolved nothing. I still knew he hated secrets, and he still knew I had them. How could I explain why he needed to disappear for a few days without telling him…what? Maybe I could at least get him to move his boat somewhere, since my Dominic-imposed vision had proved that my nemesis knew where it was currently docked. And the rental business had to be slow during the week—surely Skip could take over, at least until the weekend.

And then what? What if nothing changed by the weekend? I decided that, like they said in the country song, we would have to burn that bridge when we got there.

I brought Fred with me to the office again, even though he had been on his own most of the previous day. Sukey wasn't there yet, but I hadn't expected her to be. I managed to pull up my daily appointments without her assistance and I scanned them. There was nothing out of the ordinary, other than my first session with a teenage girl with behavioral problems, according to her mother. Whether Mommy was paying the bills or not, I wasn't going to do anything contrary to the girl's will. It was against my ethics. Which somehow still didn't seem like a hypocritical statement.

My cell phone, set on vibrate, went off during my second session of the day, showing a caller ID I did not recognize. "I'm going to step out of the room. Just relax until I return," I told the already deeply relaxed man who was looking for help sticking to his personal exercise regimen.

"Hello, this is Mercy," I said the moment I had closed the door behind me.

"It's Tino. I found Manny."

A rush of exhilaration filled me. "Where is he? Does he know you're watching him?" I would definitely hang out a *Personal Emergency* sign for a shot at Manny.

"He's at the liquor store, and I'm pretty sure he hasn't spotted me. I been playing it real cool, you know?"

I smiled inadvertently at his secret-agent-man stage whisper, and he continued. "I don't know how long he'll be here, but the thing is, I know where he's gonna be later."

"Tell me."

"He was joking with the man who sold him a lottery ticket that he's going to the casino tonight to watch the baseball game. Says if he wins at blackjack, the lottery and his baseball bet all at the same time, he gonna move to Cancún."

"Casino?" Contrary to common belief, you don't have to go to Las Vegas to gamble from Southern California, depending on what kind of games you want to play. I knew this vaguely, but hadn't been to any of the various gambling venues.

"Yeah, the Indian bingo place."

"The one on the Morongo reservation?" Which was a good hour and a half drive from Newport Beach, traffic permitting. "Do you know what time the baseball game starts?"

"If he's talking about the Angels game, it starts at four."

Damn, that was early. I would have to blow off my afternoon appointments.

"But you know baseball, the games last forever."

That was true. Surely he wouldn't leave after the first couple of innings, since he wouldn't be able to collect his winnings—provided there were any—until the game was over.

"Want me to meet you?" asked Tino. I wondered if this was still the press at work, or if he was enjoying

his undercover duty. It didn't matter—I couldn't press
him over the phone anyway.

"Yeah, Tino, I need you to point him out to me. You
ever been out there before? Tell me a good place to
meet you, where he won't see us."

"He'll be at the tables in the middle—that's where
they got the big TVs. There's a bar sorta next to it—
got built-in video poker in front of every stool. What
time you be there?"

I did a mental calculation. If I cancelled my appointments from three-thirty on, I should be able to
beat the Riverside rush on the Ninety-one freeway.
"Around five-thirty. You calling from your cell phone?"

"Yeah."

"I'll call you if I'm going to be late."

"Roger. See you there."

Roger? I ended the call, shaking my head, and
returned to my now-dozing exercise procrastinator. I
hoped Sukey would arrive in time to handle the can-
cellations, but I was leaving one way or the other.

When Sukey still hadn't shown up by five minutes
before two, I tried her cell phone, but it went straight
to voice mail. *Oh, well, I'd kind of implied she didn't
have to come in today if she didn't want to.*

I called my three-thirty appointment in the few
minutes I had before my two o'clock, and managed
to reach or leave messages for the rest of the appointments before my two-thirty arrived. At three-twenty-
five, I grabbed Fred and locked up. I left a note on the
door, just in case anyone didn't get my message,
dropped Fred in front of the apartment without getting

out of the car, watched him skitter down the alley toward the beach, then headed east yet again.

As I drove toward the town of Cabazón, situated at the edge of the Mojave Desert, something was nagging at the back of my mind. Something I had forgotten, or should have thought of. The evening traffic report came on the local NPR affiliate, and I forgot my doubts as I turned up the volume to make sure the Ninety-one was clear. Even with twelve lanes, it could become a parking lot in minutes if there was a wreck, or if the Santana winds kicked up, causing sandstorms and swaying big rigs. So far, so good.

The parking lot of the newly expanded Casino Morongo was largely empty on a Monday night, but I still counted twelve tour buses parked at the designated end of the lot. When the door opened, the unique cacophony of the slot machines assailed my ears.

White-haired women in colorful running suits sat in front of the noisy machines, clutching plastic buckets full of quarters and laughing with their companions. I looked around for the table games, and spotted signs on poles advertising blackjack, Pai-gow poker and Let it Ride. Near the edge of the area was a bar, and I saw Tino sitting on a stool, sipping a Corona and dropping quarters in a video poker machine.

"Hey, Tino," I said, taking a seat next to him.

"Hey, *Mami*." He stopped punching cards on the touch screen long enough to give me a wolfish look. "Got our boy in my sights—right over there." He nodded toward the tables, and I followed his gaze.

"Which one is he?"

"Guy in the red shirt, sitting at the blackjack table."

"Thanks, Tino. You can go home now."

"What? I just got here." He sounded hurt. "What if you need some, you know, backup or something?"

Damned if I wasn't actually starting to like this cocky bastard.

I turned to him and pressed lightly. "Tino, you did a good job. You should be proud of yourself. Now it's better for you to leave, so there's less of a chance Manny will see you and get suspicious. Do you understand?"

"Yeah, it would be better if he didn't spot me." He nodded affably.

"If I need you again, I will call you. But right now you are going to go home, okay?"

"Okay." He picked up his change and ambled toward the door.

I turned around and examined my prey.

He wasn't what I'd expected. His face was a little like Papi the bartender's, but with a few less years of gravity and booze. He was paunchy and looked like he should be running a backyard barbecue, not dealing smack. There would be no problem pressing him, but I needed to get him out of the casino.

This place may have been small by Vegas standards, but I could see from the smoked glass and mirrored ceiling tiles that the eyes-in-the-sky were just as ubiquitous. I didn't particularly want to be videotaped pressing a heroin dealer in the middle of a casino pit.

I had stopped at the ATM on my way and picked up two hundred dollars. I knew that wasn't much, and it could disappear on a blackjack table in the wink of an eye. I got off my bar stool and strolled over to the table, relieved to see the minimum-bet sign was set at five dollars. Even with my limited skills, I ought to be able to last long enough to strike up a casual conversation that would not seem suspicious to onlookers.

When a middle-aged Asian woman vacated the seat to Manny's left, I took it. I played a few hands, betting conservatively and trying not to look like I was watching Manny. He was keeping an eye on the TV and playing two spots simultaneously and still had time to notice my inexperience.

"You don't want to hit that," he told me when I hesitated over a king-and-three hand.

"It's only thirteen," I said in a surprised tone. I really *was* a little surprised.

"Yeah, but the dealer's got a six showing. Probably got a ten in the hole, means he's gonna have to hit. He's got a better chance of bustin' than you got of *not* bustin', you know what I mean?"

I made the motion that indicated I did not want a card, and the dealer moved on to the next player. Manny gave me a wink of approval. Sure enough, the dealer had a sixteen and busted with a jack, and we all got paid.

"Thanks! I would have gone over. I'm not very good at this." I tried to sound ditsy, but was probably just a little too out of character.

"Takes practice. You new around here?" Manny

looked at me more carefully as the six-deck shoe was reshuffled.

"First time." This felt like the right track, and I wanted to stay on it. "It's nice. More fun than I thought it would be."

He nodded. "Yeah, I stopped in one time on my way back from Palm Springs. Now I can't stay away."

I suppressed a shudder at the thought of repeated exposure to the constant noise of the slot machines and the garish colors, but nodded in insincere agreement. "Oh, I'll definitely be back."

The dealer finished his shuffle, and I played a few more hands. Now that we were best buddies, Manny continued to deal out advice, and my modest stack of white and red chips started to get bigger instead of smaller. I learned I should always split eights and aces and never buy insurance.

On the third reshuffle, I stood up. "I need to stretch a little. Also, I'm hungry. Is the food any good here?"

He shrugged. "Avoid the buffet—that's strictly for senior bingo tours. The real restaurant is pretty good."

I started to gather up my chips. "Why don't you join me?" I waited for his response. I had pressed him as lightly as possible, afraid he might react physically and get noticed by one of the casino's many professional observers. To my relief he drained his coffee and started to gather up his own chips—green and black.

"Sure. I'm Manny. What's your name?"

I made sure I was out of earshot of the dealer before answering. "Mercy. Nice to meet you."

Nerves prevented me from being hungry, but I hadn't had lunch and it might be a long night, so I said "Same for me" when Manny ordered a steak and fries, and then waited until the enormous Caesar salads had been served before getting down to business.

"Manny, you will tell me about your dealings with Dominic Dellarosa." No point beating around the bush. I used a press firm enough to ensure no misunderstanding, but mild enough that he wouldn't look like he was in a trance.

"I buy drugs from him," said Manny.

"Heroin?"

He nodded, and I continued. "When was the last time you bought heroin from him?"

"Almost a month ago. I was supposed to get some weekend before last, but something happened, and he didn't have any to sell." His brow furrowed. "My customers ain't too happy, I can tell you that."

Excellent. Tino had really come through for me with this guy. "Is he supposed to be getting more?"

"Yeah." He looked at his salad, probably wondering why he wasn't eating it.

I ignored his response and continued. "When?"

"Maybe tomorrow, maybe the next day." He shrugged. "I know he steps on it 'fore he sells it to me, so I guess I'll hear from him day after that."

I digested this news. If Dominic might be receiving heroin as early as tomorrow, I had better move quickly. "Where will he be going to pick it up?"

"No idea." Manny was now gazing longingly at the bread basket. Judging by the size of his gut, he was not a man accustomed to self-denial. I guess the intensity of my press had prevented him from doing anything else until my instructions were fulfilled.

The waiter came back with the steaks, and I waited until he was done fussing with water glasses and cutlery to resume. I decided to try the wording and method that had worked so effectively on Tino.

"Manny, if you were trying to find out when and where Dominic picked up his heroin shipment, how would you go about it?"

Manny's eyes clouded, and I knew he was concentrating on the question. Finally he shook his head. "I dunno. I could try to follow him, but I don't know where he lives."

Neither did I. I had checked out the Corona del Mar address on Dominic's business card and it had turned out to be a Mail Boxes, Etc. location.

I sighed, afraid the long drive and the time I'd spent in the casino had been wasted, unless I counted the blackjack lesson. I had so little time left before Dominic…did what? Who would he hurt? When would he start? I felt a sudden and urgent need to get home as quickly as possible. I needed to talk to Sukey and Sam. And Jimbo and Hilda. What about T.J. and Otis? Just when did I get so many damned friends?

And one other question—what the hell should I do about Manny? He was still looking at me expectantly.

"You can go ahead and start eating if you want," I said, and he started methodically consuming his dinner. He was a heroin dealer, and my first instinct was to press him to get into some other line of work, but the last time I had followed my instincts with regards to a drug dealer, it hadn't worked out too well. I could ask him a few questions, find out what else he was good at, but I didn't have time.

"Manny, I want you to finish your dinner and forget all about this conversation. Do you understand?"

He nodded, mouth full.

"You don't want to buy any more heroin from Dominic. You want to start thinking about—" I struggled for a safe phrase "—legitimate career opportunities. Some way you can make money without hurting anyone and without selling drugs. Do you understand?"

"Yeah." He was already done with his salad and was making a path through his steak. My meal was untouched.

"Don't forget to pay our check, okay, Manny?"

"Okay."

I stood up to leave, and Manny surprised me by putting down his steak knife and lightly touching me on the arm. "Can I ask you a question?" he said.

"Sure."

"Is it okay if I have dessert?" He looked like a little kid.

"Sure, Manny. Have whatever you want." I said, laughing. "For dessert, that is," I hastily added. Heaven only knew what else a creep like Manny might want.

I think I broke the land-speed record between Cabazón and Balboa, all the time trying to figure out who to call and what to do. I tried Sukey's cell phone and got no answer. I didn't even know if Sam *had* a cell phone, and it was too late to call the boat-rental shop. When I pulled up at my apartment, I saw Sam waiting on the patio, and my initial apprehension was tempered by relief. At least I wouldn't have to track him down.

He stood up and came around to my car. "Hi." His voice sounded neutral, and I couldn't read his facial expression in the dark.

"Hi, yourself." I found the right key on the first try this time, and he followed me in. "I'm glad you're here. I want to talk to you."

"Good." Still neutral. Well, it was better than angry.

"Probably not about what you're hoping I want to talk about, Sam." I sat down on the sofa and invited him to join me. He did, then just waited.

"You're not going to make this easy, are you?" I said dryly.

"Nope." He settled back and folded his arms.

"Okay. All right." I was stalling. "You know how last night I said there was something you were just going to have to trust me on?"

"I remember."

"Well, I know you never actually agreed. But I need to ask you to do something."

"Tell me."

"I need you to move your boat."

Whatever he had been expecting, this was not it. The careful neutrality on his face was replaced by surprise. "Move my boat?"

"Yes, Sam. I'm afraid someone might do something to harm you, and he…implied it might happen on your boat."

Sam's eyes narrowed. "Who?"

I took a deep breath. "Dominic."

"Dominic? Why the hell would Dominic want to hurt me?" He looked genuinely astonished now.

"To get at me." I hadn't intended to tell him this much, but there it was.

He was silent for a few moments. "Does this have something to do with Rocko running the ferry into my gas dock?"

Now it was my turn to be surprised. "How did you find out it was Rocko?"

"Detective Gerson came by today with a picture—a mug shot. He was calling himself something else, and he didn't have a beard, but it was the same guy."

"Did you tell the detective about Dominic coming around looking for him?"

"Yes," replied Sam.

I digested this new information, wondering if it made things better or worse for the safety of my friends.

"What does this have to do with you?" Sam asked me.

Just press him and tell him to leave the subject alone. Yeah, that would be the easiest thing to do, but I didn't do it.

I took a deep breath and jumped in. "Rocko was working for Dominic. They were selling drugs, and moving up the ladder into heroin. When Rocko disappeared, so did about half a million dollars' worth of Dominic's heroin."

"Again, what does this have to do with you?" Sam's blue eyes were getting that laser intensity again.

"Dominic thinks I had something to do with Rocko's disappearance."

"Did you?" His eyes pinned me, and I couldn't look away.

"Yes." When I could see he was growing alarmed, I went on. "I didn't hurt him, and I didn't know about the heroin, or at least not that there was a big shipment involved. But I made him leave town."

"How?"

"I—I can't tell you," I stammered.

He made a disgusted noise and looked away.

"No, Sam, I really can't. At least not yet."

He stood up, but only to pace, which encouraged me to continue. At least he hadn't walked out. Yet.

"He gave me until the end of today to get back his heroin, or he's going to start to hurt my friends. That's what he said. And he…hinted he would do something to you on your boat. So I need you to move it—tonight. And don't sleep there until I say it's safe."

He turned on me, brimming with agitation. "Until *you* say it's safe? Mercy, why the hell don't you just go to the police?"

"Because I can't prove anything. They won't be able to stop him if he decides to go after you or Sukey. Also, he claims to have contacts in the police department, which I know is true, because he knew about Rocko and the ferry. And because—" I looked up at him, trying to find a hint of understanding in his eyes "—because I'll have to explain how I made Rocko leave town and how I found out all this stuff about Dominic. And that's the thing I just can't tell anyone about right now, Sam. Not the police. And not even you."

Our stares locked, and I could almost feel an electrical current pass between us. Again I saw the restrained power shimmering below the surface. I wondered what he would be like if that careful control ever slipped. *Dangerous?* Maybe. I held his gaze and waited.

Finally he sighed, and his expression softened. "And just where the hell am I supposed to move my boat to?"

Some of my tension drained away, and one of the several giant knots in my stomach loosened. "To Hilda's. I don't think Dominic realizes she and I are actually pretty good friends, so hopefully she isn't a target—yet. But she's got a huge dock, and she sold her late husband's boat last year. I'll call her right now."

I called Hilda and told her Sam needed a place to stash his boat for a few days, promising to explain later. I was grateful when she accepted this without question, and I put Sam on the phone to get directions. As he hung up the phone, it rang again immediately.

"Hello?" I didn't recognize the caller ID, but I hoped it was Sukey, calling from a friend's house or something.

"Is this Mercy?" asked an unfamiliar male voice.

"Who's calling, please?"

"Grant." I searched my memory for a moment before I remembered Lawyer Bob's friend from the Bay Club.

"Oh, right. Yes, this is Mercy."

"You said to call you if I figured anything out about the stuff Dominic was always saying on the phone. I think I may have come up with something."

"Hold on a minute." I punched the mute button and turned to Sam. "Are you going to go move your boat now?" I asked.

"As instructed." He almost smiled.

"Look, this call might be important in this whole mess. Do you have a cell phone?"

He nodded, and I pointed to a pad and pen. "Could you write down your number? I'll let you know if anything changes."

"I was going to ask you to come with me."

I shook my head. "Not until I hear from Sukey. After I get off this call, I'm going looking for her at her apartment and at Jimbo's. I may send her over to Hilda's, too—she's got enough room for an army in that mausoleum."

Sam didn't look happy, but he headed out the door, and I returned my attention to the call.

"Sorry, Grant. What did you figure out?" I asked as I retrieved the pad and pen.

"Well, Dominic was always talking about getting shipments of *vases*. It didn't really make sense, because he never talked about styles or periods or anything. I mean, my ex-wife was into expensive dust catchers, and I know those things are valued by who made them and where and how long ago. He just talked about how many vases, and when and where he would pick them up."

"So you think vase is code for some unit of heroin?" I took notes. *Vases—when and where?*

"Yeah. So tonight I went to the Villa Nova for dinner with a lady friend, and when we were done eating, guess who I saw sitting in the bar?"

"Dominic? Is he still there?" I could make it to the Villa Nova in under ten minutes.

"No, he left. But not before he got a phone call." Grant was warming to his story. "Me and my lady friend sat down to have an after-dinner drink, and I heard Dom ask if the vases were going to all be in the same crate or in two different ones. I'd been thinking about it, like you told me, so I perked up and paid attention."

I added *in two crates?* to my notes. "Go on."

"The answer must have been two, because I heard him say he would meet the guy to pick up the crates at Sabatino's tomorrow night at eight."

Bingo. Sabatino's Sausage Company was a restaurant that really did ship sausage all over California, and it was located in an otherwise industrial part of Newport Beach pretty close to my office. Its expansion had taken over several adjoining spaces that had previously been occupied by sailmakers, boat repair shops and other marina businesses. The row still held several storage and shop-type spaces, and it shared a parking lot with a small industrial park. It had to be in one of the storage or industrial spaces that the transfer would take place.

"Thanks, Grant. I appreciate you calling me."

"No problem. Hey, maybe I'll see you again. I've

been thinking about trying some of this hypnotherapy stuff. You think it will work on me?"

"I'm sure it will."

14

I had been planning to track Sukey down as soon as I got off the phone, but I needed to take a few minutes to figure out how Grant's information would affect my next move. A Santa Ana drug dealer said Dominic was expecting a heroin shipment over the next few days, and a retired engineer had overheard Dominic, purportedly an antique dealer, arranging to meet someone to pick up vases.

Could I go to the police with this information? I had been planning to make an anonymous call, but I had hoped for something more solid. If I could sit down in front of a cop, of course, I could make sure I would be believed. But then he or she would still have to convince his or her superiors. And I didn't really have enough to interest the police.

But Dominic didn't know that. What if I called him directly? Would he call off the shipment, or relocate it? Then I would have no chance of ensuring that the police could catch him red-handed.

I knew Dominic couldn't read my mind, but he claimed to able to tell when I was hiding something. Would he know I was essentially bluffing? Maybe not, if I played it exactly right.

And so what if he figured out I was hiding something? I would *tell* him I was holding back information. Then any deception he felt or sensed—or whatever it was he did—would have an explanation. I mentally scripted a conversation with him. I looked at the clock—I didn't have time for rewrites. It was after nine, which meant Monday night was almost over. I got out my wallet and took out his engraved card. Taking a deep breath, I dialed his cell number.

He answered on the first ring. "Mercy. I was expecting your call. Do you have good news for me?"

"Actually, I have very, very bad news for you." I thought my voice held just the right touch of disdain. "When you said there was no evidence that could be tied back to you, I think you really overestimated yourself. I should have figured it would be your arrogance that got you into trouble. You've been leaving a trail all over town."

He laughed, an incongruously pleasant sound. "Come now, Mercy. Don't try to play poker with me. I'm much better at it than you are."

"You may think so," I said, keeping my tone confident, "but you're wrong. Even the drunks at the Keg knew Rocko was working for you. Did you even *try* to press him to keep his mouth shut? You said I was better at it than you, but you must really suck at it. He told half the barflies in Orange County about you letting him cut the heroin for you. Seemed to think it was some kind of a promotion."

That shut him up, but only for a moment. "This is really all irrelevant, Mercy. Rocko's not around, a fact of which we are both aware."

"Oh, but Rocko's not the only one who's been talking about you, Dominic. A lot of the dealers in Santa Ana were very disappointed when their heroin didn't show up. Apparently junkies aren't the most patient customers in the world."

I was treading on shaky ground here—if he knew I already had the specifics about his impending shipment, he would reschedule, and I would lose the only card I had up my sleeve.

"Mercy, this conversation is starting to bore me. Either you have my property or you don't." Now I was pretty sure *he* was bluffing. The words were cocky enough, but there was a tone to his voice that indicated maybe—just maybe—I was starting to get under his skin.

"I didn't call to talk about the property you already lost, Dominic. It's about the property you are about to acquire. For an antique dealer without a store, you sure do buy a lot of vases."

The silence on the other end of the phone told me I'd scored my first direct hit in this conversation. I could hear him breathing, and doing so a little too rapidly to be completely relaxed.

Then he laughed. This time there was nothing pleasant about the sound at all. "Mercy, Mercy. You *are* refreshing. For a moment there, you almost had me worried. Then I remembered, no matter what it is you think you have on me, I'm still holding the winning hand in this game."

"What do you mean?" I asked. "You don't have anything."

"Oh, on the contrary. I have something very important. But I'm not going to tell you what it is over the phone." He paused, then chuckled again. "As you well know, I have another means by which to send you a message. But you have been…blocking that particular channel as of late. May I suggest you…tune in to the frequency and see what might be playing right now?"

A chill spread through me. I didn't want to let Dominic into my head, but something in his voice told me I needed to see whatever it was he was planning to show me. "Okay, Dominic. I'm tuning in right now." I set down the phone.

It's a good thing I was sitting, or I would have fallen. I felt a rush of vertigo as a series of images rushed into my head, too disjointed to make out. Then the picture gradually cleared, and I lost my breath when I realized what I was seeing. Sukey was tied to a chair, a gag in her mouth, and her eyes wide and bright with terror. There was blood on her face and a cut on her cheek.

Sukey's face grew closer, and a pair of hands entered the picture. I realized Dominic was letting me see through his eyes, and the hands were his. Rage washed through me in waves as one of the hands touched Sukey's face and she flinched. It stroked her red curls for a moment, then roughly jerked the gag away from her mouth.

"She can hear you now, Sukey."

I heard Dominic's voice inside my head and felt the words in my own throat. I wanted to throw up.

"Mercy?" Sukey whimpered and gasped. "Mercy, I'm s-so afraid. You know I'm scared of dark places. He—he says you can hear me. If you can, get me out of here, please! Oh, God…"

The picture faded from my brain with another rush of disorientation. I picked up the cell phone and punched the redial button. It took four rings for him to answer this time. Four interminable rings.

"I take it you received my message?"

I couldn't hear Sukey's whimpers, so he must have put the gag back on.

"Yes."

"You have just over two hours, Mercy. I want my property. If I don't get it…" He let the sentence trail off.

"What if I—" I swallowed and started again. "What if I can't get it? What will happen then?"

"That would be most unfortunate," said Dominic, with what sounded like genuine regret. "I will be expecting your call before midnight. Oh, and Mercy?"

"What?"

"Don't touch that dial." He ended the call.

I staggered to the bathroom and splashed cold water on my face. *He has Sukey. Oh, God, he has Sukey.* I realized what had been nagging at the back of my mind on my way to meet Tino earlier. It was the parking lot at the boatyard. There had been an old red Mustang parked down at the other end. Sukey's car.

He must have snatched her from the parking lot on her way in to work.

I lurched back out to the kitchen to get a drink of water. I saw the piece of paper on the counter with Sam's cell number and had dialed it before I even thought about it.

"Mercy?" he answered.

"He's got Sukey," I said without preface.

"Where?"

"I don't know," I replied. Then, suddenly, I realized I *did* know. Maybe. *You know I'm scared of dark places,* Sukey had said. But she wasn't, not at all.

"Sam, are you at Hilda's yet?" I could hear the sound of his boat engine in the background.

"I'm just coming up to her dock."

"I'll meet you there." I ended the call, and was out the door and back in my car in seconds.

On the way to Hilda's, I called Tino. "You up for an adventure?" I said as soon as he picked up.

"You know it," he said. "What you want me to do?"

"I want you to meet me. And I have to tell you, Tino, it could be dangerous."

"Hey, danger is my middle name." Luckily, Tino couldn't know I was rolling my eyes.

"You got a gun?" he asked me.

"God, no." I shuddered at the thought.

"You want me to bring one for you?"

"No!" I realized I had barked at him, and tempered my tone. "Thanks, Tino, but I don't have a clue about guns. I'd probably shoot myself in the foot or something."

"Your choice. Where we meeting?"

I gave him directions to Hilda's, then hung up and called Grant. "Grant, this is Mercy again. Do you know Hilda Bennington?"

"Everyone knows Hilda."

"You ever been to her house?" I figured there was a good chance any divorced man who was a member of the Bay Club had been invited to one of her parties at some point.

"Yeah, I've been there."

"Can you be there in ten minutes?" I had no reason to think he would say yes, because it was far beyond the bounds of the instructions I had given him under the press, but to my surprise, he agreed readily.

"Sure. This got something to do with Dominic?"

"Yeah."

"Cool. See you there."

I was relieved to find Hilda still dressed when I arrived at her door, then hit her with the news that several others would soon be arriving at my invitation.

"Hilda, I can't explain everything right now, but it turns out Dominic is a heroin dealer. He's got Sukey, and he's going to hurt her if I don't find her first."

"Why don't you call the police?" To her credit, Hilda did not ask me how I knew about Dominic, or express disbelief that a man she probably found attractive could be a criminal.

"No time. And no proof." She nodded, and I went on. "As soon as everyone gets here, we're going to have to put a plan together fast, and then I promise we'll be out of your hair. I'm sorry I told everyone to come to your house, but since Sam was already on his way here—"

"Are you kidding? This is better than *Law and Order.* I'll make coffee." She went into the kitchen, and I went to let Sam in the back door.

Fifteen minutes later, we made an unlikely group of rescuers as we sat around the table in Hilda's bay-view window, drinking coffee and eating cookies.

"Dominic let Sukey talk to me for a minute," I said, neglecting to mention that there had been no phone involved. "She said something about being afraid of the dark, but she's not."

"How you know?" asked Tino. "Lotta people afraid of things, they never say nothing about it." He took a sip of the excellent coffee, and Hilda beamed at him. She seemed to think he was an Antonio Banderas movie character.

I shook my head. "Not Sukey. She and I have sat in the dark and talked a lot of times. She's even said she likes to sit in the dark and think."

"So was she trying to say she *is* someplace dark?" asked Grant.

"Maybe, but that's too general, even for Sukey. She would know that wasn't much of a clue. She's trying to tell me something else, but I just don't know what."

"Well," said Grant, "maybe it's a code. Maybe dark means something else. What *is* she afraid of?"

I thought about it. "Bugs. Sukey is afraid of bugs. If she sees one, she goes to the other side of the room and calls me to kill it."

"So, does that mean she's somewhere with a lot of bugs?" Hilda asked. "That still sounds too general."

"Is there someplace around here with *bug* in the name? Like a place that rents buggies or something?" Sam chewed thoughtfully on a cookie.

"Yeah, I think you may have something there," said Tino. "Like a Mexican bar called La Cucaracha or something."

The room was silent as we all tried to think of something obvious with a bug involved.

"Isn't there some exterminator, got a big bug on the building up on the freeway?" said Tino tentatively.

"No, that's a rat," said Hilda. "I know the one you mean."

I did, too. "That's too far away."

"Why do you think she's not far away?" asked Sam.

"Because I wouldn't have been able to—to—" I stuttered to a stop. I had been about to say that I was pretty sure I wouldn't be able to receive such a strong psychic message unless Dominic was fairly close by. Not that I had much experience—it was just a feeling. It had *felt* nearby. I realized everyone was still waiting for me to finish.

"Sukey doesn't usually stray very far from the peninsula. And she wouldn't try to give me a clue about something she didn't think I would figure out easily. I think it's something she knows I would recognize if I saw it—and that means it has to be where I would have a good chance of finding it."

"Thin. Very thin." Tino's look—like his line—was straight out of an action movie.

I sighed, looking around at the group. "If it was just me, I'd drive around and try to find something that rang a bell. But I can't ask you all to help me on the basis of a half-baked theory."

"Sure you can," said Grant, surprising me. He was the person I thought would be the least likely to want to cooperate. Sam knew and liked Sukey, Tino thought he was Zorro and Hilda...well, nothing Hilda did would surprise me. But I had only pressed Grant to call me if he thought of something, and he had already done that.

"Grant, you hardly know me, and you've never even met Sukey. Why are you helping me now?"

He shrugged. "I'm bored."

Sam looked at him. "You're sitting here contemplating joining the Balboa Scooby-Doo gang because you're *bored?*"

Grant grinned. "Twelve years ago, my wife divorced me. She said twenty years with a type-A personality was about nineteen years too long. I had never heard that before—type-A personality. She made it sound like something bad."

Grant ran his hand over his still-thick white hair. "So I looked it up. And I said to myself, 'What's wrong with being ambitious, driven and energetic?' I mean, when I was in college, that's what we called being most likely to succeed."

"You went to college?" asked Tino.

"Yes," said Grant. "But you don't have to go to college to be a type-A. You're one, too, you know."

"I am?" asked Tino cautiously. He seemed to be trying to work out whether or not it was a compliment.

"Of course you are," said Hilda brightly. "I could see it right off."

Grant nodded in sage agreement, then went on. "I read a bunch of other stuff, too, about how I was more likely to get a heart attack, die young, be divorced and get in a car accident." He shook his head. "But being stubborn, I decided to prove my wife and those psychologists were all wrong. Figured when I retired, I'd slow down with no problem at all. Play a little golf, do a little fishing. Buy a boat and learn how to sail it."

"And you ended up racing competitively," I supplied, starting to get the picture.

He nodded. "And entering fishing tournaments and getting crazy when I didn't win. And obsessing over my damned golf handicap." He shrugged again. "I realized this retirement thing wasn't really working for me, but I didn't want to go back to some office, either. I didn't know what to do. So I started drinking too much and hanging out with the assholes at the Bay Club."

"Hey!" said Hilda indignantly.

"I didn't mean you, Hilda. Not that you ever gave me a chance." Some significant look passed between Grant and Hilda, but Grant turned away and continued.

"What I miss about working is figuring things out. That's what I did—took big, complex puzzles and moved all the pieces around until they came together. I loved that part. Then working like hell until the thing, whatever it was, was built."

He took a sip of his drink, then eyed me pointedly. "What you have here, Mercy, is a helluva puzzle.

And you aren't showing us all the pieces. But I figure we've got enough to get started. So do you want my help or not?"

Wow. I had seriously underestimated this man. "You bet I want your help, Grant." I surprised myself by reaching across and squeezing his hand.

"Then where do we start?" Sam asked Grant. "You said we have enough pieces to get started. How do you mean?"

We all murmured in support of this question, and Grant reached over and picked up a pen and pad off the telephone table. A former engineer, he seemed to think better with a pen in his hand.

"Okay, so what do we know?" He put a *one* on the pad. "Dominic took Sukey from the office parking lot sometime today." He wrote this down. *Left parking lot—time unknown.*

"Then he calls you, admits he took her and lets you talk to her." He added *two*, then *Call from Dominic— Sukey conscious and okay—9:30 p.m.*

"You with me so far?"

We all nodded, and he went on. "Now, here's where it gets tricky. Sukey told you something she knew you would recognize as a lie. You concluded that she was trying to send you some kind of hint or message. This seems like a good conclusion to me." After *three,* he wrote down, *Sukey sends message. Dark? Fear? Bugs?* "The thing is, we don't know what the message actually was, and I don't think we have enough to form a definitive conclusion on that point."

I sighed. "You're right, Grant. But I just can't

imagine Sukey coming up with something…I don't know, obscure. She's a pretty straightforward person."

He nodded. "That's why I think your next conclusion is a valid one, too." *Four, Sukey's message refers to something familiar or easily accessible for Mercy.*

"Now, just because Mercy would recognize it, that doesn't mean we all would. But since we now have about—" he looked at his watch "—ninety minutes until midnight, I think we have to divide our efforts."

"What do you suggest?" I asked.

"What's the farthest point from here that you think Sukey would still consider familiar territory?" asked Grant.

I thought about it. "Maybe Corona del Mar to the south, but only the main drag. The same with Newport Boulevard, going east until it runs into the freeway. And no farther north than the Huntington Beach city limits."

"Okay, that's not too bad." He turned his piece of paper over and made an uneven cross. "Here's the Pacific Coast Highway," he said, pointing to one of the intersecting lines, "and here's Balboa Boulevard." He added a couple of shorter lines. "Also Newport Boulevard and Marine Avenue. If we take two cars and one starts here at the bottom of the commercial district in Corona del Mar, and the other starts from around the Balboa Pier, we can look for anything that screams *dark* or *afraid* or *bugs*. We stay in constant contact via cell phone, and if anything rings any big bells with Mercy, we check it out."

"I don't know," said Sam. "It seems like we're going to an awful lot of effort based on conjecture."

"You got any better ideas?" asked Tino. "We got, what, eighty-seven minutes?"

"Good point," said Sam. "We can split up into two pairs, and take Mercy's car and mine."

"What about me?" squeaked Hilda. "You *don't* think I'm just going to sit here and wait for the four of you to call me tomorrow with the gory details, do you? We can take *my* car, and I'll drive."

"Oh, yeah, a Bentley's going to be real inconspicuous," said Grant.

"I have more than one car, Grant." Hilda rolled her eyes as if this should have been obvious. "I've still got Sal's Suburban in the garage. It was his last demo car before he got sick, and I just couldn't bear to part with it."

"Hilda, I didn't really think you would be coming along," I argued, but she waved me off impatiently.

"If you think you can leave me behind, you've got another think coming. There is no way I'm going to hear about this secondhand. Besides, whoever comes with me will be able to see more if neither of you has to drive. And I've got a speakerphone setup for my cell, so you can just turn it on and chat with each other as we drive around."

She stood up and took a set of keys off a hook next to the door, then looked around at all of us. "Well? Are we going or what?"

15

We ended up taking Tino's car as the second vehicle, mostly because he refused to leave his 1968 Chevy Impala convertible behind. There was no way Dominic could associate it with me, so I had no objections. To my surprise, Grant elected to ride with Tino—the two men seemed to have formed some weird kinship—and I rode shotgun and Sam sat in the back as Hilda steered the enormous Suburban onto the Balboa Island Ferry and toward Corona del Mar.

We cruised slowly down Marine Avenue, the only street on Balboa Island with anything commercial. While we were on the ferry, Sam thought to take out a local map and review all the street names in the immediate area. Nothing to do with bugs, fears or darkness, but it had been a good idea. Since street names were out, we were probably dealing with some kind of commercial signage or business name, so we decided to avoid purely residential neighborhoods.

We didn't find anything on the island, but I hadn't expected to. It's too tiny and crowded to be a good place to hustle a presumably uncooperative hostage into a doorway or up a flight of stairs without notice. I started really paying attention once we got to where the Coast Highway becomes Main Street in the up-scale hamlet of Corona del Mar.

I dialed Grant's cell number, using Hilda's speaker-phone setup. "Seeing anything yet?" I asked them, knowing they would have called if they had.

"Nope. The Post Office, the Tale of the Whale, the Balboa Inn. We're behind the Fun Zone now."

I had already mentally traced the route he was taking in my mind and would have been very surprised if he mentioned something I had missed. I gave him a progress report for our end.

"We're just passing Fashion Island. There are some shops and restaurants in the plaza by the library," I said. I looked at the high-end plaza and dismissed it. Everything was too well lit and out in the open. I was already starting to feel frustrated, as the seconds of the clock ticked down in my mind without having to look at my watch.

"We're going to cruise up around the Newport Pier. There are a lot of little businesses and boatyards tucked around in there." I heard music start up with a thumping bass, then I heard Grant squawk in protest.

"Christ, Tino, turn that off. This big blue dinosaur draws enough attention in this neighborhood without playing that gangster crap."

"Careful what you call my ride, man," I heard Tino's voice respond, but his tone held no threat, and the music subsided. On our end, Hilda moved the big Suburban quietly along the main boulevard. Luckily traffic was off-season light, and we drew no attention with our unusually slow pace. I read the business names on the signs aloud, for lack of anything else to do. *The Quiet Woman. Wahoo's Fish Taco. California Tan and Waxing.*

Grant started doing the same, and we alternated over the next half hour. By then we had exhausted Corona del Mar's main drag and were heading toward Newport Boulevard and the western end of Costa Mesa. With more side streets and alleys to explore, Grant and Tino were progressing more slowly. As I tried to squelch my rising panic, Grant's voice continued to drone over the tinny speaker.

"*The Beach Ball. Mutt Lynch's. Blackie's.* Hey, Mercy, how about *Blackie's?* That's almost the same as dark."

"I don't know, Grant. It just doesn't light any fires for me. But we should keep it in mind."

"Yeah, well, we don't have time to—holy shit, what's that? I never saw that before."

"What?" Hilda, Sam and I all asked simultaneously.

"Oh, it's just a big mural. Up the side street from Mutt's. It's a three-story building, and the mural covers the whole side facing the street."

"Oh, yeah," said Hilda. "I heard about that. I met a guy at the John Wayne Tennis Club. His son has a custom surfboard shop. He does artwork for all these famous surfers, and he did the mural to show off his skills. His father told me where it was, and I meant to look for it when I was in the neighborhood."

"Man, would you look at that! It's beautiful!" I could hear Tino's voice. "It's like you're looking up through the wave and can see the bottom of the surfboard. What's that say on the board, man? Looks like a gang tag to me."

"It's the surfboard company's logo," explained Grant. "It says *Spyder* with a *Y.*"

"Spider!" I shrieked.

"What?" said several voices simultaneously, both in the car with me and over the speakerphone.

"That's it. Holy shit, Grant, that's it! It says spider. I can't believe I didn't remember before."

"Mercy, what are you talking about?" asked Sam.

I took a deep breath. "Hilda, speed this bus up and head toward the Newport Pier." She did as I asked, and I continued. "I said Sukey is afraid of bugs, but that's not really accurate. She's afraid of *spiders.* She told me she can't even sleep when she knows there's one in her room."

"You think Sukey is somewhere near that mural?" Sam sounded skeptical. "It seems like a hell of a stretch."

"No, it's the place. I just know it, Sam. I don't know why, but it just feels right."

"So what are we going to do?" asked Sam.

Hearing the *we,* I gave him a startled look. He must have understood, because he took my hand. I resisted pulling it away. Had anyone ever held my hand before? It felt…nice. Weird, but nice.

"We're gonna go get her," said Tino. Apparently Grant had put his cell on speaker, too.

"We need a plan," protested Grant. "We don't know enough about what's going on. For instance, does Dominic have a gun? Is he alone, or does he have someone with him?"

"He's not gonna be the only one with a gun," said Tino.

"I think he's alone," I said cautiously. "I mean, he may have other people besides Rocko working for him, but when I spoke with him, I got the impression he was alone with Sukey."

"So we go in there, we kick his ass and we grab your friend," said Tino. "Seems simple enough to me."

"Maybe not," I said.

"No, I think Tino's right." It was Sam who had spoken, and I had a hard time covering my surprise.

"Dominic thinks he's only up against *you,* Mercy. He thinks because he threatened to hurt your friends, you wouldn't want to involve anyone else."

"I didn't," I said. "But when I found out he had Sukey, I didn't think. I just started dialing all your numbers." Which really was strange, come to think of it. *Why had I done that?*

"Which proves Dominic doesn't know you as well as he thinks," said Sam. "Any time you have information someone else doesn't have, it's an advantage." He spoke with authority, and I wondered where and how he had learned that lesson.

I looked at Hilda and Sam, and I thought about the two passengers in the other car. I barely knew Tino and Grant and, even though I had known Hilda for years, I had seriously underestimated her. And Sam...

"You're right, Tino. He has no idea who he's messing with," I said.

There were a few cars parked in the tiny municipal lot near the Newport Pier, probably belonging to patrons of The Stag, which rivaled Jimbo's for the title of Best Dive Bar in the annual competition sponsored by the local paper. We pulled down an alley just beyond this landmark, and Hilda pointed out the mural—*Spyder* stood out in stylized letters—and I nodded. I looked at any doorway, window or staircase from which the sign could be seen. There were quite a few.

"Maybe you should park," I suggested, and Hilda headed down to the double row of meters that paralleled the public beach, then pulled into a spot. Within moments Tino's baby-blue Impala pulled up next to us, and we quietly got out. I looked at my watch in the light of the streetlamp. Eleven-twenty. There were still lights on at the Beach Ball, but the other businesses were closed up for the evening. The waves were quiet, which meant there would be no late-night surfers floating on their boards, shivering in wet suits and waiting for the perfect wave to give them a moonlight ride.

"It looks like there are a lot of options, but I'll bet when we get up close, we can eliminate most of them," I said to the group, once everyone had gotten out of the two vehicles and gathered where the Suburban's bulky outline blocked the illumination from the streetlights. "I was trying to see if any of the nonresidential buildings had lights on. I didn't see any."

"Which don't necessarily mean anything," said Tino astutely.

Everyone nodded in agreement—even me.

"Let's split up. Hilda, you stay with the car. If you see us coming, start the engine and get over to us." I was concerned that she would object, but she nodded. "Grant, you and Tino go around behind the Portofino Hotel and check out the places that open up into that alley. Sam and I will come around from the other side. You see anything, don't try to go in. We'll meet up by that Dumpster behind the Beach Ball, okay?"

A few moments later, we had all left the well-lit parking lot behind and were moving as quietly as possible down the alleys behind the rows of beach-view condominiums and tourist traps near the main pier. In the summer, the streets would still have held a few pedestrians, even on a Monday night. In September, it felt more like four in the morning than just before midnight.

"Thanks for doing this, Sam," I said very quietly.

"Thanks for trusting me enough to ask."

We moved slowly and quietly, moving down the alley until we could see the Spyder mural. Staying in the shadows, we carefully assessed each door and window.

There were some condominiums with garages that backed against the alley, that were rented out by the week in the summer for outrageous sums. In the winter, they were often occupied by UC Irvine students, who pooled their funds for a chance to live at the beach instead of in dormitories. From the back, it was hard to tell which were vacant. Could Dominic have rented one of them? They didn't seem like his style. Plus, all the rooms had windows. Sukey had been gagged, but he had taken the gag off. Would he have risked it if she was somewhere where screams might be heard?

The opposite side of the alley seemed more likely—mostly the back entrances for small businesses, about a third of which were vacant at any given time. The extremely seasonal nature of the local economy led many entrepreneurs to fail during their first year. I peered between the detached buildings, looking for side entrances.

I heard a noise, and looked up to see Tino and Grant crossing the side street.

"Nothing likely over there," whispered Grant. "But there seem to be a lot of entrances to the mural building."

I nodded. The surfboard shop occupied the ground floor of a three-story building. It looked like the upper floors held office space or possibly even some of the ubiquitous illegal studio apartments.

Many local people rented out single rooms where they had installed a tiny piece of countertop with a sink, a microwave and a dormitory-sized refrigerator. Add a microscopic shower stall, and you could call it an apartment and rent it out to some surfer dude for a few hundred bucks. They were in violation of local zoning ordinances, but this was largely winked at by the authorities. Commercial rents were expensive here, and a local business had a better chance of surviving if they could get someone to help defray the cost.

There was a wooden outside staircase running to the top floor but not to the second, which must have been accessed from inside. There was a fire escape, but the ladder had been pulled up and, if extended, would probably make a sound loud enough to wake the dead. The stairs to the third floor were probably creaky, too, and the surf wasn't loud enough to drown out much of anything tonight.

Tino pointed. "I think I could see in those windows from the stairs." He indicated the second-floor windows.

"Can you get up there without making any noise?" I whispered.

"Hey, I'm like a cat." His gold tooth caught the reflection of a streetlight and glinted. He started up the stairs, and I could tell that Sam, Grant and I were all collectively holding our breaths. As he climbed up on the stair rail of the landing to peer into the windows, I heard the wood creak and I almost peed my pants. After a few minutes, he came back down.

"It looks like an office," he said. "Bunch of surfer stuff in there—must go with the store."

We all looked up at the third-floor landing. There were no windows near the stairs, which led to a plain wooden door. Grant pointed to the building next door and said, "If someone could get up on the roof over there, they could look in the windows."

"I'll go," said Sam. The building next door was a bar and restaurant that had changed hands at least three times since I had lived here. It was currently unoccupied, and I wondered how Sam planned to reach the roof, but he was down the alley before I could stop him. He disappeared around the corner of the building, and I followed. To my astonishment, he appeared above the roof over the back door of the building, climbing up the telephone pole like a monkey.

He dropped down on the roof of the building almost silently, then I saw his head sticking out from the edge of the roof. From his silhouette, I knew he was trying to see into the darkened third floor. He was silent for a long time, and I had to grit my teeth to prevent myself from calling out to him. Then his head disappeared, and within a few moments he was coming back down the alley.

"Man, how you learn to climb like that?" whispered Tino. "Breaking into houses?"

"Working in boatyards," said Sam. "I'm not sure, but I think we may have found the place."

"What makes you think so?" asked Grant, which was good, because I didn't trust my voice not to rise.

"Well, it doesn't look like anyone is living there. There's some debris in the corner like someone painted the place and never really cleaned up. There's no real furniture. But there's something just out of my line of sight—I thought it might be the toe of a shoe. And there's some stuff lying on the floor. The light's not very good, but I think it might be that big suitcase Sukey always carries."

Apprehension stabbed through me, and I nodded. Sukey's oversized purse, out of which she was likely to pull just about anything, was legendary. "So she's probably in there," I whispered. "What do we do now?"

"We go in after her," said Tino. "Old building like

this, that door's gotta come down with one good kick." He sounded like he had some experience in these matters.

"Remember, Tino, someone starts shooting and the police are going to come," whispered Grant. They must have spoken about this in the car on the way over.

"I may not have been able to go to the police, but if we catch Dominic in there with a tied-up hostage, I think we'll have a little credibility."

"We may, but Tino's got a record and an unregistered handgun." Grant gave Tino a pointed look, and the other man had the grace to look embarrassed.

"Look, I'm not gonna start shooting at nobody," said Tino. "Someone starts shooting at us, that's a whole other thing."

"No one is going to start shooting at us. Dominic doesn't think he needs to use a gun to get people to do what he wants," I replied crossly.

"What do you mean?" asked Sam.

"No, she's right," said Tino, and I silently blessed him. "People are scared of Dominic, but I never seen him with no weapon or nothing. He's just...I don't know, someone you don't want to fuck with."

"Who's going in first?" asked Grant.

"I am," said Sam and Tino simultaneously.

Tino turned to Sam. "You ever kick down a door?" There was a challenge in his voice.

"Yes." Sam's voice was very quiet, but there was no question he was telling the truth. Tino looked him up and down—Sam probably had five inches and forty pounds on him—and stepped aside, gesturing toward the stairs like a maître d' offering the best seat in the house.

"Grant, you stay down here—keep a lookout." I didn't know anything about Grant's general health, but his shape and his red face made me think of heart failure, and I didn't want him on the steep stairs.

We crept up the wooden structure as silently as possible, considering its probable age. I was in the rear—Tino's Chicano chauvinism might allow Sam to precede him, but walking into danger behind a woman would have been too much to ask. When Sam was positioned on the landing, he looked down to make sure Tino and I were ready. I saw that Tino had one hand on his gun but hadn't drawn it. He nodded, and so did I.

Sam drew himself up visibly with a deep breath, then kicked so hard and fast that the motion was a blur. The door sprang open and crashed against the wall, and Sam leaned back behind the open frame as if getting out of the line of gunfire. *Just like in the movies,* flashed through my mind. *He really has done this before.* The impact sounded incredibly loud in the quiet alley, and I waited for windows to open and voices to inquire, but stillness returned. Sam peeked his head around the doorframe, then stepped inside, motioning for us to follow.

Enough light filtered in through the dirty windows for us to see that nothing was moving inside. It was indeed a studio apartment, recently painted, according to the smell. My hand found a light switch, but nothing happened when I flicked it. Tino had better luck with a chain hanging from a bare bulb in the tiny doorless bathroom. As light spilled into the room, I gasped.

A chair sat against the center of the windowless wall, the ropes that had been used to tie Sukey still hanging from its back, arms and legs. I recognized her purse, one shoe and a sweater lying on the floor. A folded piece of paper lay on the empty seat. I rushed over and picked it up.

Still staying tuned? was all it said.

I crumpled myself along with the note and landed in a heap on the floor next to the chair. "Too late," I said. "We're too late."

"Mercy, you don't know that he's really going to do anything to her," said Hilda, handing me a glass of Crown Royal. I sipped it reflexively, then put it down. The last thing I wanted to do was get drunk.

We were back in Hilda's commodious breakfast nook. Hilda was drinking coffee, but everyone else had some kind of alcoholic beverage in front of them. "I still don't understand what the note means," said Sam.

"I think it means Mercy should expect his call," said Grant. "Or she should call him."

"Do you think he'll answer?" asked Hilda.

"Don't hurt to try," chimed in Tino.

I was ready to strangle all of them, which wasn't even remotely fair. They had no way of knowing what Dominic really meant—that I should let him into my head—and I wasn't about to do that in front of other people. But I realized Tino was right—I might as well call Dominic. Sighing, I pulled out my cell phone.

"Mercy," he purred after the first ring.

"Where is she?" I blurted without preamble.

"Even if I knew what you were talking about, which I don't," he said in that hated purr, "you know I wouldn't talk about it on the phone."

"But—"

"But you can't talk in front of all your friends. I know."

I was stunned. How did he know about my friends? Had the son of a bitch been lying about his ability to read my mind?

"If you're wondering how I know about your little posse, the answer is simple. I saw them. I was watching."

"Watching?" *With his eyes or with his mind?*

"Yes, watching. From my car. No, not the Jaguar— you didn't really think it was my only vehicle, did you?"

"So you were expecting us?"

"Oh, yes. Well, I was expecting *you,* anyway. I was a little surprised when you showed up with reinforcements. I didn't think it likely you had many friends."

"Tell me what you did with her."

"Not on the phone, as I've said." He sighed dramatically. "Look, Mercy, when you figure out how to break loose from your band of merry men, just turn on the station and wait for a broadcast. Until then, I really have nothing to say to you." He hung up.

"What did he say?" came a chorus of voices.

"He said he—he would call me back later."

"I thinks it's time we went to the police," said Sam.

"If you're calling the cops, let me get out of here first." Tino got to his feet. "I'm already pushing it, just driving my ride around this neighborhood after dark."

"I'm not calling the police," I said tersely.

Sam threw up his hands. "Look, Mercy, we know he's got her. There may be some kind of evidence back in that apartment—his fingerprints or his name on the lease. Something."

"You know he's too smart for that," I argued.

"Well, I don't know what the hell else to do!" He raked his fingers through his hair impatiently. "We can't just wait to hear from this asshole."

"That's exactly what we *have* to do." I stood up and faced the group. "And I am going home to do it." Everyone gaped at me, and I continued. "Look, Dominic played us—played me. He probably wants us exhausted and terrified. We have to try to rest." I turned to Grant and Tino. "You two have already done more than I had any right to ask. You should go home and get some sleep."

"No way," argued Tino. "What if he calls and you need backup again?"

"Then I'll call you. But in the meantime, you need to get some rest."

"You could all stay here," said Hilda. "I have seven bedrooms, not counting the guesthouse."

Sam shook his head. "I have to get back to Dad's. Usually he's fine, but I don't like him being alone this long."

"And I'm going home," I replied. Seeing everyone was about to protest, I raised my hands. "Look, Dominic might be watching my place. He might not call me until he's sure I'm alone."

"If he's watching your place, then that's all the more reason you shouldn't go home," said Hilda reasonably. "He might snatch *you* next."

"No, he doesn't want me. He wants what he thinks I can bring him." I hadn't told them the whole story, but they knew some of Dominic's drugs had disappeared with Rocko, and that Dominic thought I knew where to find them.

"Sam, I'll give you a ride back to your car if you want," I said, "but I'm going home, one way or the other."

"All right," he said, with the air of someone who was reserving the right to say *I told you so* later. He stood up.

"I think Tino and I will accept your hospitality, Hilda," said Grant. "I'm pooped, and I don't think Tino should be driving around Newport Beach at one in the morning in a convertible cop magnet with an unregistered firearm tucked into his jeans."

One in the morning. The morning *after* my deadline. I hoped Sam wouldn't change his mind about going to his father's house. We said goodbye to Hilda, Tino and Grant, and Sam was silent on the walk to the car. During the ride, he only spoke to give me directions to where his car was parked.

As we pulled up next to his parking space, he turned and looked at me. "You're sure about this," he said. It was not a question.

"Yes."

He looked at me for another minute then nodded. "Okay," he said. "Call me when you know something."

I waited until I heard his car start up, then went home.

As soon as I was inside my house, I walked carefully to the sofa and sat down in the exact center. I closed my eyes for a moment, then opened them and picked up my phone. I punched in the number and waited.

"Hello, Mercy."

"I'm listening." We both knew I wasn't talking about the phone call. I hit the end button and waited. Again a feeling of vertigo swept over me, to be replaced by a wavy picture of Dominic. I realized he was looking in a mirror.

"I may not be able to read your thoughts, but your friend Sukey was much more transparent. I knew she was trying to hide something from me." He smiled at his reflection, and I felt a rush of hatred so strong it seemed my chest would burst.

"I don't know what she said that made her so sure you would understand, but I knew she had given you some kind of message about where I had taken her. She trusted you to save her, you know. Unfortunately for her." He smirked at the mirror, and I longed to wipe that arrogant look off his face.

"I realize now that you really don't know where my heroin is. Also very unfortunate."

I was about to dial the phone again and tell him to quit stalling when the room seemed to spin. He was

turning his head to look at something behind him—
something on the floor. At first I couldn't see what he
was showing me; then the picture suddenly resolved
itself.

Sukey was lying on her side, her head at an impossible angle, her glazed eyes staring sightlessly at
nothing. The last thing I was aware of was Dominic's
horrible laughter as everything faded to black.

16

"Freak! Freak! Freak!" The high voices of children chanted the refrain as I walked stonily past the playground on my way to the bus stop. "Mercy's a freak! Freak! Freak! Freak!" The words echoed against the brick walls and through my brain. As the bus door opened and I got inside, I could still hear the voices, muffled now but still clear. "Freak! Freak! Freak!"

The bus drove away, and the voices faded, but I could still hear them reverberating in my brain. "Freak! Freak! Freak!" I was still listening, my eyes squeezed tightly shut, when the bus arrived at my stop.

"Mercy," said the bus driver. "Mercy, wake up."

"Nooo," I said. If I kept my eyes closed, I wouldn't have to look at his face. I wouldn't have to see what was in his eyes—that he knew what the chanting voices said was true.

"Mercy, wake up!" He shook me.

I was confused—wasn't he supposed to be driving the bus? I opened one eye. Sam was standing over me.

"Sam" I said, sitting up. "What time is it? How did you get in here?"

"Almost noon. Your patio door was unlocked." He sat down on the bed next to me. When had I gotten into bed? I still had most of my clothes on. "I take it you're not opening your office today."

"Oh, shit! I'll just call…" I groped for my phone, then remembered. *Sukey. Oh God, Sukey.* My hand dropped. "There's no one to call."

"What's the matter with you?" Sam tried to help me as I struggled to disentangle myself from the bedclothes.

"Sukey's dead." I stood up and walked into the other room. Sam seemed to wait a beat, then came after me.

"What do you mean, she's dead? What makes you think she's dead?" He grabbed me by the upper arm and tried to turn me toward him, but I jerked away.

"I can't tell you." I walked through the living room, ignoring the empty vodka bottle on my coffee table. Opening the sliding glass doors, I stepped out onto the patio. Sam followed, and when I curled up in a ball on the lounge chair, he towered over me.

"You can't tell me," he echoed. "This is getting real old, real fast, Mercy."

"So sorry to disappoint you," I said, and the coldness in my voice even made *me* shiver. "He killed Sukey, Sam. She's dead, and it's my fault. The last thing I give a shit about is whether your goddamned feelings are hurt because I can't tell you how I know."

"Fine. Don't tell me. But are you going to call the police now?"

"No."

"What do you mean, *no?* You're going to let Dominic get away with murder?"

"I didn't say that." Honestly, I'd just woken up with the hangover of death. My best friend was dead, and Sam wanted to argue with me about it? Just who the fuck did he think he was?

"Look, Sam, I can't go to the police and tell them, because I don't have any proof and I don't know where he is—or where she is."

"Then how can you be so sure she's dead?"

"I can't..."

"Tell me," he finished. "Yeah, I get that."

He raked his fingers through his hair, which I was beginning to recognize as a gesture of extreme frustration. Like he was doing something with his hands to keep from strangling me. As if he had given up, he slumped in the other patio chair.

"If you're not going to the police, then just what *are* you going to do?"

"I don't know yet." I pulled tighter into my ball.

His fingers raked his hair again. "Well, I can't just leave you here like this."

"Sure you can."

He snorted. "Mercy, you should go take a look at yourself in the mirror. You look like you've been through a war."

"I have."

I knew I wasn't being fair to Sam, but I didn't care right then. I just wanted him to go away and leave me alone, so I could poke at my wound. I wanted to think hard about how much it hurt, and I didn't want to share the pain with anyone. It was my pain. Mine.

I slowly got to my feet. "Sam, I need you to go now."

"No way." He folded his arms.

I looked at him. He was the most beautiful man I had ever seen, and the stubborn concern on his face broke my heart. I could love this man. And in so doing, I would inevitably destroy him.

I did the only thing I could do. I pressed him. "I need you to go now."

"Okay." He started for the patio gate. I saw that he was trembling. It was as if his inner resolve was at war with what the press was forcing him to do. Again I wondered what he would be like if he was really angry. I would probably never find out.

"Sam?"

He turned back. I was going to say, *and forget all about me.* But I couldn't quite get the words out.

"Nothing. Go ahead now." He went through the gate and headed down the sidewalk toward his shop.

After he left, I took his advice and looked in the mirror. He was right. Twenty-nine years old and I looked forty. No, fifty. I got in the shower and stood there until the hot water ran out. I put on my terry-cloth robe without drying off. Unable to concentrate enough to make coffee, I lay on the sofa and stared at the cracks in the ceiling.

I thought I could be normal. And look where it got me. That was the first coherent thought that entered my mind, and things went steadily downhill from there. The cell phone rang a few times, but I never even picked it up to see who was calling.

I should probably go down to the office and put up a Closed Forever *sign,* I thought idly. I was too afraid of what might happen to my clients if I made some kind of mistake, and they went off and hurt themselves. I had no business fucking around in anyone's head, and I had been deluding myself in thinking I could use my ability to help people.

I drifted in and out of a fitful sleep in the semi-darkness of the living room—I had drawn all the blinds sometime in the wee hours before I finished the bottle of vodka.

I slept all day and into the evening. I kept hearing Sukey's voice in my dreams. *I really wish I had more confidence, Mercy. Like you.*

"No," I moaned. "No, Sukey, you don't want to be like me. I only hurt people." I tried to break away from the dream, from the voice, but I couldn't.

That's not true, Mercy. You helped me.

"I killed you," I argued. "You're dead because of me. I thought I could help you, but I was wrong. I can't help you. I can't help anyone." I struggled toward the surface of consciousness, unable to reach it.

Help me, Mercy. Sukey's voice was plaintive.

"I can't. I can't." I moaned incoherently and tried to hide my head under the sofa cushion to get away from the voice.

You have to help me. No one else can hear me.

I lifted my head. I was awake. I could no longer see light filtering through the blinds, but the room wasn't completely dark. I wasn't dreaming anymore. Why was I still hearing Sukey's voice?

Mercy, I don't know if you can hear me, but I have to try. Dominic left. I'm in some kind of storage unit, and I can smell something cooking. I'm gagged, so I can't scream. No one else can hear me. I don't even know if you can hear me. You have to help me, Mercy. I don't know when he's coming back, and I'm scared. This time I think he really will kill me.

Sukey! With all my might, I tried to send a message to her, not even bothering to question why she thought it was even possible for me to hear her thoughts. *Sukey, I can hear you! Sukey!*

Sukey's voice in my head droned on. *I don't know if you're getting this message, but I need your help. I'm in some kind of storage unit, and I can smell food. The walls must be thick, because I can't really hear anything. Maybe…maybe boats. But I'm not sure. Come find me, Mercy. Come find me before Dominic gets back.*

A storage unit…food cooking… "Sabatino's!" I shouted aloud. Dominic didn't know I had found out where his shipment was coming in. He had her in one of the empty industrial spaces at the pier next to Sabatino's Sausage Factory.

This time I wasn't calling anyone else. I had screwed up everyone's lives enough already. I was dressed and in my car before I had a chance to change my mind, and was approaching Sabatino's less than ten minutes later.

I turned around and parked in a bank parking lot a few blocks away. Dominic said he had more than one car, and he could be sitting in one of them looking for me again. I looked in every parked car I passed as I walked toward Sabatino's but didn't see anyone sitting in any of them. I stood in the corner of a building next to a palm tree, which afforded some cover from the streetlights, and scanned the several rows of shipyard-style buildings where merchants could rent industrial space. Which one would Dominic be using?

I had no way of knowing.

Sukey, can you hear me? Answer if you can hear me. Sukey's *"voice"* had fallen silent, and I was afraid that might mean Dominic had come back. So far she had been unable to hear *my* messages, but I had never really tried this before and kept hoping I would break through.

Choosing a row of industrial workshops for no reason other than it was the one closest to the water, I started slowly down the alley where the back doors opened. Some had *For Rent* signs, others, small placards with information about the occupants, and a couple were open, revealing people working inside. I avoided them, but thought I might come back and ask them questions later if I had no luck.

Suddenly I heard her voice again. *Mercy, help me! I don't know if you can hear me, but I'm somewhere I can smell food. And hear boats—I think. Come get me. Please! I'm scared.* Food! I mentally kicked myself for wasting time. She had to be in the same building as Sabatino's, or somewhere directly down-wind. *Which way was the wind blowing?*

I risked stepping away from the buildings to assess the wind direction. Some sailboats were tied up in front of a restaurant on the opposite side of the small channel, and they had wind indicators on the tops of their masts. I took note of the way they were pointing, then gauged which buildings were in the right direction from the delicious odors emanating from Sabatino's kitchens.

There were two short rows of buildings that were more or less downwind. Unfortunately, their exteriors were extremely well lit. I went around to the far side of the first building. Each unit ran the width of the building, which stood between two narrow drives. On one side there were wide roll-up doors that could function as storefronts or loading docks, depending on the needs of the occupants. None of the roll-ups were open. A trip around to the other driveway revealed a single high window and door in each unit. The building was about sixty feet wide, but I could glean no hints of the interior floor plan.

Mercy, can you hear me? I'm getting really scared now. I've been trying to think about how brave you would be if this were happening to you. But I'm not as strong as you are. Please, please, come get me. Her voice fairly thundered in my head, almost staggering me. I must be very, very close.

I stood with my back to the windowless end of the building farthest from the main street and willed my hammering heart to slow. I breathed deeply, trying to force everything from my mind as I had been taught in the daily yoga classes that were part of my course load at the Institute. When I felt a measure of calm begin to take possession, I concentrated as hard as I could on the thought of Sukey. Not her body, but her mind. Her essence. The thing that made her what she was.

"Sukey, can you hear me?" I said the words aloud

as I pressed—not the way I did with my clients, but into the very air around me.

Mercy? The thought came back immediately, crashing into my skull with enough intensity to snap my head back.

"I hear you, Sukey. I'm trying to find you. Can you hear me?"

I hear you! I was afraid I wasn't getting through. Where are you?

"I'm right by Sabatino's, Sukey. I think I'm very close. You said you could smell food. Could it be Sabatino's?"

I don't know. I could feel her frustration but didn't know what to do to pin down her exact location.

Suddenly the motor yacht docked in front of the Cannery gave a loud blast with its air horn.

"Did you hear that, Sukey? Did you hear the horn blow?"

Yes! came the excited reply. *Hurry, Mercy. Hurry!*

Screw it. I didn't care if anyone heard me now. I looked around desperately for something I could use to make a loud noise. At the edge of the parking lot, a bearded man was loading some coils of rope into a battered pickup truck. I could see the rusty toolbox built into the bed. I ran toward him.

"Do you have a tire iron or a crowbar in your truck?" I asked, panting.

"Yeah," he said cautiously. "Why?"

"Give it to me!" I pressed him so hard he jumped, fairly leaping into the truck's bed and throwing the toolbox lid open with a crash. He handed me a crowbar, and I ran back to the row of roll-up doors on the first building.

As I ran, I again spoke aloud and with my mind. "Sukey, I am going to bang on all the doors. If you hear the banging, let me know." I began pounding on the first metal door with the crowbar.

"Can you hear anything?"

No, I don't think so. Hurry!

I ran to the next door and slammed the crowbar against it. "How about now?"

I think I hear something.

"Is it close?" I swung energetically.

Yes. No. I can't tell.

I moved up to the next door and crashed the crowbar against it. I was leaving dents. I didn't care.

I hear something! It's closer!

Encouraged, I banged the door like a drummer doing a solo.

"I'm going to move now. Tell me if it's closer or farther away." I moved up to the next door and swung for the outfield.

Farther away!

"Yes! I know where you are now. All I have to do is get the door open. Don't worry, I'll get in there one way or another."

I tried inserting the end of the crowbar into the large padlock that held the roller in place, but it wouldn't fit. I tried to pry under the bolt that led into the concrete lip of the door, but it was too firmly anchored. I ran around to the other side of the building to where the door and small window faced the alley.

Seeing no way to get a purchase on the tightly sealed door, I aimed at the window and swung.

I hear glass breaking.

"That's me. Hang on, I'm almost inside." The window was above my head and, although my energetic swings soon had the glass in splinters, the window frame was still in place, preventing me from fitting through. I looked around for something to climb on and saw nothing.

I ran back to the parking lot and saw the crowbar man still loading his truck, as if hysterical women demanded his tools every day. I ran over to him again, calling, "Hey, you! I need you to drive your truck over here."

"Okay." He dropped the box he was loading onto the pavement and got in the driver's seat. He started the truck and headed toward me.

"Stop!" He did, and I got in the passenger seat. "Pull up behind that building. See that window? I need you to park so I can stand in the bed of the truck and climb through."

He did exactly as instructed, and in a few moments I had a much better angle to smash, pry and yank out the window frame. I pulled a piece of canvas tarp out of the truck bed and threw it over the bottom of the frame to protect me from the fragments of broken glass that still protruded. Then I dropped the crowbar and pulled myself up and into the window, wiggling through and landing in a heap in the dark on the other side.

I was in a washroom, and had banged my shoulder

and ribs on the industrial sink on my way to the floor, where I was slumped next to a toilet.

"Sukey!" I called.

"Hmm uhnnn hrrr!" This time the voice wasn't in my head—it was in the next room. On my feet in moments, I sprinted around the corner and found a closed door. Luckily, it wasn't locked. I flung it open and groped for a light switch. A bare bulb came on. And there was Sukey.

Her hair was a snarled mess; there was dried blood on her mascara-streaked face; and a filthy gag was in her mouth. She was the most beautiful sight I had ever seen. I yanked the gag out of her mouth and threw my arms around her.

I hadn't realized I was sobbing, but must have started while I was still trying to get through the window. "Oh, God, Sukey, I thought you were dead. Dominic sent me a—a vision and showed me your body."

"I know, he told me." She was sobbing, too, and her nose was running freely. "Untie my hands before I suffocate on my own snot," she said, and I laughed through my sobs.

"Very attractive, Sukey," I said, as I went around behind her and started working on the knotted cords.

"I know," she said. "Don't tell my mother I said snot."

We laughed and cried at the same time as I gradually loosened the bonds on her hands and her feet.

"How did you know to send me a message like that?" I asked as I struggled with an especially difficult knot.

"Dominic said he was a telepath and could send you a message. He said you would get it because you're a telepath, too. So I thought if you could get *his* messages, maybe you could get one from me." She started to cry again. "Oh, Mercy, I didn't know if I was getting through, but I didn't know what else to do."

"You did great," I said as the last knot gave and her foot came free. "Now let's get the hell out of here before Dominic comes back and finds us."

As if my words were a signal, a sound came from the opposite end of the building. It was the sound of a metal door being lifted.

Dominic was back.

17

I reached over and switched off the light, and we were plunged into darkness. I didn't have to tell Sukey to be quiet, but she gripped my arm so tightly it hurt. "Back door," I whispered, and we edged into the hallway.

I could hear a car engine running and thought it was the crowbar man's pickup truck, then realized it was coming from the front of the building. Headlights suddenly shone partway down the hallway, and I pressed against the wall to get out of their beams. Someone was driving a car in through the roll-up door.

Dragging Sukey with me, I scooted crablike down the hallway, until we reached the open bathroom door. I pushed her into the room, out of the range of the lights, then looked at the door to the outside.

There was a deadbolt above the knob, the kind that you needed a key to open. There was no key in it, but maybe it wasn't locked. To find out, I would have to reach my hand out into the beam of light. I inched as close as I could before snaking my hand out and trying the knob. No luck.

I pulled my hand back. There had been no change in the sound of the car, and no other movement. I backed up into the bathroom next to Sukey. Faint light showed through the busted-out window.

"The door's locked. Climb out the window," I whispered into her ear. "There should be a truck parked under it, but even if it's gone, jump anyway."

I felt her nod, and helped support her as she climbed up into the sink. I hoped it was anchored well—if it came crashing down, we were both screwed. I saw her head and shoulders silhouetted against the frame. Then she paused.

"Mercy," she whispered, and leaned down toward me.

"What?"

"There's something important I need to tell you, in case we're separated and Dominic catches one of us."

"There's no time. Tell me later." I shoved her toward the window, and this time I saw her hands rise to pull herself up and through the frame. I listened anxiously until I heard a thump outside—crowbar man must have left the area.

I had started to climb up myself when a sound directly behind me froze me in my tracks.

"Hello, Mercy." The light flashed on, temporarily blinding me. When my vision returned, I wished I still couldn't see. Dominic was holding a very big, very black pistol, and it was aimed directly at my chest. "I guess my little illusion didn't fool you after all."

"Hello, Dominic. I wish I could say it was a pleasure to see you, but you claim to be able to tell when I'm lying."

He laughed. I heard the sound of a key turning in a lock, and the back door opened. A man I did not recognize pushed Sukey in the door in front of him. "She was coming around the corner like a bat out of hell," he said to Dominic. "I invited her to come back to the party."

"Thank you, Sergio," replied Dominic. "Why don't we escort our guests out to the front room, so we can all be more comfortable?"

"Let her go," I told Sergio. I might not be able to press Dominic, but I'd wager his friend was another matter. Confused, the man let go of Sukey's arm. She wheeled and stomped on his instep, then leapt for the back door.

"Stop or I'll shoot Mercy!" thundered Dominic, and Sukey skidded to a halt. She turned slowly and glowered at the two men. Sergio was bent over, a grimace of pain on his face. The look he gave Sukey did not bode well for a convivial evening.

"Countermand your instruction or I will be forced to hurt her," said Dominic curtly.

"Never mind what I said," I told Sergio. He grabbed Sukey's arm again, and pushed past Dominic and me to escort her down the hall. He was limping badly, and I mentally chalked up a point for Sukey. Too bad it wasn't his balls.

The roll-up had been closed, and the front room held Dominic's Jaguar and a Mercedes I didn't recognize. An overhead fluorescent shed a harsh light on the otherwise empty room.

"This where you get your *antiques* delivered?" I attempted to sound scathing but could hear the nervousness in my voice.

"Sometimes. Although there's nothing to tie my name to the place, so don't start getting any ideas." Dominic used the gun to gesture at me to move toward the wall, where I stood next to Sukey. She grasped my hand and held it tight.

"Sergio, I need to keep an eye on our guests here. So if you wouldn't mind getting things ready to make the transfer…" With his free hand, Dominic removed a set of keys from his pocket and tossed them to Sergio, who opened the Jaguar's trunk. I could just see the top of a canvas duffel bag, which Sergio opened. He started taking out stacks of money.

"I can assure you it's all there." Dominic's voice held irritation.

"I always count. Nothing personal." Sergio examined each stack quickly, then put them back in the bag. When he was done, he walked over and opened the trunk of the other car, putting the bag in. He took out two paper-wrapped parcels and put them in the Jaguar.

"You want me to hold the gun on them while you check this?" he asked.

"You didn't bring your own gun?" Dominic asked Sergio, who shrugged.

"Didn't think I'd need it. You didn't mention these—" Sergio gestured toward Sukey and me "—complications."

Dominic shook his head. "Alas, I'll have to trust you. I'm afraid if I hand you the gun, I can't count on

Mercy here not to attempt her powers of persuasion again. She'll probably tell you to shoot me."

Damn. Exactly what I had been thinking.

Sergio looked confused again, but didn't argue. He was probably used to Dominic being cryptic.

Sergio shrugged and slammed the Jaguar's trunk.

"Could you do me a favor, Sergio?"

"Depends."

Dominic smiled, nodded slightly at me, then shifted his gaze to the other man. I could see I was still in his peripheral vision and didn't move. As he spoke to Sergio, I could actually feel Dominic's press, like something brushing past but not quite touching me. It was familiar, yet different.

"You will put Sukey—the redhead—in the trunk of your car and take her out of here. You can do whatever you want with her, as long as you kill her when you are finished. I don't want her to be able to identify either one of us later. Do you understand, Sergio?"

I shivered. It was too much like the way I led my clients, although even from the outside looking in, I could tell his ability wasn't as strong as mine. Either Sergio was highly susceptible, or he just liked the idea, because he responded, "Yeah, I understand. What about the other one?"

"Ms. Hollings and I have some unfinished business. I will…dispose of her myself." Dominic's tone was caressing, and I tasted nausea.

"Nooo!" shouted Sukey as Sergio tried to pry her hand from mine. He lifted a big fist and hit her in the face with it, cutting off her protests.

"You son of a b—" Dominic's gun in my side silenced me. Sergio pulled Sukey around the side of the car and forced her into the trunk. It wasn't an easy task. I could hear her muffled cries from inside the well-insulated Mercedes, but they would probably be lost even in light traffic noise.

I looked at Dominic, wondering if he had been eavesdropping on my mental conversations with Sukey and that was why he'd arrived when he did. Fuck him—it didn't matter if he heard what I was about to say.

Be strong, Sukey, and pay attention to anything that might tell me where he takes you. I'll come get you as soon as I figure out some way to kill this son of a bitch.

I'll try, came Sukey's reply. I saw no sign on Dominic's face that he was tuned in to our conversation. He motioned me away from the light as the door opened and the Mercedes pulled out. I memorized the license plate—just in case I lived through this. I didn't plan to go down easily.

The door closed again—Sergio must have had a remote control—and I was alone with Dominic. Again. I hadn't enjoyed it the first time, either.

"So what am I going to do with you, Mercy?"

"Gee, I figured you'd just kill me, Dominic. Getting squeamish?" Maybe baiting him wasn't the best idea, but I couldn't help it. Even if four out of five verbal barbs never landed, knocking that smile off his face even once in a great while was worth the trouble.

"Oh, I'll kill you. Probably. It's just that I don't often meet someone with whom I can communicate so effectively. Someone who has…insider insight, you might say." He chuckled at his double entendre.

So I'm not the first you've met? I asked him the question mentally, as I had finally learned to do with Sukey. There was no reaction. Odd. Was he able to switch it off or something? I restated my question, this time verbally.

"So I'm not the first insider you've met?"

"Oh my, no. Although—" his smile grew wide and unpleasant "—I am apparently the first *you've* met." He seemed very pleased at this conclusion. "It really is a shame we have come to…contretemps."

I snorted at the understatement. "Yeah, a dammed shame. I'm just sure we could have been bestest buddies under other circumstances."

"We could have been a great deal more than that." I was sure he had understood the sarcasm, but he was choosing to ignore it.

"Tell me, Mercy. Do you even know who your real parents are? *What* they are?"

I wanted to say yes, but my lie would have been obvious. I shook my head. "It really isn't relevant right now, Dominic."

"Oh, but I think it is. You see, Mercy, I know precisely what they are. And where they are, for that matter."

I must have reacted physically, because he went on. "Oh, so it *had* occurred to you that they might be alive, had it? Just waiting to meet their long-lost offspring?"

The long-suppressed fantasy sprang into my mind, whole and tangible and smothering. Parents—real parents—alive and wanting me. *Oh, my darling child.*

We didn't want to give you up, but we were forced to. Thank God we've found one another. You'll never be alone again. Never be different. Never be a freak.

I shook myself. I hadn't allowed myself to have such thoughts since I was a teenager—had thought they were a thing of the past. But one line from this…this monster, and there they were again.

He was looking at me with an amused expression. All my longing and despair must have flashed across my face like a billboard. I felt a rush of hatred and revulsion so strong I had to swallow my bile. *How dare he?* How dare he treat my innermost longings, my most secret pain, as something casual? "Look, Dominic, I don't—"

Mercy. I was interrupted by Sukey's voice. *Mercy, I think we're out near the Wedge. I think we only made left turns.* I looked at Dominic swiftly, but his expression showed only curiosity.

"You don't what?" he asked.

"I don't think you really know anything about my parents." It wasn't what I had been planning to say, but Sukey's voice had made me remember I needed to keep him talking. Long enough for me to—what? To think of something, I supposed.

I sent a quick thought to Sukey. *Dominic may be listening in.*

No, Mercy, that's what I was trying to tell you. He can't hear me.

"…don't you agree?"

I realized I hadn't been listening to what Dominic was saying. "I—I have a hard time agreeing with anything you say, Dominic." This answer seemed safe, and I returned my concentration to Sukey.

How do you know?

He told me. The answer was immediate.

Dominic was speaking again. *Hold on, Sukey, I have to concentrate on Dominic for a minute.* This was like freaking call-waiting.

"…not interested in prolonging your life, then I suppose there's nothing I can do about it."

"Of course I'm interested in prolonging my life." I hoped I hadn't missed something that rendered this response a non sequitur.

"Then you might be a little more cooperative, Mercy." He raised his eyebrows expectantly. Had he already explained what he wanted me to cooperate with and I had missed it? I decided to hedge.

"Look, Dominic, I just saw my best friend stuffed in the trunk of a car on your orders. Forgive me if I seem a little hostile."

"I take your point," he said. "But it's not too late for me to call Sergio and tell him to bring her back."

"How are you going to do that? You pressed him, Dominic. You can't reverse your instructions over the phone."

"No, probably not. But I also told him he could do whatever he wanted with her first. Knowing Sergio, that could take some time. And I have a pretty good idea where he's taken her."

"So call him."

"Not unless you agree."

"Explain precisely what it is I'm agreeing to."

He sighed. "Do you really want me to repeat myself?"

"Yes. Just so I have it clear in my mind."

"It's your mind I'm interested in, Mercy. All right, I'll say it again. I need your press. I need to learn why yours is so much stronger than mine, and whether I can use that knowledge to strengthen my own press. And I need you to use your ability on my behalf until I do so." His theatrical tone held patient weariness.

"Enlighten me. I would want to do this because—?"

"Because if you do, I will tell you everything you've always wanted to know about yourself. Who you are, *what* you are, and how to find others like yourself. Including your real parents."

Could he really know? I had wanted to believe he was lying, trying to play me. But what if he wasn't?

Mercy? Jesus, I had almost forgotten about Sukey.

I'm here. But I don't know if Dominic is listening. I hoped he would believe I was considering his offer, which would buy me a few moments to communicate with Sukey.

He's not. He can't block you and listen at the same time.

I kept my face neutral. *Are you sure?*

Yes. He never stopped talking when we were alone. He loves the sound of his own voice—it was driving me crazy. He told me everything that came into his mind.

Where are you?

I'm not sure, but the car's stopped. I can hear waves crashing.

Do you still think it's the Wedge? Even on quiet days, the artificial barrier built to shelter the end of Newport Harbor created a dangerous triangle of tall-faced waves that broke into inches of water. Bodysurfers and Boogie board riders came from all over the world to challenge the dangerous surf. It would be much louder there than on the relatively calm south-facing beaches.

Maybe. I think so.

"I appreciate you may wish to give my offer some thought, Mercy, but I am not going to stand here and wait all night." Dominic's voice was impatient.

"I'm not doing anything until you get Sukey back," I said.

"I'm not getting Sukey back until you concede to my wishes," he countered.

"And just how am I supposed to do that? How can I demonstrate my willingness to do what you want in some way you will believe?" An idea was beginning to form. *Hang on, Sukey, I think I may be on to something. Don't send any more messages until I say it's okay.*

Dominic seemed to consider my challenge. "I suppose I could take you out right now and have you press someone for me."

I shook my head. "I don't know if Sukey has enough time. How about if I *show* you something, Dominic? If I let you into my head long enough to see how it works—what it feels like when I press. I can do that, I think. I've felt your press, and I know how you do it. Mine's different. You'll be able to see it. To feel it."

I knew I was on the right track. The hunger in his eyes was so tangible, so intense, I could almost taste it. I turned the screw. "What's it going to be, Dominic? Sukey's time is running out and, if she dies, I don't care what you promise me. I'll never make this offer again."

"Show me." His voice was almost a whisper.

I dropped my shield and let him in.

Where is it? I heard him say. His lips didn't move. I smiled. If what Sukey had told me was correct, his shield was down now, too.

"Right here," I spoke aloud and pressed harder than I ever had before. "You are under my control, Dominic. You will do anything I want. Do you understand?" I held my breath. *Had it worked?*

"Yes, anything you want." The hunger was gone from his eyes, to be replaced by the vague glassiness I sometimes saw in my clients. Dominic was mine.

18

Holding on to my control of Dominic's will was like riding the mechanical bull at a country–western bar. The glazed look in his eyes lasted only moments before I had to reassert my dominance. "You will do as I instruct. Put the gun down on the floor and kick it away."

He did so, then turned to me. I felt him trying to pull away from my influence.

"You must do as I tell you. Open the garage door."

He stepped to the Jaguar and opened the driver's door. I realized he was reaching for a remote control, and I quickly added, "Get into the driver's seat." I ran around to the passenger's side and jumped in. As the big door rolled up, I said, "Close your door." If I gave commands continuously, he might have less time to struggle, but it would give me less time to figure out what to do in between.

"Take out your cell phone." He did as I told him, holding it in front of his body. I felt his mind coil and flex like a giant anaconda, but did not release my grip. "Call Sergio."

He didn't move. I almost panicked—was he already figuring out how to avoid my control? "You will do as I tell you! Call Sergio!"

He seemed to be struggling to speak.

"Tell me why you are not calling Sergio," I said, gritting my teeth. Sweat was starting to trickle down my spine.

"I don't know his number."

"What?" I shouted, and saw Dominic wince. I didn't know whether my shout had hurt his ears in the close quarters of the car, or if the intensity of my press had momentarily peaked. I felt him strain against me and tried to tighten my grip.

"Tell me why you said you would call him."

"To trick you." Not being able to lie to me was taking a toll on him. I could see drops springing out on his forehead, too.

"Were you telling the truth when you said you had an idea where he would take her?"

"Yes." He almost squirmed loose then, and I realized I didn't have the luxury of asking him questions. Everything had to be phrased in the form of a command.

"Tell me where you think he has taken her."

"He has a house near the Wedge."

"Start the car. Drive to the Wedge—normally and in a way that won't get attention." I wasn't sure this was even possible, resisting me as strongly as he was, but maybe it would take enough of his concentration off fighting me that I could breathe. I felt like my chest was wrapped in tightening bands of steel, and I could feel my pulse pounding in my temples. I had no idea how long I could keep this up.

"Turn left." Dominic obviously knew the way to the Wedge, but I was afraid of what would happen if I slowed my commands. "Stop for the red light." There might have been the slightest easing of pressure from his attempts to break free, and the ringing in my ears seemed to subside slightly. "Don't drive over the speed limit."

It's less than seven miles from the Lido Island Bridge to the Wedge, and traffic was light at this late hour, but the strain of hanging on to Dominic's slippery will made it seem like an epic journey. By the time we pulled up to the tiny public park at the base of the breakwater, I was drenched and shaking.

"Tell me which house is Sergio's." Luckily it didn't matter if my voice shook or sounded hoarse with exhaustion.

"I don't know."

I almost screamed with frustration. "How can you do business with the man and know so little about him?" Almost too late, I realized I had asked another question. He nearly slipped free.

"Tell me what you know about Sergio and where he is! And why you haven't pressed him for more details," I pressed.

"He calls me when he has business to conduct. I know he lives down here somewhere near the Wedge, on the water on the ocean side. I haven't pressed him because I haven't needed to yet."

I pounded my fist against the dashboard. If I was

going to find Sukey, I would have to do it the same way I had before. But if I took my mind off Dominic long enough to communicate with her, he would break free. He was probably strong enough to kill me with his bare hands, and even if he failed, I would never get to Sukey in time.

"You will do as I say." I threw this statement in to buy myself some time. I didn't have any idea what to tell him to do. Drive me around and look for Sergio's Mercedes? In this neighborhood of multimillion-dollar homes, the cars would be in garages. And the sides of the buildings that faced the alleys were usually windowless or shuttered.

But the sides that faced the Pacific were all glass.

Would I be able to keep control of Dominic during a trek down the beach? There was no boardwalk in this exclusive neighborhood. Front decks opened onto a row of dunes that afforded some privacy from the hardy surfers who parked in the rare public spaces and hauled their boards toward the Wedge's legendary shore break, and the photographers and groupies who came to watch them. I would have to crawl over and around the sandy barriers to peer into the over-priced fishbowls, hoping to see something that would give me a clue as to which house was Sergio's. I could not imagine attempting this with an unwilling Dominic in tow.

"You are under my command." I was starting to feel light-headed and, even with my full concentration, I was beginning to doubt my ability to maintain my grip on him for much longer.

I would have to do something permanent.

No! said my abandoned child who still lurked deep, deep within. *I'll never find out about my parents. About what I am.* With deep regret, I silenced my inner child. My parents were a possibility—a dream. Sukey was real. I knew I had the strength for only a few more minutes, and I couldn't waste any of them on a pipe dream.

"Dominic, you are going to do exactly what I tell you. Roll down the windows."

He did so, and I got out of the car and leaned in the passenger window. "Listen carefully."

I went quickly around to the other side of the car and got as close to the driver's window as I could without touching him.

"Look at me." I felt the reluctance as he turned his head to stare into my eyes.

"When I tell you to go, you are going to hit the accelerator of this car and drive it directly at the seawall." I pointed to a spot across the park, where the breakwater joined the shore. "Look where I'm pointing. Can you see what I'm pointing at?"

"I see it." His teeth were gritted, and I felt him heave against me.

"Look at me!" His face snapped back to mine, and there was no glassiness. He could not break away, but I could feel his hatred right through my tenuous control. "Stop fighting me!" I felt the pressure drop but knew it was temporary.

"You are going to drive the car over the breakwater and into the water. You are not going to try to get out of the car and swim to the surface. You want to die. Tell me what you want, Dominic."

"I want to die."

I was shaking so hard I thought I would fall down, and I leaned against the roof of the Jaguar.

"Tell me what you are going to do when I give you the command, Dominic. Tell me what is going to happen."

"When you say go I am going to drive as fast as I can—over the wall and into the bay."

"Tell me you will not try to get out of the car. Tell me you want to die."

"I will not try to get out of the car. I want to die." A wave of nausea threatened to overwhelm me, but I swallowed and continued.

"Fasten your seat belt, Dominic."

He complied, but I felt a wavering as his will started to reassert itself. With my last strength, I shouted, *"Go!"*

I fell back against the pavement as the black Jag roared into life. Tires squealed as the motor moved faster than the wheels could get a purchase on the pavement, then the powerful car shot like a rocket toward the low spot in the rock barrier that I had indicated. Within moments there was a metallic bang as the car hit the wall and went airborne. The sound of the splash was drowned out by the pounding of the surf from the opposite side of the breakwater. I lay on the pavement, outside the circle of light from the nearest streetlight, and felt Dominic's mind fade into oblivion. I nearly followed it there.

* * *

Do no harm. Do no harm. Do no harm. The fourth rule of my carefully crafted code of ethics was a drumbeat in my head. I closed my eyes, but the sight of Dominic's taillights disappearing over the edge of the breakwater seemed imprinted on my eyelids like an indictment. *Do no harm. Do no harm. Do no harm.*

Somehow I had managed to get to my feet and move along the farthest edge of the park from the breakwater and onto the sand nearest the Wedge. I could hear shouts coming from the breakwater. Even on such a quiet night, someone had probably been fishing out there or smoking dope or doing whatever it was people did at midnight on a finger of piled stones extending into the Pacific.

The house facing the bay closest to the breakwater, formerly owned by Dick Dale, aka King of the Surf Guitar, showed no lights. But chances were that someone had been awake in one of the houses on the opposite side of the inlet or a commercial fishing boat had been passing through. The police would be around before too long, and I didn't have time to talk with them right now.

Officer, forget the car and help me find my friend, who's being held hostage by a psychically controlled drug dealer with no last name, by knocking on the doors of the most powerful people in Southern California and asking them if there's a woman tied up in the back of their Mercedes.

Right. Even if I had enough strength to press someone, which I didn't think was the case right now, there was no way I was going to be able to handle the number of cops, ambulances, harbor patrol boats and Coast Guard vessels that would no doubt arrive in the next twenty minutes.

I crawled between two sand dunes and sat down. *Sukey!* I tried to call out with my mind. *Sukey, can you hear me?* It was like being in a nightmare, when the monsters are chasing you and you can't call out or scream. I could form the thoughts, but I couldn't seem to get enough momentum behind them to propel them where they needed to go. *Sukey, can you hear me?*

Mercy? The volume almost shattered me. *Did you say something—I mean think something? I thought I heard you, but I'm not sure.*

Yes, Sukey. It's me.

Are you far away? I can barely hear you.

No, I'm close. Or at least I think I am. I'm just… tired. I took a deep breath of the cool air, trying to pull in strength along with the sharp scent of the Pacific. *Where are you? Are you still in the car?*

Yes, but I'm in a garage. I heard the door roll up and close. Then a regular door slamming—I think he went into the house.

I breathed a sigh of relief. If Sergio had left her in the car, it might mean he was preparing for whatever it was he had planned for her. I hoped it would take a while. *Dominic said Sergio's house faced the ocean near the Wedge. I'm here on the beach now, and I'm going to try to figure out which one it is.*

What about Dominic?

I hesitated before answering. *He's out of the picture. Sukey, I need to save my—my mental strength now. Send me a message if you hear anything, okay?*

Okay, Mercy. Please hurry.

My heart ached at how brave she was being. I had to save her. What I had done to Dominic—to *myself*—if I didn't save Sukey would all have been for nothing. I struggled to my knees and crept between the dunes toward the first house.

One of the older houses had not yet been bulldozed in favor of the floor-to-ceiling glass-fronted monuments to capitalism. It was nevertheless a beautiful home, even if its New England style seemed a little out of place in this center of all things modern. There was a raised deck leading down to a bricked courtyard, from which stone paths disappeared between two dunes, toward the surf. Someone must have swept that courtyard every day to keep it from disappearing beneath the shifting sand.

Lights flickered in the windows, indicating that someone was watching television within. Hunched over, I walked to the edge of the deck and peeked over. Suddenly, lights flashed on. *Shit. Motion detectors.* I fell flat and rolled up against the edge of the deck, hoping no one would walk all the way out to investigate. I heard a sliding glass door open.

"Is someone out there, Henry?" A querulous female voice came from within, and I heard the scrape of footsteps on the deck.

"I don't see anyone. Must have been a raccoon or a cat."

The steps went back to the door, and I heard it slide closed again. I let out my breath. Both voices had sounded elderly, with cultured accents. Definitely not Sergio's place. The lights flicked back off, and I cursed myself for not moving faster. How was I going to get back off the patio without turning them on again?

I wriggled along, keeping my head below the level of the deck, until I felt sand under my hands. Then I crawled toward the line of the dunes, where I collapsed in relief.

I sincerely hoped every house on the row wasn't equipped with a motion detector, although I should have considered the possibility beforehand. I wondered how many houses I would have to investigate before I would no longer be considered to be *close to the Wedge*. I supposed when the pounding of the surf grew too quiet to be heard from the trunk of a car in the alley, I would have gone far enough. Sighing, I got to my feet and edged toward the second house.

Twenty minutes later, I had only made it to the sixth house on the row. Two more sets of motion detectors, cyclone shutters and a near stumble into a hot tub where two people were luckily too occupied with one another to notice me had slowed my progress, and I wanted nothing more than to lie down in the sand and sleep for a week.

Mercy? Sukey's voice startled me, and I almost let out a squeak.

Yes, Sukey?

I hear sirens.

I listened, and realized I heard them, too. *They*

should pass right by. Tell me exactly what you hear as you hear it. I might be able to figure out which house she was in.

They're getting closer. I think…I think something just passed by. There's more than one.

I wasn't sure how accurate I could be from the opposite side of the buildings, but I didn't think the first siren had passed directly by me yet. I shot out from between the sand dunes on the beach side and started running—or trying to—through the soft sand heading away from the Wedge. *Keep talking, Sukey. I hear more. Have they passed you yet?*

A second one just did. And I still hear more coming.

Cursing the drag of the deep, moist sand against my shoes, I kept moving north along the beach. This time I happened to be even with a break in the buildings— some kind of narrow alley—when the second vehicle flashed past.

Here comes the third one. As she sent the message, I heard the deep blast of a fire engine horn—one of the big ladder trucks was coming down the street. I heard Sukey's thoughts continue. *Closer…closer… now! The last one's moving away.*

I had been able to see the glow of the flashing lights above the buildings, and when she had said *now,* I was pretty sure she was in one of two houses. I headed back up to the dunes, frustrated when there seemed to be no direct break where I needed to go.

Okay, Sukey, I have it narrowed down to two houses. I'm trying to get up to the first one now. Keep talking— half the emergency vehicles in Newport Beach will probably go by in the next few minutes. I found a narrow break in the dunes and half climbed, half crawled through. *Just hang in there, Sukey. I'm almost there.*

Mercy! The door just slammed. He's coming back out.

I cursed under my breath. If Sergio took Sukey somewhere in the Mercedes, I'd never find her.

19

Is he getting in the car? I sent this question to Sukey even as I halted in my tracks. From where I stood, I could see the windows of both likely houses. They were impressive, even by Newport Beach standards. Glass rose three stories and intricate staircases abounded. Multitiered decks, built for the kinds of parties that made the society pages, competed for the title of Most Likely to Host a Republican Fund-raiser.

I don't know. I can hear him walking around. I edged toward the first deck, expecting motion detectors to set off anything from lights to a mortar attack. I was surprised there wasn't a moat.

Sukey's voice sounded again. *He's opening the trunk. I can't see...the light is too bright.*

Shield your eyes, Sukey. Tell me everything you see and don't leave out any detail.

Okay. Even though, technically, what I heard wasn't her voice, I could discern unsteadiness. The terror she must be experiencing almost made *me* want to pee my pants.

He's got a gun. He's making me carry the bag with the money and walk through the door in front of him.

Try to get near the front windows, Sukey. Can you tell if there are any lights on that I would be able to see from the beach side? I eased up to the lower deck, which was at about the level of my head. A flight of stairs led down to the sand, but I was afraid to step onto it.

I don't know. We're going up a staircase right by the garage. I can't see the front of the house. There was a pause. *God, Mercy, he's saying things…really terrible things he wants to do to me.*

I tried to peek over the edge of the deck at the windows above. There were no lights in the front rooms, but there might have been toward the back. I simply couldn't tell. *He's not going to get the chance, Sukey. But stall him if you can.* I changed my tactics and peered into the gloom beneath the decks. Could I get close that way?

Okay, Mercy. I'll try.

I ducked under the deck but soon met a barrier—foundations built to support the upper deck against earthquakes and erosion blocked the route farther back. I retraced my steps. Holding my breath, I tiptoed up the flight of steps onto the lower deck. Nothing happened, and I cautiously crept onto the upper deck, near the darkened windows.

I'm looking into the first house, Sukey. Can you give me any hints? She'd said she had been on a staircase. I could make out the dark shapes of furniture inside but couldn't tell much about the upper stories.

We're in a bedroom. I don't think it faces the water. He...he says I have to take off my clothes.

Stall! I looked around desperately to see if I would be able to view the sides of the house from the deck. No longer cautious of noise, I sprinted toward one railing and was rewarded by a view of the long side of the house that ran between the deck and the alley. *Are there any lights on in the room, Sukey?*

Yes, he— Her thought was abruptly cut off.

Sukey, what happened? There were no lights visible on this side of the building, so I headed back around to the other side.

He hit me. He was mad because I wouldn't take my clothes off.

I paused and squeezed my eyes shut. Had my advice caused her to be hurt? *I'm sorry, Sukey. Do what you have to do. But...*

It's okay, Mercy. Her response was immediate. *I'll try to go as slow as I can without making him too crazy. I can stand being hit if I have to. Just hurry.*

I inwardly took back every disparaging thought I had ever had about Sukey. I just hoped Sergio had underestimated her as badly as I had. There were no lights on this side of the house, either.

Okay, Sukey, I can't see any lights, so I'm going to try the other house. Just hang in there a few more minutes. I ran back down the deck steps and practically threw myself over the dune to the next house. As I started up the second set of stairs, this time not even thinking about motion detectors, I was stopped by a low growl. A very close, very serious growl.

I read somewhere that if a guard dog barks at you, he's a watchdog. It doesn't mean he won't attack, just that it's not his first line of defense. It's when a guard dog *doesn't* bark that you're really in trouble.

I froze in my tracks. I could hear the growling, but the shadow of the upper deck prevented me from seeing its source. "Good dog," I tried. The snarling got closer, and I almost did pee on myself. The head that moved into the light was enormous, and I could see moonlight glinting on eyes and teeth. The sound ceased, and I saw the outline tense, as if he was about to spring.

"Stop! Sit!" To my astonishment, the big dog froze, then sat. *Holy shit. I just pressed a dog.*

What was that, Mercy? I hadn't realized I was still channeling my thoughts toward Sukey.

I think this must be the right house, Sukey. Just let me figure out how to get in. I moved toward the dog, who was watching me carefully but not moving. A rottweiler. Seemed exactly like Sergio's style.

"You're a good dog," I told him. "You like me. I'm your friend."

Still sitting, he whined, and I stroked the big head. "Are you a good dog?" He held out a paw, and I shook it.

"Okay, doggie. Let's go in the house."

Released from his position, the dog joyfully ran up the stairs to an upper deck, then through a dark, rectangular hole low on the house's front wall. I came closer and investigated. It was a dog door. I pushed against it, but nothing happened.

"Come here, doggie." The big head popped back

through the opening, and I heard a *snick*. I realized it was one of those doors that was locked unless triggered by a magnetic chip in the dog's collar. These devices keep the whole neighborhood from having a pet party in your house while you're out.

"Okay, go inside now." This time I caught the door flap with my hand before it could close and pushed my head through. The dog door opened into some kind of mudroom. In the glow of a night-light, I could make out a Boogie board leaning against a wall, along with some swim fins and other assorted beach paraphernalia.

While my new best friend panted in my face, I managed to squeeze first one shoulder and then the other through the small opening. Unfortunately, it wasn't possible to move my hips one at a time. I rolled around until I had them at an angle where the widest part of the door was lined up with my hip bones, then grabbed onto the edge of what turned out to be a shower stall. My butt slipped through with only the loss of a belt loop. I never wore belts anyway.

Sukey, I'm inside. I'm going to try to find you now. Can you make some noise? Scream or something? The door of the mudroom led into a breakfast room that reminded me of Hilda's. I moved into the kitchen, followed by the dog.

He said he'll shoot me if I scream. Oh, God, he's taking off his pants.

It's okay, I'm almost there. "Provided I'm in the right damned house," I whispered to the dog. "Do you live here with your daddy?"

He whined and butted his big head against my hip.

"Is Daddy home? Let's go see Daddy."

Obediently, the dog padded out of the kitchen and into a dining area. I followed him and saw an ornate criss-crossing staircase that led up from the back of the lower living area. The dog went to the foot of the staircase, then sat down, whining.

"What's the matter, boy? Not allowed to go upstairs?"

The whine came again, and I wondered whether I should press him to accompany me. He might distract Sergio long enough for me to assess the situation and take control. I was still feeling mentally weak, and it would presumably take a lot more effort to press a man than a canine. Not that I had any previous experience by which to judge—maybe Fido here was just crappy at being an attack dog.

A sudden crash upstairs startled me. *Was that you, Sukey?*

Yes. I knocked over a lamp. He's mad, but he didn't shoot me. He's picking it up. God bless her for being resourceful.

Be ready, Sukey. I'm on my way up the stairs. With a new friend.

I turned to the pooch. "Come on, boy. You can come upstairs. Go see Daddy. Go!"

The dog leapt past me up the stairs, and I could see the stump of his tail wagging. I ran to catch up, figuring the thumping paws would mask any noise I made. He made the second landing and was out of sight before I reached the first. I heard him thunder down the hall, and then a male voice raised in protest.

"What the hell? Bad dog, Cujo. *No!*"

I heard a thump and a whine. Sergio must have hit the dog with something big enough to hurt it. Like maybe a telephone pole.

"You know better than to come up the stairs!" The furious voice advanced, and I made the second landing just in time to see Cujo streak around a corner, followed by an extremely hairy naked Sergio, holding a pistol by the barrel. The asshole must have hit the dog with the butt of his gun. It probably would have crushed a lesser creature's skull, but the important thing was that Sergio was holding the wrong end of the gun, giving me plenty of time.

"Stop, Sergio! Drop the gun." My press felt puny and fragile, but it was enough. He stopped in his tracks and dropped the revolver, which landed on his foot.

"Ow!" he yelled, and jumped backward, falling directly on his hirsute ass. He grabbed his injured toes, giving me an unwanted view of his balls. I almost laughed aloud.

"Mercy?" Sukey ran from the bedroom, pulling a sheet around her. Cujo, who had returned from wherever he had fled, growled at her, and she gasped.

"It's okay, Cujo," I said quickly. "Sukey is good. Sukey is our friend. We like Sukey, okay?"

The big head turned toward me, then back to Sukey.

"Nice doggie?" she said tentatively. Cujo sniffed her, then stuck his head under her hand. "Nice doggie," she repeated with audible relief.

"Go get dressed, Sukey. We need to get out of here as soon as I figure out what to do with this jerk."

Sergio had stopped rubbing his foot and was sitting up. He looked confused, and I realized my feeble press would wear off before too long. I was so very, very tired, but I had to think carefully about what to do next.

"Sit still, Sergio. Don't move."

He froze, and I watched him as I waited for Sukey. It didn't take long.

"I'm ready, Mercy. What are we going to do with Sergio?"

"I'm not sure. I don't think we can call the police. There will be too many questions I can't answer."

"About what?" she asked.

"About a lot of things. I'll tell you later. Right now, we're going to take this piece of shit into a room somewhere and tie him up."

"Why? Can't you just make him hold still with that…that thing you do?" Apparently Dominic had done a whole lot of talking.

"Yes, but it takes a lot of effort and I'm tired. I need time to think, and I don't want to worry about him while I'm doing it."

She nodded her understanding.

I continued to press Sergio until we had maneuvered him down the stairs and into a heavy upholstered chair with wooden arms and legs, that we moved from the head of the dining table and into the living room. Automatic controls closed all the shades so we could turn on a few lights. We secured him with duct tape retrieved from the garage. Cujo watched the entire process with apparent interest and no evident concern about his supposed master. Who could blame him?

Before Sukey stuffed the gag made from a dish-towel into his mouth, I gave Sergio one last press and asked a question. "Do you live alone? Is there a maid or anyone else who's likely to show up here in the next several hours?"

"She don't come on Wednesdays," he said. "I ain't expecting anyone else."

I nodded, and Sukey fitted the gag in place.

We sat in the breakfast room with the lights off and listened to the occasional siren that still rolled past. Sukey went into the kitchen and found what she needed to make coffee. As it brewed, the aroma almost made me dizzy. When it was joined by the scent of buttered toast, I moaned aloud.

"I might just have the will to live after all," I told her as she appeared with a tray bearing two steaming mugs and a plate piled high with cinnamon toast.

"What are we going to do? Where's Dominic?" She handed me one of the mugs and took a bite of a piece of toast.

"Dominic's dead." I waited for guilt to wash over me, but I was too numb with relief and exhaustion. I tried a bite of the toast. It was delicious.

"Did you…?" The question trailed off, but Sukey's expression finished the sentence for her.

"Kill him? Not technically. But, yes." I took a gulp of the coffee, almost scalding my tongue. My eyes almost rolled back into my head from the ecstasy of fresh-roasted Colombian beans and the promised rush of caffeine.

"You made him do something?" Sukey wasn't going to let the subject drop.

"He drove his car into the bay. He didn't get out." I ate more of the toast, savoring the flavor of butter caught in the crevices of the cinnamon-laden raisin swirls. It was the best thing I could remember eating in my entire life.

"I see." She was silent.

I wondered idly what she was thinking but couldn't summon up the urge to care. I just wanted to sit there until the sun came up, eating toast and drinking coffee. Cujo came into the kitchen and put his paws up on the bench beside me. I fed him a piece of toast.

"Good dog," I said, and registered a feeling of satisfaction as I saw the stumpy tail wag. "We need to give you a new name, doggie. What shall we call you?" I rubbed the bony planes of his head, and he whimpered slightly as my fingers found a raw spot with a raised ridge, which must have been where Sergio's pistol connected.

"I think he looks a little bit like Rocko. What do you think, Sukey?"

I wasn't able to read her expression in the dark, but she didn't answer. I went on.

"But you're too much of a sweetheart to name after a moron like Rocko. Yes, you are! I think we'll call you—" I fondled the velvety ears "—Cupcake! Would you like that, boy? Can we call you Cupcake?"

His happy panting told me he approved, and I felt gratified. At least I had improved one life tonight. Or this morning. Or whenever it was.

"Stop it, Mercy." Sukey's tone surprised me, and I looked up.

"Stop what? I'm just giving Cupcake here a new name. Cujo's a terrible name for a nice dog like this."

"Stop pretending nothing is wrong," said Sukey. "You're avoiding talking about what we're going to do about Sergio."

I sighed. "Nothing wrong? Oh, a lot of things are wrong. Too many things for me to count right now. But you're right. We have to do something about Cupcake's daddy." The dog perked up his ears. He already knew his new name. I was delighted.

"Well, that's why I was asking you about…about what you did to Dominic. I was wondering if we…if you, I mean, should do something like that to Sergio."

"Kill him? No, I don't think so." My lighthearted tone belied the sick feeling threatening to creep back into the front of my consciousness. I pushed it down—hard.

"Our fingerprints are all over his house, and yours are all over his car. We could try to clean everything up, but we might miss something. And if someone were to turn up dead who lived less than two blocks from the scene of another suspicious death, the Newport Beach police department would launch their biggest investigation in years." I was actually thinking pretty rationally for an insane, quasi-human, freak-azoid killer. I almost congratulated myself with another piece of toast but saw it was all gone.

"I'll just make some more toast." I got to my feet and headed toward the kitchen.

Sukey followed me. "We don't need toast, we need a plan." She sounded exasperated with me, and I couldn't really blame her. I opened cabinets, looking for the bread.

"Where'd you put the rest of the loaf?" I asked her.

"That was the last of it," she said.

I felt a wave of disappointment, then investigated the contents of a deli bag.

"Oh, look, bagels!" I gave one an experimental squeeze. "Not fresh, but probably from yesterday. They'll be okay if we toast them. Has Sergio got any cream cheese?" I opened the refrigerator and started shuffling containers around.

Sukey gave up and reached past me to open a container marked Dairy Keeper. *Ahh, the motherlode.* Cream cheese, lox and caviar soon littered the counter. Seeing the frightened look on Sukey's face as I turned, searching for something to use to slice the bagels, I relented.

"Look, Sukey, I haven't eaten since…" I tried to remember. Oh, yeah, the cookies at Hilda's. "Well, since too long ago. And neither have you. We're going to make a plan and get out of here, but we may as well eat while we're at it. And we probably shouldn't leave until the excitement over Dominic's unscheduled swim dies down, so it wouldn't hurt to get some rest. No one is going to come looking for Sergio for a while."

Sukey winced at my flippant tone, but sighed and took a bread knife out of a butcher block and began slicing the bagels.

We found red onion and capers before we were done, and sat down for a feast we shared with Cupcake. "I didn't kill Rocko, you know," I said as I licked cream cheese from a finger.

"I wondered," said Sukey.

"I just told him to get out of town and never come back. I didn't know he had Dominic's drugs at the time."

She nodded. "Maybe you could tell Sergio the same thing."

I shook my head. "No, if he owns this place—or even if he's just borrowing or leasing it—someone will notice if he just disappears. It will be just as bad as killing him, as far as getting the police's attention. That's why I need to take my time and make sure I'm fully alert when I...instruct him." I poured myself another cup of coffee.

"Maybe instead of drinking that—" Sukey pointed at my mug "—you should try taking a nap."

"As tempting as that sounds, I don't think I can sleep until I get this handled. And am lying in my own bed. With you in the guest room." I reached out and took her hand. "Sukey, I'm so sorry all this happened to you. If I hadn't made Rocko..."

She pulled her hand away. "We'll figure all that out tomorrow. Tonight you saved me. Let's leave it at that." She got up and started clearing the plates. It seemed pointless—we were hardly houseguests—but it gave her something to do. She turned and eyed me speculatively. "Mercy?"

"What?"

She put down the mugs she was holding and gave me her familiar little-girl smile. "When we leave, can we take Cupcake with us? Please?"

I actually laughed. "Of course we can."

Sh ... ...
... for the Bastille ... ... "When we leave, can
... take Carlos with us?" There ...
I smiled. Sweetly. "Of course we can.

20

In the end, it was a lot easier than I expected. After a lot of questioning about Sergio's business, whether he owned the house or the car, and the source and location of his current assets, it was decided he would quit the drug business, pay off the lease on his house and move back to New Jersey to take care of his sick mother. He could live on what he had in the bank and the duffel bag—I'd briefly considered taking it, but quickly abandoned the idea as distasteful—for the rest of his life, and he didn't owe any money to any of his narcotics contacts. He believed he would be allowed to quietly retire.

It had taken hours to cover all the details, but I thought my suggestions were strong enough that by the time they wore off, he would be so deeply ensconced in his new life that it would be too late to pick up where he had left off—at least in Newport Beach, California. He was also going to feel a strong urge to seek counseling for some of his more deviant sexual leanings.

By the time Sukey and I pulled the big Mercedes sedan out of the garage and proceeded down the alley toward Balboa Boulevard, it was full daylight. Cupcake was sitting in the back of the car, and the trunk was full of premium dog food. We had found cases of it in the garage. We even had his papers, his diploma from guard-dog school and a bill of sale showing he now belonged to Ms. Susan Keystone.

A police car drawn across a traffic lane gave us a momentary stab of apprehension, but it turned out he was questioning people in arriving vehicles and letting only those with legitimate business through. We joined the stream of exiting cars, presumably residents on their way to a normal weekday at the office, and were ignored.

I pulled the Mercedes into my driveway and popped the trunk so we could unload the dog food. As soon as we were out of the car, the side door to my apartment slammed open and Sam came rushing out. Cupcake growled, but I calmed him with a word.

"Where the hell have you been?" he demanded, then stopped dead in his tracks when he saw Sukey coming around from the other side of the car. "Sukey, you're—"

"Alive. Yes, I know. And Mercy saved me. So you aren't going to give her a hard time right now, okay?" She looked absolutely fierce, and I almost laughed at the stunned expression on Sam's face. She opened the trunk and took out a case of dog food. "Help me with this, wouldja?"

Sam came out of his stupor in time to grab the heavy carton Sukey swung his way.

I walked through the door Sam had left open,

followed by Cupcake. Fred took one look, then arched his back and hissed. His fur stuck straight out, roughly doubling his size. Cupcake woofed, and I said, "Settle down, you two. Fred, this is Cupcake. Cupcake, Fred." Unconsciously, I pressed both animals as I went on. "Make friends. Cupcake is going to be staying here until Sukey can move into someplace with a yard or a patio."

The two were sniffing tentatively at one another's tails when Sam walked in, laden with two cases of jumbo cans. He put them down on the kitchen counter and stared at me. "We need to talk," he said, just as Sukey followed him in with a third case.

"Oh no, you don't," she said in a tone that brooked no argument. "You need to finish unloading the car, then go home and come back later. Mercy will answer all your questions then, but right now she's going to take a long, hot bath and sleep for about ten hours. And I'm going to do exactly the same thing."

"Your phone's been ringing off the hook. There are about twenty messages on there," Sam argued.

"Then call them back," I contributed. "Tell them Sukey's fine, I'm going to bed, and I'll call them all tomorrow." I no sooner spoke than my cell phone, which I had apparently left on the coffee table when I fled the house, chirped. "And turn that thing off." Turning on my heel, I walked into the bathroom and closed the door, not quite slamming it in Sam's face.

Soaking in the tub about twenty minutes later, I reflected that Sam deserved better—a lot better. I had probably burned my bridges with him, and my heart should be broken. Probably would be when I was awake enough to feel it and this protective numbness wore off. Right now, all I wanted to do was sleep.

A knock on the door interrupted my thoughts, and Sukey entered. She sat down on the toilet next to the tub. "I know you're exhausted, but there's something I just have to ask you, or I probably won't be able to get to sleep."

"What's that, Sukey?"

She paused, brow furrowed. "Well, it's this…this psychic message thing we've been doing. It's so… well, it's so *easy.* Can you hear everyone's thoughts in your head all the time or what?"

"Nope. So far, just you. And Dominic, of course, but he's dead. I…I was sort of connected with him when he died. I felt him…fade out." I shivered despite the steaming water.

"Well, I never did anything like this before. I mean, I always joked around that I was psychic. You know, like when I'm thinking about someone, and then the phone rings and it's them. Stuff like that." She looked at me inquisitively, and I nodded to let her know I understood.

"But when you send me a message, it's like having a telephone conversation or something. I hear everything you say, and I know you hear everything I say. Why is that, Mercy? And why now, all of a sudden? I mean, we've known each other for five years."

I thought about it before I answered. "This is totally new for me, too. Not the press…" Seeing her puzzled look, I explained what I meant. "The thing when I compel people to do as I instruct—I call it *pressing*. I've known about it since I was a kid. But this tele- pathic instant messaging is something else." I shook my head.

"I think...I think the reason it didn't work for us before is because I wasn't *listening*. It's like I had the volume turned off or something. But Dominic was powerful enough to force his way into my head. It's like he switched the whole thing on for the first time. Once I knew what it felt like, it was completely natural."

Sukey nodded. "Well, I didn't have any idea if I could do it. He told me he could send you thoughts and you could hear them. So I decided to try it. I mean, it seemed crazy, but I was all tied up and gagged and didn't have anything else to do, so what the hell, you know?" She laughed.

"So I concentrated really hard, like when I was a little girl and saying my prayers and I wanted to make sure God was paying attention. And I thought about you and just started—I don't know—talking in my head. I guess you couldn't hear me, because I did it for a long time before you answered."

"I was sleeping, and I heard you, but I thought I was dreaming about you." I thought about the first time I had successfully sent her a message. "But you turned out to be better at it than me, Sukey. I heard you for a good half hour before I finally managed to say some- thing back."

Her eyes widened. "You mean I'm more tele- pathic than you?"

I shrugged. "Maybe."

"You know when you did your first session on me? The trial run?"

"Yes. What about it?"

"Well, I think maybe it started then. I mean, I started feeling more confident. I guess you did that press thing on me, didn't you?"

"Yes." I swallowed. "I'm sorry, but you said you wanted me to—"

She interrupted, waving off my protests. "No, it's good. I mean, I'm glad you did it. But I didn't just start feeling better about myself and that I deserve love and all that. I started feeling more...more tuned in. Especially to you. Like I could figure out when you were tired or hungry or worried. It was like you opened some kind of channel or something. And the more I was around you, the more open it became. Like...like Drano."

"Drano?" I laughed despite my tiredness and the seriousness of the conversation.

"Yeah, you know. Like the pipes were clogged, but then you poured some drain cleaner in them. And whatever was blocking them started to break free. And the more...stuff that ran through them, the clearer they got. Like Drano." She shrugged.

This was a sobering thought. I had been pretty sure the clients I pressed had no residual effects from the sessions, other than the suggestions I gave them. Was I opening up some kind of mental pipeline between them and myself? "Jeez, Sukey, I wonder if it's happening to anyone else I've worked with. Like Hilda?"

"Did you ever press Sam?" she asked.

I closed my eyes and nodded. "Once. Just really quickly, to get him to leave so that I could be alone to talk to Dominic." *And maybe a little by accident while we were having sex.*

I groaned and ducked my head under the water, which was starting to cool. I had also pressed Tino, Manny, Rocko's two wannabe friends, and about two dozen lowlife scumbags in Costa Mesa and Santa Ana in my search for info on Dominic. Cupcake, Fred, Lawyer Bob, my impromptu chauffeur—it gave a whole new, scary meaning to the term Psychic Hotline.

When I came up for air, Sukey was on her feet. "Look, I'll let you finish your bath. But as soon as things get back to normal, you and I are going to try to figure this out. Do some experiments or something. See how it works." She got up and left, closing the door behind her.

Wonderful. Now I had a whole new area to obsess over. I sighed. *Well, I had wanted minions.* I groaned. Something else to keep me awake at night.

In fact, I fell asleep in the tub and might have drowned, except that Sukey awakened me and practically dragged me in to bed. And then I slept for twenty hours. Straight.

"Hey, Mercy! How you doin'?" Tino's familiar voice almost shocked me out of my stupor. I was standing in the open sliding glass door, blinking my eyes against the morning light on my patio. The two small tables had been pushed together, and seven people were at work on an enormous stack of pancakes. It was the mingled smells of sizzling hotcakes and coffee that had finally pulled me from my comalike slumber, and the sound of voices that had caused my feet to detour from the most direct path to the kitchen.

Across the table sat Hilda, flanked by Tino and Grant. Otis was spooning some kind of fruit onto a stack of pancakes on Sukey's plate, and T.J. was stroking Fred on his lap with one hand and drinking coffee with the other. Sam was at the end of the table, with Cupcake's big head on his knee. His empty plate was pushed back, and a stack of newspapers was on the table in front of him.

"What is everyone doing here?" I asked blankly.

"We got tired of waiting for you to wake up," said Hilda. "Sukey wouldn't let anyone disturb you last night, so we came over for breakfast. It's a good thing I already reached my goal weight, or I wouldn't have been able to try Otis's heavenly pancakes."

I eyed Sukey suspiciously. *How much did you tell them?* I asked her.

Almost nothing. Just that you figured out where Dominic took me, and came and got me out. They think the dog was his, and we borrowed the car from a gentleman friend of mine.

"Sit down, Mercy." T.J. put Fred down as if preparing to relinquish his chair. "Otis just brought out a fresh batch of pancakes and some more coffee."

"No, take my chair," interjected Sukey quickly. "I

have to get a change of clothes from my place and get to the office before nine. I'll call everyone and explain you won't be in until tomorrow." She stood and picked up her empty plate, which was quickly replaced with a full one by Otis, who took the empty in trade.

Good luck with them, Mercy. Don't let them push you around. Sukey smiled and stepped out through the patio gate. Grant handed me a cup of coffee, and I sipped it automatically. Perfect. I looked for my fork, found it and cut into the pancakes. They melted in my mouth, and I was taking another bite when I looked up. Six faces were staring at me. Eight, if you counted Fred and Cupcake.

"Do you mind if I finish my breakfast before the interrogation?" I asked dryly.

"Of course not," said Otis, and everyone else chimed in. Everyone except Sam. He sat quietly at the opposite end of the table, his eyes on the papers before him. He didn't seem to be reading them, just avoiding looking at me. I gave up and put down my fork.

"Never mind, let's get it over with." A clamor arose as everyone tried to ask questions at once. Grant banged on his orange juice glass with a knife, and the cacophony subsided.

"Just let her tell us what happened at her own pace," he said, and when voices started to interject, he raised his voice again. "Let her get through it once, and then we can start asking questions, okay? Back off!"

This time his suggestion held, and the group remained silent. Sam was still staring at the table, but all other eyes waited eagerly. I took a deep breath and began.

"How much do T.J. and Otis know?" I asked.

Otis spoke in his rumbling, James Earl Jones baritone. "People started coming by when you didn't show up at the office and your car wasn't here. Knocked on our door. Grant here said some drug dealer had made off with Sukey and you all had been out the night before trying to find her with no luck. Thought you were missing, too. I wanted to call the police, but Sam wouldn't let me."

"Sam?" At the surprise in my voice, Sam finally looked directly at me.

"I would have called them myself if you hadn't shown up by yesterday morning. But I knew you didn't want me to. So I held off." He went back to staring at his newspapers, and Otis went on.

"Then I came down yesterday morning, and Sam said you and Sukey were both fine and you had gone to bed. He said we shouldn't disturb either of you until you got some rest."

T.J. cut in on his partner. "I got tired of waiting last night and called downstairs, but the phone was off the hook, so I came down and let myself in. Sukey heard me, and got up and said we should let you sleep, and that I should come back in the morning."

"Which is what she told the rest of us when she returned our messages," put in Hilda. "So here we are."

I looked around at the eager faces. Less than two weeks ago, I had never had a guest over for a meal and I could count my friends on one hand. Make that one finger. How had I gotten from there to here in—I mentally calculated—twelve days?

"It all started with Dominic's note," I began, and I wove the story as best I could, leaving out any mention of telepathy or Sergio. It was a thin, unconvincing story without the power of the press behind it, but I was not going to use my abilities today. No matter what. Tomorrow, I'd see, but today the very thought of it made me queasy.

As I explained how Manny's information and Grant's deductions had combined to point at the rental spaces near Sabatino's, I said I saw the Jaguar pull into the garage—almost true—and waited until it pulled out again to break a window and get Sukey out. I said Cupcake had been guarding her, again not a complete lie, and we had befriended him and decided not to leave him in a criminal's care.

When asked about the Mercedes, I said I had been afraid Dominic might be watching my car, so we borrowed one from a friend of Sukey's who lived nearby. I was expecting problems with the timeline, but Sam was the only one who knew how late we really got home, and he never spoke up.

"What about Dominic?" asked Tino. "What happened to him?"

"I—I'm not sure."

"I am." Sam's voice was very quiet, but every head swung his way. He picked the first newspaper off the top of the stack and tossed it toward the center of the table. "Read this."

Heroin Found in Mystery Jaguar. Drug Deal Gone Bad? I blinked at the headline, then looked at Sam.

"Mystery Jaguar?" My heart beat wildly. Dominic

had to be dead. There hadn't been time for my command to wear off. Not with his seat belt fastened and the frigid Pacific water streaming through the open windows. I'd felt him die. "What does that mean, Sam?"

"Read the article." Our eyes locked, and that laser-blue intensity poured into mine. I broke away first.

Newport Beach police have confirmed that the substance found in the trunk of the Jaguar XJ that plunged into the harbor early Wednesday morning is heroin. There is still no news as to the identification of the body found still belted into the driver's seat. A Newport Beach Police Department source told the Orange County Register that the identification in the glove compartment of the car and the wallet of the deceased, while issued by the California Department of Motor Vehicles, both turned out to carry a false name.

I looked up from the article. I would want to read it in more detail later, to see if witnesses had reported seeing anything. Like a tall brunette with a ponytail leaning into the car's window moments before its driver accelerated toward certain death. But right now, I needed to see Sam's face.

"It sure sounds like Dominic," I said cautiously.

"Let me see that." Hilda snatched the paper and read the article aloud, with Tino and Grant both trying to look over her shoulders. I saw that Sam had several other papers but did not interrupt.

"'Police arrived at the scene minutes after receiving numerous 911 calls from the passengers of a charter fishing boat, returning from its regular late-night trip down the coast south of Newport Harbor. "It just came out of nowhere," said George Jensen of Mission Viejo. "It landed about thirty feet from the boat. It went down like a stone, and we could see its lights for a few seconds, then nothing." Kevin Welper of the Orange County marine patrol said…'"

I tuned out Hilda's droning voice. If I had been seen, it would have preceded the bystander accounts. My cell phone rang from the living room, and I stood up to get it. No one noticed except Sam, whose eyes followed me. I saw my office number on the caller ID and answered. "Hello."

"Hi, Mercy. I just wanted to see how it was going before I called up the rest of today's appointments and rescheduled them." Sukey sounded out of breath, as if she had run up the stairs. I turned to see Sam still watching me, while everyone else's attention was riveted on the still-reading Hilda. I walked back toward my bedroom.

"Maybe you should just cancel them altogether, Sukey."

"What are you talking about?"

I sat down on the edge of my unmade bed. It smelled of sweat and despair, and I wrinkled my nose. "After what's happened in the last few days, I don't know how you can ask me that. We haven't talked about it yet, but you know perfectly well none of this would have happened if I hadn't been fucking around inside someone's head."

"I know no such thing," said Sukey. "Rocko was an asshole, and he would probably have given me heroin that night anyway. And if you hadn't chased him out of town, he might have given it to more people, too."

"Maybe," I conceded. "But—"

"But nothing. If it wasn't for you, I'd be dead right now."

"I killed a man, Sukey," I said brutally. "He was scum personified, but that still didn't give me the right to end his life. And I used my…my abilities to do it. I swore I would never use those abilities to harm anyone. I made a solemn promise to myself. And look how long that lasted."

"If he wasn't dead, I probably would be," said Sukey. "What you did was…well, it was *heroic*."

I snorted, but she went on. "No, I mean it, Mercy. You helped me. Not just with Dominic, but with believing in myself. And you've helped other people, too. All your clients just rave about you. Mrs. Winston called you an *angel*. Just now, when I called her. She said she's been sleeping soundly at night for the first time in twenty years since she saw you last week."

I remembered Mrs. Winston, who was so consumed by groundless worries that she could barely function. I had been so moved by her distress, and pleased when the session went well. "Yes, but—"

"No buts, Mercy. I'm rescheduling. Now, how's it going with the gang?"

The gang? Since when did I have a gang? Well, it was better than minions. "Okay, I guess. But Sam's still pretty pissed."

"Well, un-piss him. He's too good to let get away." Good old Sukey. She might not be willing to do just anything to get a boyfriend anymore, but that didn't mean it wasn't still high on her list of priorities.

"I'll try, Sukey. But I don't know if I can do it."

"You could use a little…you know. That thing you do."

"No," I said flatly. "If I have to resort to that to keep him, then he's not mine to keep."

"I guess not. Oops, gotta go…the other line is ringing. Someone's calling me back. Good luck!" She disconnected.

I walked back out to the front of the house, to find Grant clearing the table and Hilda and Tino in the kitchen, where Hilda was tying an apron around Tino's waist and explaining that real men could indeed wash dishes. Sam was sitting alone on the patio.

"Where are T.J. and Otis?" I asked.

He gestured to indicate they had gone back upstairs, and I sat down on a lounge chair.

"So," I said, then hesitated.

"So…what?"

"You said we needed to talk." I stifled a gulp. "So I'm ready to talk."

He stared at me for a moment with those amazing blue eyes. Then he stood, walked across the patio and sat next to me on the lounge chair. He waited until I turned to face him, then spoke.

"I've had a lot of time to think, over the last twenty or so hours," he began. "And I decided the first thing I had to do when you were ready to speak to me was to tell you I can't live with secrets indefinitely. I just can't. So I have to ask you to tell me everything."

I took a deep breath, not breaking eye contact. "I can't." His eyes dropped from mine, and he moved as if to stand up. I grabbed his hands.

"I'm not saying I can't ever tell you, Sam. It's just that…" I struggled, trying to make my own thoughts clear so I could convey them to him. "It's just that there's something important I need to find out first. Something I need to know before…before I can tell you the rest. It may change everything I believe to be true about…about things." Even I could hear the inadequacy of this speech, but Sam was still sitting next to me and was again looking at me closely.

He spoke more quietly. "When I decided I was going to ask you to tell me everything, I also considered the possibility you might refuse. I told myself if you did that, I'd have to walk away. And stay away."

I felt something suspiciously like a sob try to well up in my throat and bit it back.

He went on. "Tell me, Mercy. Just how long do you think it will take you to find out…whatever it is?"

"I don't know," I said honestly. "It's something I've needed to do for a long time. But I never really…never really tried very hard before. Now I know I have to." *Or you won't be the only thing I lose.*

Sam was silent for what seemed like an eternity, but

his eyes still searched my face. A tiny glimmer of hope ignited somewhere in my chest, and I realized I was holding my breath. Finally, he spoke. "I should walk away, Mercy, and I could do that. But I'm pretty sure I wouldn't be able to stay away."

I could see tension in his jaw, and I had a sudden flash of him kicking down the door, his movements a blur. "Not knowing you were right around the corner. Not running into you around town. I may have the will, but I don't think I have the strength."

Slowly, I nodded. "Okay." It was all I could think to say. Was he really going to let me keep my secret for now? Was he really going to give me the time I needed? I was afraid if I said too much, he would change his mind.

"Okay?" he asked. "Does that mean we're going to try this?"

"Try what?" I asked.

"Try to be…whatever it is that we are," he finished.

"Yeah," I said, exhaling slowly. "Yeah, I think it does mean…that." I tried a smile, but it probably came out as a grimace. "I'm not promising I won't really suck at it, though."

"Hey, you two!" Hilda stuck her head out the door. "Do you think Sukey will be gone all day?"

"I doubt it," I answered. "Why?"

"Because it's a glorious day, and Grant has invited everyone out on his boat for lunch and a sail. And he wants the whole gang to come."

I guess I do have a gang, I thought ruefully. Cupcake bounded out past the sliding glass doors and put his huge paws on my lap. I grabbed him under his chin and gave him a serious look. "How about you, Cupcake? You ever been on a boat?"

He woofed loudly, and everyone laughed, even Sam.

This is going to take some getting used to, I thought. I got to my feet, and Sam rose with me. As he slipped his arm around my waist, I stepped through the door to talk to my friends.

Author's Note

Those of my readers who live or have spent a lot of time in Balboa, California, will know that I've taken some creative license in writing this book. I know the Balboa Island Ferries dock on the island side of the harbor when they're not running, but I needed to leave one on the peninsula side so it would be available for Rocko to steal. I also know that there are no longer live-aboard yachts at the Balboa Marina, as there were when I first moved there in 1986. Although it has been some years since I made my home in Balboa, I recently visited there and was delighted to see that, although some of the businesses have new names and there are many faces I didn't recognize, the character of the town remains substantially unchanged. Million-dollar homes still sit next to tear-downs inhabited by college students, tourists still dance to steel bands and the locals who hang out in the dive bars are still known by nicknames that invoke old jobs or new habits, such as Sailor Sally and Barbecue Bill. You can still play Skee-Ball at the Fun Zone and buy a frozen banana from a stand. It all made me a little homesick and happy that I had chosen this place for Mercy and her friends to live and work, perhaps as an excuse to continue my connection to a place where I loved living.

* * * * *

Turn the page for an advance look at
ANGEL OF MERCY,
the next Mercy Hollings adventure
by Toni Andrews,
available in May 2008
from MIRA Books

1

I killed a guy last month.

A horn sounded behind me, and I jumped. A quick glance told me the light had turned green, so I shook myself out of my reverie and put my foot on the gas pedal. What passed for rush hour in Balboa, California, wasn't over yet, and I was interfering with the morning commute.

My office was only about two miles from my beachfront apartment and the route had less than five traffic lights, so you'd think I'd be able to make it to work without getting sucked into a spiral of self-doubt and terror. *I killed Dominic. Deliberately.*

I wasn't afraid I'd be caught. I was pretty sure I had dodged that bullet. No, what woke me from a sound sleep almost every night was the cold dread that I would lose control again. Harm someone again. Put people I cared about in danger again. *I have no business doing this. I've got to stop kidding myself. I've got to—*

Yet another horn blared, and I jumped. Two trances in two lights. A new record.

Waving apologetically at the driver of the BMW hugging my bumper, I put the Honda into gear and sped out of his way. I probably should have walked or ridden my bicycle to work as long as the perfect Southern California fall weather was holding out. But walking gave me too much time to think, something I was lately trying to avoid. And my one attempt to ride the bicycle with Cupcake in tow had been a disaster.

To distract myself as I drove the last few blocks to where I rented a parking space from a boat builder on the Lido Peninsula, I pondered the problem of Cupcake, who was standing in the backseat with his face squeezed against the window's narrow opening. I had acquired him less than a month ago—on the same day that I killed Dominic, actually—and I had sort of a joint-ownership agreement with my office manager. My apartment was bigger and had a patio along the boardwalk and the beach, so at the moment the 135-pound rottweiler was bunking with me.

Cupcake, formerly known as Cujo, had been previously owned by a sleazeball who had not only thought it would be a great idea to have him trained to attack, but to do so using obscure voice commands. Nothing obvious like "kill" or "dismember" for him. The two commands I had accidentally stumbled across so far were "nail file" and "bumblebee." Neither discovery had been made at a particularly convenient time, and I was living in fear that someone would say something like "hopscotch" and the otherwise mild-mannered canine would tear some innocent bystander's throat out.

I pulled into my parking space a few minutes early, got out and opened the back door. Cupcake obediently waited for the leash to be snapped onto his collar before tugging me toward the stairs to my office. He knew what was waiting behind the door marked *Mercedes Hollings, Hypnotherapy.*

New York Times Bestselling Author

ERICA SPINDLER

Five years ago, three young victims were found murdered, posed like little angels. No witnesses, no evidence left behind. The case nearly destroyed homicide detective Kitt Lundgren's career—because she let the killer get away.

Now the Sleeping Angel Killer is back.

But Kitt notices something different about this new rash of killings—a tiny variation that suggests a copycat killer may be re-creating the original "perfect crimes." Then the unthinkable happens. The Sleeping Angel Killer himself approaches Kitt with a bizarre offer: he will help her catch his copycat....

"[A] bloodcurdling romantic thriller."
—*Publishers Weekly*

COPY cat

Available the first week of September 2007, wherever paperbacks are sold!

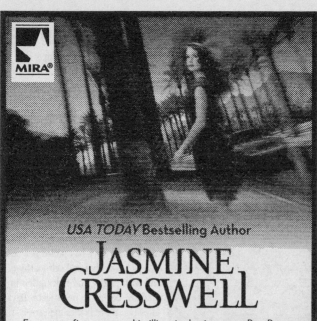

REQUEST YOUR
FREE BOOKS!

2 FREE NOVELS
FROM THE ROMANCE/SUSPENSE
COLLECTION PLUS 2 FREE GIFTS!

YES! Please send me 2 FREE novels from the Romance/Suspense Collection and my 2 FREE gifts. After receiving them, if I don't wish to receive any more books, I can return the shipping statement marked "cancel." If I don't cancel, I will receive 4 brand-new novels every month and be billed just $5.49 per book in the U.S., or $5.99 per book in Canada, plus 25¢ shipping and handling per book plus applicable taxes, if any*. That's a savings of at least 20% off the cover price! I understand that accepting the 2 free books and gifts places me under no obligation to buy anything. I can always return a shipment and cancel at any time. Even if I never buy another book from the Reader Service, the two free books and gifts are mine to keep forever.

185 MDN EF5Y   385 MDN EF6C

Name   (PLEASE PRINT)

Address   Apt. #

City   State/Prov.   Zip/Postal Code

Signature (if under 18, a parent or guardian must sign)

Mail to **The Reader Service:**
IN U.S.A.: P.O. Box 1867, Buffalo, NY 14240-1867
IN CANADA: P.O. Box 609, Fort Erie, Ontario L2A 5X3

Not valid to current subscribers to the Romance Collection,
the Suspense Collection or the Romance/Suspense Collection.

Want to try two free books from another line?
Call 1-800-873-8635 or visit www.morefreebooks.com.

* Terms and prices subject to change without notice. NY residents add applicable sales tax. Canadian residents will be charged applicable provincial taxes and GST. This offer is limited to one order per household. All orders subject to approval. Credit or debit balances in a customer's account(s) may be offset by any other outstanding balance owed by or to the customer. Please allow 4 to 6 weeks for delivery.

Your Privacy: Harlequin is committed to protecting your privacy. Our Privacy Policy is available online at www.eHarlequin.com or upon request from the Reader Service. From time to time we make our lists of customers available to reputable firms who may have a product or service of interest to you. If you would prefer we not share your name and address, please check here. ☐

BOB07

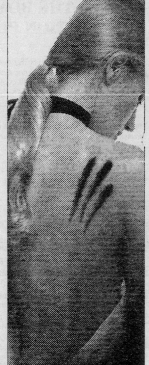